BREAKING KAYFABE

BREAKING KAYFABE

A Novel

Wes Brown

Bluemoose

for Mum and Dad

Copyright © Wes Brown 2023

First published in 2023 by
Bluemoose Books Ltd
25 Sackville Street
Hebden Bridge
West Yorkshire
HX7 7DJ

www.bluemoosebooks.com

All rights reserved
Unauthorised duplication contravenes existing laws

British Library Cataloguing-in-Publication data
A catalogue record for this book is available from the British Library

Paperback 978-1-915693-08-2
Hardback 978-1-915693-07-5

Printed and bound in the UK by Short Run Press

'Men   are broken things   breaking things.'

Joelle Taylor

There are bad guys and good guys in pro wrestling, *heels* and *faces*, and Dad was a bad guy. They rode in different cars. Changed in different dressing rooms. Drank in different bars. Wrestlers played their characters straight, inside and outside the ring, no matter how stupid. Despite every wrestler having their own gimmick, usually something archetypal, a simple piece of macho gimmickry – a cowboy, Indian chief, Samurai, or in Dad's case, a sailor – the wrestlers of Dad's era portrayed staged events and personas within wrestling as 'real' in a code of honour known as *kayfabe*.

Part One

I threw myself at the dark canvas. The impact rippled through me in stop-motion, as I imagined myself gut-wrenched and bouncing off the mat, cheeks flapping and the ring in shock. Dad said doctors told him getting bumped in the ring was like getting rear-ended by a car travelling at 20 mph.

As you slapped the mat, the spring beneath the ring compressed, the girders flexed, and the stack of your spine belted the canvas like a whip. I looked up for Trev's approval. He just motioned for me to do it again. This was the way in pro wrestling. An education through a repetition of violent acts on the body. I got up, raised my fists, quarter-squatted and launched myself backwards.

Earlier in the day, I had sat on a wall in the spring heat outside the corrugated shutters in a business park in Brixton, waiting for Trev the coach, and the other trainees to arrive, before entering an archway that was about the size of a large garage.

A dismantled wrestling ring lay in a heap at the far side of the space. Near the door were some green mats, a rickety bench and a few weights. The chalk walls were dank with grime.

I heard footsteps and turned to see a guy in white jeans ducking his quiff under the shutter.

I gave him the last strong handshake I ever would.

Everybody changed. Two big guys, both over twenty stone in the early-nineties brightness of old-school purple Macho Man and yellow Hulkamania T-shirts, then some guy in stretch Lycra, small and looking like an old man in a child's body, who chatted with Trev like he knew him. A waiver was handed round and I signed away any liability the gym had for my protection. Macho Man wore a spotted bandana and signed with his tongue sticking out. He had thick dark hair that was already sweated into a wild mullet around his stubbled face. The one in the Hulkamania shirt was bald and had a goatee; his skin was pale, and he wore a pair of gigantic baggy shorts with football socks pulled up to his knees.

When we were done, Trev gathered us around him and said, 'Who are we? What are we doing here?'

People mused on their favourite wrestlers. Said they had loved wrestling since they were kids. This was all they had ever wanted to do. We were told that hundreds of trainees walked through the door every year, each convinced the business owed them something and they would live out their dreams, but barely anybody made it onto shows, fewer had careers and if they did, they were often short, hard and lonely.

If we were willing to work hard and pay our dues, we would be given every opportunity to succeed.

When it was my turn to share I said my dad had been a wrestler, but nothing about the summers spent learning to fall in a field. I stared over at the disassembled ring, laid out before us like a puzzle.

I said nothing of my desire to become somebody else.

The first task was to construct the ring. This took up much of our three-hour session: guys wandering round aimlessly with beams, wooden planks and foam padding. The old-man-child hoisted a plank over his shoulder, whilst Macho Man and Hulkamania hauled a girder into place, and I stood there with some bungees. The other guy, well-groomed and tanned, I think was called Adem, was doing his own thing trying to organise some of the mats. The planks were numbered but this only suggested a design none of us were capable of working out. Trevor said nothing, just smiled, sucking through his teeth as he presumably made mental notes while we struggled to assemble the squared circle. Eventually, with some intervention from Trevor, a wrestling ring stood before us like a monument. It had an aura like a stage, and as I stood beside the others gawping at it, I could barely conceal my excitement and wanted to slide in and act out a thousand scenarios I had watched on TV or fantasised about as a boy.

Before we could get in the ring, we had to perform a hundred squats. I had spent six months in the gym preparing my body but fifty reps at my own bodyweight was already doing me in.

My quadriceps cramped as Hulkamania was barely able to get himself back up from the hole of a deep squat, bandana rank with sweat.

'Oh dear,' Trev snorted. 'We're gonna have to get fitter than this.'

A few more reps in and Macho Man was on the floor. 'I can't do it,' he panted. 'This was a mistake.'

'You sure? No refunds,' Trev said matter-of-factly, then smiled, shaking his hand with a weary glint in his eye.

The course cost eight hundred pounds.

Macho Man said okay and then ran out to vomit.

I willed my body to keep going against the injections of lactic acid and tight breaths and my heart boxing its way out my chest, sweating across my body, dying to give in.

The shutter opened and a guy ducked in wearing a leather jacket over a hoodie; he had a long black crow's wing of a fringe drooping down over his face and an undercut. It was Marilyn Draven, the Renegade Pro Champion and biggest *heel* in British wrestling.

'Fucking hell,' he shouted over to Trev and started laughing. 'Where the fuck did they find you lot?'

Nobody answered.

I wiped the sweat from my forehead. Hulkamania was still rolling around on the floor. I heard the other dude still heaving outside.

The guy who looked like an ancient child, Owen, who said he had trained before, already seemed to know everybody and everything, and he was keen to show it and tell *me* about it. He squatted deeper and faster. Even the way he did this was annoying, his sticking-out arse and the self-regulating up and down movements that were more adept than mine. He was just a lean guy, built like a thirteen-year-old, but acted as if he was a veteran with his sage advice, bobbing up and down with an ease that seemed effortlessly superior at this moment, stroking his open palms to the floor on each descent as if they were blessing the dusty ground.

When we made it through the warm up, I ran over to my bag and drank a bottle of water, ran over to the taps, refilled it and drank some more. I bent over with my hands on my knees. I knew I was making a target of myself but I had to breathe, chest heaving, barely able to stand.

The workout was one hundred squats, push-ups, sit ups and burpees and I was already nearly maxed out on the squats.

Hulkamania now ran off to spill his guts somewhere beyond the shutters. When he came back, he was complaining of an ankle injury and unable to move. The guy with the quiff was struggling as much as I was, stiffening into stop-motion.

'I'm fucked,' I said while sweat slid down my face and eyes. 'I don't know what's wrong.'

Trev spoke slyly out of the side of his mouth in the way South Londoners did, 'Fatigue makes cowards of us all.'

Marilyn had taken up a seat at the far side of the ring and, watching it all unfold, he cackled and shook his head.

Owen turned to me without breaking his rhythm.

'Gym fit isn't wrestling fit,' he said.

Well, if he was such a pro, why was he here?

I pushed harder and deeper, focusing on moving the ground away from me rather than the nausea, completing the motion to standing no matter how gassed I was.

Dad used to tell me honesty was the most important thing in a man, that people didn't want to hear the truth because they don't want their illusions destroyed. Within an hour of training I had no idea what I had been thinking. What Dad said was starting to make sense.

Marilyn stalked the room and then moved toward me. My head dropped. He swooshed the fin of his undercut and eyed me up.

He lifted my face with his thumb.

'And what's your fucking story then?' he asked.

'I'm Wes,' I said, still panting, extending my hand.

Marilyn brushed it aside.

'I didn't ask you for your fucking name,' he snarled. 'I don't want to shake your fucking hand. I asked why you are here.'

He knew why I was here. I had been researching the British wrestling scene because an editor had seen me at a one-off session Dad ran for a promotion and was willing to pay me to write about it. At the time, I was depressed, had nothing better to do and thought it would be better than drinking myself into oblivion.

Marilyn Draven was entertained by the sight of his own blood. He had been thrown through tables and off balconies; he had had his body stapled, thrashed with barbed wire, smashed by light tubes, lemon juice poured into the cuts. He said he was afraid of being set on fire until he did it.

A few weeks before, I'd bumped into him in a pub in Covent Garden, told him about Dad and he was happy to chat to me when he thought I was just a fan until he realised I had signed up to become a pro wrestler. *I'll be a cunt,* he said. *But that's how I am with everybody.*

Now he fixed his eyes on me.

'Did you not fucking hear me or something?' he said. 'Why are you here?'

My squat slowed.

Down.

Up.

'To be a wrestler,' I said. 'Like my dad.'

'Who was your dad?'

'Earl Black.'

'Who?'

'Earl Black. He wrestled in Stampede for Stu Hart in the seventies.'

Everybody looked at me.

Stampede Wrestling was a legendary promotion based in Calgary. Fans were hard-working miners and lumberjacks who favoured a no-nonsense, realistic style and it was seen as the 'missing link' between the showmanship of American wrestling and the realism of 'Strong Style' Japanese *puroresu*.

Marilyn tilted his head like a raptor.

'Whatever your old man has done means nothing,' he said with evil eyes. 'You are a fucking nobody. Do you get that? This business owes you nothing.'

Looking over his shoulder I saw that everybody had stopped. Trev eyeballed me.

'What do you do for a living?'

'I don't know.'

'What do you mean you don't fucking know?'

My palms were wet.

'I'm supposed to be a writer,' I said. 'But I haven't written anything in a while.'

'What do you do for a living?'

'Teach creative writing.'

'Fucking hell,' he said. 'And you're gonna be a pro wrestler?'

'I am.'

My squat froze in agony.

'Fucking looks like it,' he said. 'I've seen enough.'

I wiped the sweat from my head, had a gulp of water and sat down on the mats with the others.

*

When I was growing up, Dad worked nights as a bouncer and slept in the attic. He was in his forties, with one leg fused and the other poisoning his bloodstream; he was struggling to make it up and down the stairs of the four-floor nightclub in Leeds where he had been head doorman, and had begun illegally taxi-driving punters he had often beaten up.

He had tried doing things the legitimate way before being put off by the regulations and licensing.

Turning up in a red Ford Cortina with a boot full of knocked-off tapes was more his thing.

He would work all night, come home, turn his wage over to Mum, then sleep into the afternoon while Mum cleaned, prepared Marks & Spencer's ready meals and redecorated the house. Woven wicker fans on white walls, *pot pourri* that lingered an odour of petal and peel. The distances between the thinking man and Buddha ornaments were tape-measured. Nothing was to be touched, not even the cushions.

One day when I was about four, she decided the house wasn't right and, like her mother who changed the layout of her living room every week, ripped the carpets from every floor, tore down the wallpaper, stripped the doors of handles and the handrails from the stairs. The bare walls were thick with coats of paint; the brushstrokes bore the slashes of hard bristles on cracked plaster.

Until eventually she gave up and the house remained like this for the rest of my childhood. I stood at the foot of the attic door. One of the floorboards had a worn eye of darker wood that creaked when I wasn't careful enough to miss it. Because there was no handle, I pushed against the door hoping it would spring back as if by ghostly assistance.

On a previous journey to the attic, I had seen the outline of a skeleton in a rocking chair after watching *Ghostbusters* and ran screaming all the way downstairs. The staircase leading up to the double dormer was sanded down the middle and cream strips remained on the outside like white slime. When you climbed to the top, there was a small landing partitioned by a thin panel and a shell-coloured door that slid open like a hatch.

Inside was a single bed pressed against a wall. The window was as long as the room but too high to look out of. No nets or curtains. The light was bright. A picture of clouds fixed above the room. Sometimes I would crane my head up and see only roof-tiles and red-brick chimneys of back-to-back terraces under a sky that was always wet and grey.

I slid open the door and crept inside.

Dad's grade-1 buzzcut was smoky in daylight. His breaths were slower than an ordinary man. His lungs required a deeper trawl for air. The slow intake gradually inflated his chest and hung a moment before being driven out in a long snort.

All the air returned to the room.

I inhaled deep as I could, filled the small chamber of my chest enough to show the feathery ridges of my ribcage, and exhaled a wheeze.

By his bed were a tub of Vaseline, one of his two pairs of jeans, and a shell-shaped cup he wore for work.

Dad's washed-up bulk lay there, snoring beside me, while I reached in slowly for the gold.

The soaring breaths sucked up the air and thundered it back out while the slow drum loop of his heart blasted blood through to the rest of his body. I could almost hear the beat.

Sometimes I could prod him without waking him up, explore the contours of his nose with a pointed finger; his skin was thicker and browner than mine. He hadn't lived in Australia for ten years, but he was still tanned and still sometimes spoke in a Sydney accent. His skin looked foreign. His false teeth floated in a glass of water; without them, his face had an imploded look. His mouth puckered like an asterisk and grey eyebrows furrowed. He slept in a thin shawl that barely contained the geography of his bulk. His huge belly was tattooed with a snarling tiger's face and one shoulder and arm were illustrated with Japanese emblems, with a winged rose across his chest beneath an eagle zoning in for a kill under a red sunset. On the other arm was a ring of skulls, with an eagle, a black dog and a native American woman above them. The muscular canvas of his back was painted with a wrestler called Hamanasuke fending off bandits in a Japanese jungle before a huge waterfall. The aged green inks and red-green scales decorated the dense musculature like a leviathan. From a distance it looked as if he was wearing a T-shirt. His tattoos stopped at the elbows so they wouldn't be seen when wearing a kimono. It was considered disrespectful for outlaw *irezumi* to be visible when clothed. His scalp was scarred and his knuckles were smoothed by violence.

The only evidence I had that Dad wrestled around the world as 'Sailor' Earl Black was the wreckage of his body, a nylon mask, the stories he told of personas authored by his own devising, and a scrapbook of clippings and promotional pics.

Usually, it was the books I'd come up here looking for. I'd sit cross-legged on the bare floorboards, examining the cracks for dust balls, silvery in the light, or beetles marching down the groove in their dark shells, get myself comfortable, then gaze upon the pages of the scrapbook.

I liked the glossy book about American Football with the unreal green pitches and helmeted players in wing-like shoulder pads, but the game didn't make sense to me. The closest thing I had known to anything like this was an afternoon spent sitting on a cold terrace watching Leeds Rhinos. Dad had books by Lucretius, Cicero, Caesar, and a series about monarchs, but they were too complex and dense for me to read. They had yellowed pages, thumb-worn, smelling deeply of something unusual – not quite perfume or aftershave, not quite moss or damp, but something like that: a deep curdled manliness I learned to associate with books and took to be the odour of knowledge. The wrestling scrapbook was what drew me up here. There was only a handful of clippings and copies of posters and promo pics, but they were enough: I would look through each time in the same order; the memorabilia still pulled me in as if I was reading a match programme.

This was Dad. This was me.

There was the promo photo he was most proud of first: it was him with a blond quiff that seemed audacious and full of bravado, so out of keeping with who he was now: bald, no-nonsense, macho. This was masculine in a different way. The caddishly smooth jawline and sturdy old-style strongman body with his fists pressing into his hips and flexing his back big enough make his entire upper body into a V-shape. Around his waist he wore an intricately welded championship belt that would be small by Wrestle World USA standards and looked more like the belt of a boxer or martial artist. Some of them showed him in his black facemask from when he performed as Mr X and kayfabed the character in and out of the ring. There were depictions of him as Earl Black, Mr Tiger and himself. Clippings of the riot the wrestlers started in Jakarta airport. Posters for shows which he had main-evented. Other pictures were just memories of his time as a wrestler. Dressed in a sharp suit in the sixties, slim black tie and a Tony Curtis quiff, laughing over dinner with a date or masked in a club with his arm around Miss Indonesia. Then there were the promo pics in various poses or action shots performing in the ring. The prints from *Team Germany vs The World* where he wore black tights and singlet combination with swastikas on the shoulders. One showed him above a black man, Jack Claybourne, holding the ropes snarling while Dad jackbooted his throat. In another, he was barring the arm of Claybourne in front of thousands of Singaporeans. I turned to the last page where one wrestler was biting another in the head, blood around his eyes.

'Wesley?' Mum called up the stairs, 'Dinner's ready.'

I closed the book and slid it back under the bed.

*

We went to Peasholm Park in the summer holidays one year. Tension had been building along the motorway as we neared the coast because Mum wanted to go out for lunch and Dad had made corned beef sandwiches.

Mum's sister, Louise, was sitting in the back seat beside me and my little brother, Cal.

'I'm not eating that fucking shit,' Mum said.

'Shirley,' Louise said. 'He's only trying to help. You don't have to eat them.'

The sandwiches were squares of crusty brown bread filled with corned beef and wrapped in five pounds worth of foil. No salad or sauces, just wet beef between bread and margarine. The appearance of corned beef itself reminded me too much of Dad's leg to enjoy it and the thought of him preparing them made the connection too apparent. Cal didn't mind. He'd eat anything. When he was born, he was bull-necked and weighed over a stone and, as the family story went, when Dad rolled in after his shift, the midwives turned around and knew immediately which boy was his.

Every five years or so, the migrating bone chips in Dad's leg would flare into osteoarthritis, his leg doubled in size, marbled and purple like hung beef, secreting poison into his bloodstream.

Dry-cured, the plasma rushed to the surface in crusts.

The doctors had said on more than one occasion that he didn't have long left.

'What's your obsession with spending money?' he said.

'Frank, we're having a fucking family day out.'

'Nothing wrong with a sandwich.'

Mum took a deep breath and gasped.

'Nobody wants to eat your fucking sandwiches, Frank.'

I could see the side of her sneering face from behind and knew that her anger would soon become rage.

There would be the hissing, the overenunciated expletives, screaming and thrashing about like she was trying to escape herself. All the rage in her one good eye.

Dad pulled into the carpark.

'Turn this car around,' she said. 'We're going home.'

'Nay, Shirley. We've only just got here,' Louise said.

'I need to go home,' Mum said.

I wished Louise would just keep quiet. Cal stared out of the window. I was terrified for whoever Mum would lose her temper with and if I would also be blamed. Nothing seemed to affect Dad. He found her tantrums hilarious and would try to wind her up, to watch her explode.

'You look like a bulldog chewing a wasp,' Dad said.

Grinning, he waited for his comment to colour her expression. Then rocked with laughter when she started screaming.

'Turn the car around,' Mum said. 'You fucking dick.'

'Have I to take Wesley in?' Louise said.

'He's staying here. In this car. We're going home.'

'We're not fucking going anywhere,' Dad said.

He opened the door and Louise followed.

Mum was in the front seat, kicking the dashboard. How could I get out without her killing me?

I didn't want to antagonise her. So I sat there, seatbelt across my chest, wondering how I could be better. If I was better, I wouldn't upset her. It was my stupid big ears. My weird-shaped knees. The fact that I couldn't pronounce my r's. The shyness that made it near impossible to wave hello to a friend I saw in the street.

Then I thought she would know what I was thinking and rip it apart.

Louise walked up to the car and said, 'C'mon boys, we'll take you in.'

Cal shouted *yay* and I prayed for him to not draw attention to himself.

'He's not fucking going anywhere!' Mum screamed.

Louise had learned to ignore her. She opened the door, released my seatbelt and pulled me out onto my feet. Cal followed. We walked toward Dad, who was smoking with his sunglasses on.

I couldn't help looking over my shoulder at the shaking car, all Mum's rage.

We walked toward the entrance to Peasholm Park. People laughing at us was easier to deal with than people judging us, those who would mutter things to themselves with their eyes on the floor. I didn't look at the people looking at us. Didn't listen to their mutterings about how my family conducted itself.

Dad stubbed his butt on the floor with the heavy sole of his unbending left leg.

Louise put her arm around me, but I shrugged it away, not wanting to betray Mum.

'She'd start a fight in an empty room,' Dad said

He was standing the way he stood in the pictures I had seen of him on the doors: hands by his sides, bolt upright, cradling the mass of his belly. Cal ran up and stuck his face into the bouncy flesh.

'I don't want to get in trouble,' I said.

'You've got nothing to worry about.' He put his hand on my shoulder. 'You're with your dad.'

We walked around a man-made lake overlooking a Japanese-style pavilion. The reflection of a wooden arch shimmered when a boat passed. Carp had been added for realism and they swam around the bandstand in the middle of the water. The sea breeze swept up and gulls dive-bombed for chips. Faraway screams, seagull chatter and organ drone came from a fairground on the beach. Dad hobbled over to a kiosk, pushed into the front of the queue and bought ice-creams for the three of us. By the time he had limped back they had begun to melt; he licked the edges of the cone before passing one to me.

I examined the saliva on the cornet.

'You can't spend your life worrying about your bloody mother,' he said.

'But she's my mum,' I said.

'And I'm your dad.'

He rested his palm on my shoulder again, false teeth chomping on a cone. When he had finished, he thought it was a good time to tell me about the only memories he had of his father. One was walking the churn of grandad's ice-cream maker round in circles all day. The other was following him out into the land in Berkshire where he would point his shotgun up beneath rook's nests and shoot, covering them in a discharge of blood, shell and shot.

When grandad died, my father and his siblings were shipped out to boarding schools, the armed forces or the merchant navy. As the youngest of six siblings he had spent most of his childhood wandering around woodland, kept company by a pig in a wheelbarrow that he won in a raffle.

While he passed his eleven plus, he struggled to interact with people and failed the interview. When he left school he was given a discharge book and sailed across the sea.

I ate my ice cream. The top first, and then from the bottom up, avoiding the bit that Dad had licked.

Cal had ice cream up his nose. Dad spat on his thumb, rubbed it off and patted it down with a napkin. 'Mucky pup,' he said.

By the time we got back to the car Mum had calmed down. Her window was pulled down and she swept her hand through her short blonde hair. I was still fearful of repercussions when I opened the door and sat down on the back seat. Louise got in the other side with Cal and held my hand. Mum looked at me.

She smiled. 'Did you have a nice time?'

'Yeah,' I said.

'Are you hungry?'

'A bit.'

With one knee unable to bend and the other swollen from the burden of bearing his whole weight, which was almost thirty stone – he liked to make a point of telling us – Dad held onto the roof with one hand, pointed his unbending leg into the car and swung himself in, hoisting his body into the driver's seat. The car rocked. Nobody spoke, then Dad turned to Mum and grinned.

'Hello darling,' he said.

I had never seen them come to violence with one another but there always seemed like the possibility it might happen. Mum had charged at him with a kitchen knife once and he had deflected her into the stove. I didn't think Dad would ever lay a fist on her, only that he might do it in retaliation. Mum was crazy, I had seen her throw pots and pans, hissing with rage.

My heartbeat thrummed under the strap of the seatbelt. I squeezed my aunt's hand more tightly.

'Shut up fatman,' she said. 'You fucking *prick*.'

Then they laughed.

She took such delight in elongating the k sounds and rolling the r of prick; they both burst out laughing and were friends again. When they were getting on, they exchanged insults that were pretty much the same as when they weren't getting on, the only difference being the tone of the word, how they stressed the phrases and that the insults would be followed by laugher. Mum liked to call Dad fatman, prick or *dense* while Dad liked to call her a fat one-eyed dyke, slag or *bastard* in West Country English, extenuating the 'bar' sound which somehow exaggerated their differences and made it personal.

'Anybody fancy some fish and chips?' Mum asked.

'Anything you ask for, darling.' Dad said.

So we drove to the road lined with semi-detached houses, where railed fencing divided the road from the seafront and an elderly couple were sitting on a metal bench looking out at the blue waves in the early evening sun.

The seafront hotels were painted in alternating shades of pastel green, blue and cream, long faded in the sea air. Wash foamed at the shore as we turned down toward the water and the sea that seemed greyer up close; the black figures of surfboarders in the distance collapsed on waves that rippled and crashed, smaller as they billowed further into the tide until the sun glittered the surface and the horizon became the sky.

After we ate, I put all Dad's change into a coin pusher machine and had a few goes racing against Louise and Cal on *Daytona USA* and shooting bad guys on *Time Crisis*. In the car on the way home, I listened to the disco song Mum played - Viola Will's 'Gonna Get Along Without You Now' - and tried not to focus on the implication of the lyrics.

For years I had overheard conversations about when Mum and Dad would split up. Other than laughing when they insulted one another, there was almost no affection in their relationship. They didn't hug or kiss. No gifts were exchanged between them. There was a frankness in their discussions. Dad was twenty-four years older than her, stable in his views and widely read, if eccentrically, and had a capacious knowledge without being incisive, while Mum was cunning, understood how people worked and had a sense of irony that cut through most situations, though she lacked confidence and depth of field. Some of the things Dad was expert in were kooky for a meathead, like his encyclopaedic knowledge of birds, wildflowers, trees and leaves; other things he knew about were the history of the British monarchy and the constitution of the UK government, pro wrestling, weightlifting, ancient civilisations. He liked to use Latin phrases he had taught himself with an Italian bouncer who had worked the doors with him in Leeds. The thing Mum most wanted to learn from him, though, was his understanding of lesbian culture, or dykes as he called them. Before he had moved in with Mum, Dad had lived with five lesbians in his house in Armley, who he knew from working on the doors of gay bars. Many of his ex-girlfriends were bisexual or outright gay. I would overhear conversations from the attic while they watched *Prisoner: Cell Block H* after I was supposed to have gone to bed, my ear pressed to the door. Mum talked about how me and Cal would need to be older. Her plan was for me to be in secondary school, and she would then lose weight and get on a dating site.

I accepted this, like everything else, with a sad inevitability. What else could I do?

I had known for a long time that Mum and Dad's relationship was held together for the sake of us, and they weren't a real couple. They didn't love one another the way a married couple should.

For the first few times I listened to them, I wasn't entirely sure of what a lesbian was; all I could think about were scorpion-like creatures with claws. I understood from the tone of the conversations that Mum was interested in women in a more than friendly way, though I was still puzzled as to how this would work in practice.

I thought of the word lesbian again, scorpions in a cloth bag, serpents.

'I've got a thing for older women,' Mum said. 'I like strong women, somebody stern with steely grey hair.'

Dad laughed.

'I like my women younger,' he said.

So here it was. At some point in time, Mum and Dad would separate and a girlfriend would be moving in. I couldn't think of where Dad would go or how he would look after himself. He could cook and wash dishes, but I had never seen him clean anything, wash any clothes or vacuum the floor. How would he get by?

Despite sometimes feeling ashamed by the age gap of my parents and the dramatic arguments they had, I had a happy childhood and loved us being together. I spent most nights watching TV in bed with Mum and Dad. When Dad was out, Mum and I would look through the latest Argos catalogue at all the toys and games and she would buy me them, like WWE Superstars on my Gameboy; we'd have treats from Marks & Spencer's, go shopping and watch movies.

She could be explosive, but for the most part she was the one who kept everything going, ran the house, fed and clothed us, while Dad handed over his wage to her and napped in his wicker chair.

There was nowhere he wouldn't take us, though, nothing he wouldn't do for his boys.

Both of them encouraged me to read and make the most of myself. Each time we went out for a drive in the countryside or for a McDonald's, or a birthday passed, I considered it our last, waiting for the moment Mum decided I was settled into secondary school, and she was independent enough to come out, and leave Dad.

A year later, when I returned home from school one day, not long before my eleventh birthday, Mum sat us down at the top of the steps and told us that Dad had moved out. And in the coming months, Mum re-invented herself: she started working as a manager in a video game shop, sprinted away every night on her exercise bike until the broad planks of her floorboards pounded, and became interested in travel, yoga and reading. She had poshed up the house with praying Buddha statues and soapstone thinking men. Bought herself a bookshelf and filled it with classics, biographies of famous lesbians, popular Buddhism and other books that she didn't read.

'Don't worry,' Mum said. 'Your dad will always be your dad and I'll never stop you seeing him. He's got a lovely flat and you can see him every weekend.'

'Yeah,' I said without any breath.

Even though I was mostly pretending to be surprised, when of course I wasn't, the enormity of what was going to happen was unbelievable. However, no amount of foresight could have prepared me.

'I'm having a friend move in soon.'

Cal touched his palm to her face and stared at her through blue eyes, 'Who's your friend, Mummy?'

'She's called Salma,' she answered. 'She's really fun and loves cats. Her house is like a zoo, it's full of animals.'

'Can we get a cat?' I asked.

'Course we can. Soon as she moves in.'

*

On the first few Saturdays Dad would turn up, stubbled grey, shrunk into himself. He took us to Burger King, where we decided the fries were crisper than McDonald's because they were cooked in peanut oil. We ordered sundaes and talked about how things were going. He was in his fifties and sleeping in his car. Eyes watery and pale.

I watched him almost lose a plastic spoon in a swirl of ice cream.

'I swore I'd never leave my kids,' he said.

One Saturday morning he turned up as he usually did at about midday, but without the Astra hatchback his mobility entitled him to. Instead he was spending the money on smack and driving a yellow banger held together by sellotape. Staring out of the window, he looked older than he was, like a mug shot faded to a point that I could barely recognise.

Why couldn't we be normal?

Dad didn't deserve this. I had always been good. While Mum was slim and going on weekend trips to art galleries and looking into doing a degree, we were going to drive-throughs and shopping centres for something to do. His frame was a carriage of bone. The vitality had gone. The skeleton showing in the face, around the eyes, the slim bone of his forearm apparent in the wastage.

His forearms had once been bigger than my legs. His car looked and smelled like an ashtray. His face was the face of some old guy. A few months earlier, he would haul himself from the car, sunglasses on, and strut into the newsagents and strike up conversations with strangers because he couldn't bear not being noticed.

With one leg fused together and a chunk of spine missing, Dad could only move awkwardly, so he leaned his skull out through the window.

'Hello, darling,' he said in a suave camp style borrowed from Leslie Philips, which in turn was a pastiche of somebody else, 'It's *so* nice to see you.'

Mum walked to the end of the yard and stopped at the end of the gate. Cal was smashing two Action Men into one another, *pow, pow, pow* he was saying as they made bloodless contact.

'What happened to your Astra?' Mum asked Dad.

'It's in for repair.'

'Still?' she said in a high pitch.

'You don't get a courtesy car?' She looked over at Cal. 'Can you be quiet for a minute, bullet head?'

Dad opened his mouth and his tongue felt for the air.

'You always had a suspicious mind,' he said.

She held the gate. 'Is it safe?'

'Of course it's bloody safe,' he growled. 'I'll get it back next week. Anyway, where's Fanny-Anne?'

'She's inside.'

'What is she, terrified of men?' Dad asked.

'No,' Mum said. 'But she's not keen on them.'

'Keeping her from me?' he laughed.

I opened the door and climbed across the backseat on my knees. Cal got in beside me. The upholstery was nicotine yellow, smelling like an old man's suit.

'You'll look after them, won't you Frank?' Mum asked.

Dad flashed a grin, turned on the ignition, put the car in gear and we rolled down the slope of our street onto another road that curled around the back of the pub.

The end terraces had all been shops at one point. When I was little, my gran, mum and aunts took us 'down the road', as it was called, to break up the day. Dad did the same but would drive round the corner to buy *The Daily Mail* and a Mars Bar. There was still a newsagents left, run by my schoolfriend's dad; Dad called him 'Saddam' due to his resemblance to the Iraqi dictator, with his moustache and sideswept hair. The streets were cobbled with Yorkshire stone slabs that were being stolen at night, one slab at a time, and sold to poshos in the other half of town, as Mum said.

I was getting used to this zombie version of Dad, unblinking eyes and corpse-stubble.

'Now then,' Dad said. 'How've you been, young man?'

'Fine.'

He laughed. 'A man of few words. You keep your cards close to your chest.'

I shrugged. 'What does that mean?'

'You don't like to give anything away.'

Further down the street, the houses became semi-detached, which tradesmen could afford, unlike the single mums in the terraces near us.

'And what about you, bullet head?' he asked my six-year-old brother.

'I miss you, Daddy,' he said.

'Make sure you don't listen to any of the bullshit your mother says about me,' he said.

'No,' I agreed.

'I could strangle her for kicking me out. I waited a long time to be a father, I was forty-two by the time you were born. I never thought I would leave you.'

I looked over at him in the driver's seat with his glazed eyes. Every so often he would almost fall asleep and then jerk awake. The clothes he was wearing were always versions of the same theme: a black T-shirt, turned-up jeans, sturdy shoes and his leather belt with an 'M' buckle, because the 'F' for Frank was too tight around his waist. Frank wasn't even his name. Justin was. But he had changed it because it wasn't manly enough. Dad wanted to call me a real man's name like Wolfgang and sometimes still did, whereas Mum settled on Wesley Justin.

Above the suburban housing I saw the two dun-coloured towers of Grayson Heights.

'Is it as bad as people say?' I asked him. A few years ago, the place had made the news after some boys pushed a concrete block off the top and shattered the skull of a woman who worked in the bakers down the road.

'I've seen worse,' Dad said.

'What floor are you on?'

'Eleven. One from the top.'

Cal asked, 'What can you see?'

'Everything,' Dad lied. 'You can see the whole world from up there.'

'Mum said it was really nice,' I added.

'How the fuck would she know?' Dad said.

Telegraph poles linked down the street. The car moved at a creep and the towers of Grayson Heights emerged above the smaller tenements in the grey sky. The ascent steepened. Then came the maisonettes facing the heights in a semi-circle with gates and panels that were regularly painted in what Mum said was the council's attempt at caring.

She was outraged. It was something for nothing. Who was painting her fence?

Painting over the cracks didn't stop them being scum.

We pulled up a street between the shadows of the towers. Clouds hung above the high rooftops. Dad parked by the ground floor entrance. I didn't know where to go and stood at the foot of some steps, waiting for Dad to lead us inside. Dad unlocked the door and Cal ran into the foyer. The place smelled like the fluids that congeal in a bin, all baby shit and burnt hair.

I stepped into the lift and held my nose.

The doors closed.

The ascent began.

The metal tank of the lift was stainless steel, doused in piss, and I felt like crying as we moved up through the floors.

When the doors opened we walked through a rotten fire door and into a flat. The floors were all paint-speckled lino. Dad said he got all the furniture from charity shops, and he wasn't kidding. There was fat congealed like candlewax on his frying pan, awaiting heat. Everything smelled *used*. I opened a window, looked out across the city and saw the area I had grown up in.

I stopped and listened in the hallway to a conversation my dad and brother were having with somebody, a man's voice in the living room.

It took me time to stake out strangers. Often I just wouldn't speak, or I kept things to a minimum. Dad was the only adult

I could speak with, otherwise I struggled to make eye contact and was too anxious to say what I thought about anything, even with Mum. Dad loved me for whoever I was. Mum had a vision about what she wanted from me and who she wanted me to be.

I didn't want to make any statements that would define me.

I went back into Dad's bedroom. There was a view of Burley running all the way to the edge of town. The windows once again didn't have curtains. The room was bare inside, like his room in the attic, just his bed and some off-white bedsheets like a prayer shawl.

I ran my hand under the bed for the spine of the wrestling scrapbook and pulled out a ball of spandex that turned out to be Dad's wrestling mask, beside a riding crop and an eight-ball.

I loosened the knots of the mask with hurried fingers, pulled it over my head and was barely able to see through the eyeholes that were embossed with a black material. It was close, layers of stench released by the humidity of my own breath, the smell of fetid breath and aged fabric.

I snarled into the mirror, barely able to believe that this was the same mask that had been worn in the ring when Dad hailed from 'parts unknown'. When I pulled it from my head my hair was charged and stood on end. I looked from the window at the ground plan of the neighbourhood. The River Aire bent like a neck through the valley and the Leeds-Liverpool canal ran almost alongside it. An almost straight line from here down Argie Road to our street.

Dad was calling.

I went into the living room where he was laughing with a man with a beard and long dark hair.

'Hey, man!' He reached out his hand and I took it. 'Your old man has been kind enough to let me stay here for a few weeks, that cool?'

I nodded.

His drained red eyes were framed by long black bangs. He wore a chinstrap beard like the wrestler X-Pac.

'Yeah,' I said.

'Drew's helping me pay the rent and get back on my feet,' Dad said.

'Yeah.'

I had never known Dad have a friend before and was glad he wasn't alone. Drew was high-fiving my brother and seemed friendly enough and I got a good feeling about him. But his skin was pale, and he hadn't stopped sweating since I had walked in the room. He smelled like the flat. The same greasy, unwashed stench I doubted could even be corrected with a bath or a deep clean. Did he know he smelled this bad? Sometimes I would catch an unwashed stench from Dad, all folds of fat and excess muscle that had slackened in circles of flesh about his armpit. After we sat and watched WWE Heat on the TV, Dad and Drew said something about scoring and pulled out the cushions on the sofa, looking for change for the telephone box.

Dad pulled on his coat.

'You two gonna be alright if I pop out for a minute?' he asked.

I nodded. He patted me on the head and said I was a good boy.

This was the moment I had been waiting for. As Dad and Drew turned and walked out through the hallway, as we heard the latch go on the door, we pulled the cushions from the sofa and the duvet from Dad's room to make a ring.

I took my shirt off and came back into the room with a replica wrestling belt.

'What do you want to do?' I asked my brother, who was blonde and about four foot tall, with a thick back and round belly. I was taller and skinnier but could do all the moves on him; he could barely do any on me.

'I want to be the good guy,' he said.

I removed the plastic caps from my skateboarding knee pads and pulled them around my elbows to look more like a wrestler. Cal was too small to be able to lift me and I spent most of our wrestling time doing moves on him but what I wanted was to wrestle somebody my own size. I wanted to take bumps. Horrible dives like Mick Foley, who would put his body on the line to entertain the fans and show his love for the business. There was almost nothing he wouldn't do. In Japan, he took part in 'Death Matches' without any rules, where the ring ropes were replaced by barbed wire, and he took bumps on planks of wood coiled in barbed wire, with CS explosives beneath that exploded upon impact in a plume of smoke. Foley wasn't a physical specimen, nor was he a great in-ring worker; what set him apart was his willingness to sacrifice himself for our sins, our perversion, our admiration, I don't know. In the WWE, he had been thrown sixteen feet from the top of a roofed steel cage onto a table below, the moment broke kayfabe as the commentator, Jim Ross, legitimately believed Foley was dead and shouted, 'That killed him! As God is my witness, he's broken in half!' Somehow, Foley gathered himself enough to climb atop the structure, only to be slammed through the cage roof onto the canvas, the impact knocking a tooth through his nostril. This is why I did my stunts at school – letting people do wrestling slams on me on the common room floor, doing flips over people's shoulders when the impact was hard, so I could show everybody just how much I loved the business.

'We'll start off with a brawl,' I said. 'Then I'll be on top, and you have a comeback, but I stop you. Then you have a big comeback and give me the stunner, but I knock into the referee and try to hit you with my belt. Except you duck it, and hit me, then I'll blade.'

Blading was a term I had learned in *Power Slam* magazine. Dad had always described wrestlers bleeding as the result of blunt force. Imagine a sheet of paper over a rock and how the impact would slice the paper. When the skin split on the skull, blood will pour. This was known as *hardway*. A wrestler would draw blood from a legitimate strike, a *potato*. Whereas I knew most wrestlers bled by slicing their foreheads open themselves with broken ends of razors they kept taped under wrist wraps or in the referee's pocket. I didn't have a razor blade but had dismantled a pencil sharpener and had sharpened the end of the blade.

Of course, before the match could begin, we needed to make our *entrance*. We left the room to walk back in through the door in the manner of our characters with our entrance songs played from *WWE: The Music, Volume 1* on a knocked-off portable stereo. I stood in the doorway, looking down, then raised my arms as the beat dropped and I leered at an imaginary crowd.

The wrestlers in a faction called D-Generation X were a gang of rebels who insulted everybody, had a crude sense of humour and liked to point their hands at their crotches to make a V sign which meant *suck it*, a gesture I was embracing in the living room.

I announced myself as Wes 'The Hammer' Brown and Cal 'D'Lo' Brown, me shirtless and him wearing Mum's swimming costume we smuggled out earlier – a grudge match a lifetime in the making between two second-generation brothers, like the feud between Bret Hart and Owen Hart in the WWE between '93 and '96.

The same Hart brothers who carried Dad's bags in Calgary in the '70s.

I made the sound of the bell ringing to start the match and, this being a grudge match, we began with a flurry of pulled punches and took it in turns to trade blows.

When we reached the climactic moment in the match, with the imaginary referee down and hearing the boos of the crowd, I swung for my brother with the belt . He ducked it and rammed it into my forehead.

While Cal spoke to the referee on the floor, I lay face down on the stinking cushions, scoring two or three times across my forehead with the sharpener blade. I made it to my feet and a drop of blood wept from a sting, Cal hit a stunner, snapping my neck downward, and I was down for the count.

*

When Dad got home it was getting dark and we showed him our match. This time it felt even more exciting because Drew was commentating and acting as a referee. The match happened as it had before and when I took the belt shot to the head, I lay face down trying to dig as much blood out of my head as I could.

'What the bloody hell are you doing?' Dad said.

'I'm trying to juice.'

There was thunder in Dad's eyes and Drew started laughing so I laughed too. Then stopped after seeing the chuckle had not loosened the look on Dad's face.

'Where the hell have you got that from?' Dad asked.

I held the sharpener blade to the light.

'My pencil case,' I said.

'Come here,' he said. And I took up a seat next to him while he tossed my blade into the bin and a resigned look came over him. 'If you want to do a blade job, you're gonna have to get a better blade than that. Abdullah the Butcher was the best at it. He used to blade every match. He had matches with knives and forks and the fans thought he was fucking crazy. But what he'd do is put a blade between each finger and swipe across his forehead.'

I touched the scratch on my forehead.

'Did it hurt?'

'No,' he laughed. 'Not if you do it right. It's just the same as shaving: a little nick can produce a lot of blood.'

When he told me to stand up, I did, he pushed me, and I fell over.

'You're a pushover,' he grinned.

'I wasn't ready,' I said.

'Exactly. An athlete needs balance and wrestlers are on balance all of the time.'

I looked over at Drew who was rolling a cigarette and nodding a wry smile.

'Stand like this,' Dad said. 'With your feet apart. This is a split-legged stance. Now watch what happens.'

He pushed me and I didn't move.

'You see?' he said. 'Balance.'

He snatched the back of my hand in his and pushed it downward. I winced. With a flick of the wrist, he sent me tumbling to the floor.

I held my hand and looked up at him.

'Second lesson,' he said. 'It doesn't matter how big or strong you are, leverage is the basis of all joint manipulation.'

'Wow.' I said, 'Can you show me again?'

'I'll teach you everything you want to know,' he said. 'Looks like you're smartened up to it, and better I teach you than you end up bloody killing yourselves. The first thing a wrestler learns is how to fall.'

'Can we do that now?'

'Not in here. Not really.'

'What about next week?'

'Yeah.'

I exchanged a stunned look with my bother.

'How do wrestlers throw punches?' I asked.

Before I could see it coming he clubbed me in the face with his hand. It made a loud cupped slap.

'Did that hurt?' he asked.

'No.'

'Trick is not to throw too many. The more you throw, the less impact they have.'

'How did you do it?'

He showed me how to make a cup shape with his open palm and curled fingers, then punch the sweet spot between the fault line of the jaw and the neck to effect a loud lop when full contact was made.

Dad cooked a curry he had learned to make when he was living in a Japanese mountain monastery. For the rest of the evening, me and Cal clubbed one another in the face with open-palmed strikes and Dad broke kayfabe for the first time. When he trained, he was taught a few basic holds, some reversals and how to fall. The classic kayfabe line when training new wrestlers was that you had to learn how to fall to protect yourself, it was safer to go with the throw or slam than to try and resist it.

When Dad had his first match, he was thrown in with a veteran who began telling him what to do, where to move, when to respond to the crowd and when to sell.

There were still tough guys in wrestling though. Many wrestlers were legitimate athletes and fighters, as WWE itself was often at pains to stress. Wrestling itself could be tough. On Hulk Hogan's first training session, his leg was broken by Hiro Matsuda just to see if he would come back. Obviously, he did and the rest is history.

The promoter of Stampede Wrestling, Stu Hart, the guy Dad worked for in Calgary, would 'stretch' wrestlers in the gym under his house known as *the dungeon* to toughen them up.

There was time for one last match before we went home. We began by wrestling this time and not what Dad called 'Cowboys and Indians'. A punch should mean something and be protected. We went back and forth while Drew narrated the action in an American accent, All Saints' 'Never Ever' playing on mute on the TV; he was commentating one minute, on his knees the next, to count like the referees did in the WWE, with a quick count shouted out every time our shoulders were pinned.

After getting beaten down with a flurry of pretend kicks and punches by my brother, I began my comeback, found the *fighting spirit* to block two of Cal's haymakers to return with my own before body slamming him onto the cushions, the woman from downstairs began beating her ceiling with a broom handle, and I climbed the top of the sofa. As I looked out, I was at Madison Square Garden, standing on the top turnbuckle in front of twenty-thousand fans at WrestleMania as I torpedoed through the air like a snapshot in a pro wrestling magazine and drove my elbow down into the chest of my brother. A haze of dirt billowed from the cushions and as the crowd roared, Drew counted the three.

I waved the plastic belt we bought from Toys R' Us above my head as if it was the world title. The banging from downstairs carried on and I began to get dressed. I touched my finger to the sting on my forehead to find the blade had barely left a scratch.

Dad said I was allowed to pull out the poster of 'Bone Collector' Bruce Logan, who was out in Japan representing the best of British, from my Power Slam magazine, and stuck it up on his wall. He had his own pose, one hand grabbing the wrist of the other, gurning into shot. Then we got our things together, descended the lift, and drove back down the valley in the dark.

When we got home, there was no way to sneak round Mum and her new girlfriend. Salma had moved in, but without the cat as promised. She was an opera singer whose self-restriction and entitlement could be heard in her tightly controlled enunciations. When Mum wasn't around, we weren't allowed in the same room as her. She read *The Guardian* and had very strong views about things we liked, things like wrestling and football and being a man. But also the food we ate and the TV we watched: nothing was up to her standard. Most of the time she would end up in vicious rows with Mum, plates and dishes would be thrown and when things got really bad they would buy us chocolate and promise us a day out.

When I came into the living room, I tried to skip past them while they sat there drinking and kissing.

'Hello, boys,' Mum said, pleased with herself.

'Did you have a nice time at your dad's?' Salma asked with red lips, wine glass in hand.

'Yeah,' I answered.

Cal nodded and I stared at him to check that the pink knuckle strikes beneath his jawline had faded. They had.

'Did you do anything?'

'Not really,' I said. 'Just watched TV.'

Mum's eyes rolled and when she did this, you could see the small crack of her real eye beneath her contact lens.

'That it?'

'I don't know. Just normal stuff. We went to the park,' I said.

Salma added in her strangled way, 'You can join us if you like? We're about to put a film on.'

I didn't want to watch a film with her and neither did she.

'No, it's alright.'

'Are you sure?'

'Yeah, I'm really tired,' I said.

'Night.'

Then I ran upstairs.

I went to my room first, chased by my brother and placed my replica wrestling belt in prime position on my bookshelf. Then I leapt down the stairs three or four at a time using the handrail and slinging myself like Spiderman.

I ran downstairs into the bathroom, took off my scum-scented clothes and ran a bath. Mum knew dad's place stunk but never said. The fabric was filled with a greasy stiffness. It smelled of cooking oil, tobacco leaf, farted-on sofas, food waste, sour hair and other men, and clung to me like my shame.

It was on my fingers. Dried beneath my hangnails. Smoky hair. I took my clothes off, stuffed them in the washing basket on top of Salma's purple polka-dot dress and still smelled of it.

How did Dad live like this?

I had never thought of Dad having emotions.

Not in a normal, *human* kind of way. He didn't spend hours on the phone like Mum did. Dad didn't have friends, not the way I did, nobody he socialised with had anything in common with him. No emotional connection. He was almost entirely self-contained in a way that made my need to share my feelings and talk about other people feel effeminate and wimpy. Where I was anxious and self-aware he was assured and oblivious. I had never seen him cry. I had believed he was indestructible. When I was five I had been desperate for him to take me to a monster truck show I had seen on posters plastered onto lampposts and shop windows. On the evening before we were due to go, he was glassed with a bottle of Champagne and had to spend the night in hospital.

When I woke up Mum sat me down and holding onto my shoulders, stared into my eyes and said, 'I'm sorry Wesley but Daddy was hurt last night. I don't think you'll be able to see the monster trucks.'

I began to cry.

'It'll be okay,' she said. 'Your dad is tough.'

I knew that. Dad had wrestled the toughest guys in the world, had been hit by chairs and slammed through tables. Nothing could stop him. I was crying because I would miss the monster trucks.

At eleven am that morning, Dad discharged himself with a bandage across his head and took me to the show.

Later in the afternoon he dropped me off, bought a knuckle duster, went round to the house of the person who had glassed him and beat him up. And everybody else who lived there.

Presently the water in the bath was only ankle height, only deep enough to redden around my skinny shins while trails folded in between my legs. The bathroom mirror was too high for me to see my torso from the floorboards but here I could see the misted image of my skinny body.

I practiced my poses. Double bicep. Side chest. Compared to Dad, my arms weren't even the size of his wrists. I was lean and, if I tensed up I could trace the outline of a six-pack on my abdomen. The segments of my stomach muscles didn't align exactly and formed two uneven stacks. The dream was to have a six-pack that was visible even without tensing. That and about ten stone more of solid muscle, arms and a chest I could be proud of.

I flexed my biceps and lunged into a most-muscular pose, hands clasped, bringing out the small arch of my neck. I was built like a boy, with thin slivers of muscle growing over my boyish frame, and a man-sized dick. Some of the other guys in year nine at school were already six five; I would never be a giant, but I was more ripped than anybody else.. I flexed the bridge of my neck and my biceps until the mist clouded my image, practicing for the man I might one day become. I wouldn't have to hide in my room, away from people like Salma. I wouldn't be afraid to express myself, I would be strong and heroic like Dad, I thought, as I disappeared into mist.

*

The next Saturday morning I went downstairs to the kitchen and poured myself a bowl of Rice Krispies. The balance between the crisped rice puffs and the level of milk had to be just right, otherwise they would be too dry, or I would be left with mush. I sloshed the milk at a deft angle and stopped just as I hit the sweet spot. It was an intuitive feeling. An instinct born of judging the splash every day. I listened to the happy medley of the snap, crackle and pop, then opened the door to the fridge, put the milk back and bent over to place the cereal alongside whatever posh shit Mum was eating these days. Granola, muesli, bagels.

These weren't foods we ever ate.

They sat there like the books on Mum's shelves or the ornaments she still measured the distances between with a ruler. The house itself was still in a state of near disrepair; Mum's bedroom had been decorated and was open and airy, while the floorboards in the rest of the house were still browned and paint-licked and our attic bedroom was filled with toys but also bare.

There was an iMac on an antique desk at the corner of the room. Mum had convinced my grandad to lend her the money to buy it, based on educational reasons. Nobody used it other than me. I had begun writing surrealist passages on existential themes.

I had shown the piece to my English teacher Mr Firth, who had got me interested in reading and delivered his classes in a downbeat, cynical, blokey way that I connected with. He liked it. And I was now writing a sequence of stories called *Tales From the Opium Farm* in the gothic excess and psychological horror of Edgar Allan Poe, the way life itself seemed infused with dread, the suffering in simply *being*, to his mind; the hideousness of mysteries and the horrific burden of conscience filled him with despair. One of my stories, called 'St Anger', was about a guy who went around late at night engaging strangers in Socratic dialogues and beat some sense into the ones whose answers were too stupid.

This was exactly who I was.

It was a work of profound genius, there was no doubt about that, and I would become a writer to channel these energies and I would get the respect I deserved. Despite being a nerd and a loser, deep down I knew I had something special in me and when my book was published people would see who I really was.

I went into the living room and sat down on the new red futon Mum had bought. There was a bottle of wine left out by the sofa, which was unusual for her, as her need was to always control and tidy and which naturally led her to enrol as a mature student on an Environmental Science course. She talked about how much she would enjoy going into restaurants in her uniform and enforcing the law.

I thought of them kissing and then got distracted by a bullfinch bungeeing from the windowsill outside. The Battenberg slabs we had grown up with in the yard had been smashed up and replaced by a lawn with cherry blossom. I lifted the spoon to my mouth. I didn't want them to get up. How good would that be? When they were together, they both played a version of themselves that they didn't when they were with me or my brother alone. Mum suddenly relaxed from the pretence of this aspirational self and all of Salma's contrived warmth disappeared.

Most days after school, Mum wouldn't be home from work until about six o'clock and Salma would shout at us if we came downstairs or wanted to engage her in any way. One day I would be a wrestler, and everybody would respect me. I would be too big and strong for Salma to fuck me about, or the kids at school who shouted 'Jew' at me and had created a whole anti-Semitic character for me simply because I liked saving my money and had dark hair.

I heard heavy, flat-footed steps down the stairs. It was Cal.

'Hello, bum head,' I said.

'What you having?'

'Rice Krispies,' I said.

'No Coco Pops?'

'Don't think so.'

'Smackdown's on soon,' he said.

'I know.'

With some money from Dad, I had made a gym in the cellar which I liked to call 'The Dungeon' in honour of Stu Hart. I went downstairs and had a mid-morning workout, a circuit of upper body exercises amidst the chalky walls and hard stone floor. When I was done, I drank a protein shake, took two amino acid pills and went back to the attic to watch WWE Smackdown with Cal.

The opening match featured my favourite stable, *The Radicalz*. These were an upstart team of smaller, technical wrestlers who had jumped ship from rival promotion, WCW, because the old guard of Hulk Hogan and his cronies on the booking team thought them too small to be pushed as main eventers.

The tag match began with chain-wrestling, actual hold-for-hold grappling rather than pulled punches, between Chris Jericho and Dean Malenko. Dad had said you can tell how good a worker was simply by watching them move. Malenko's transitions were so smooth. I watched him, not looking at his opponent, just his movements and his feet were full of waltz, and jive, and tango.

'Dean Malenko's head looks too big for his body,' Cal said.
I laughed, 'Yeah. He's good though, isn't he?'
'One of the best.'
'I want to know how to do that reversal,' I said, seeing the smoothness with which he worked.
'His dad was a wrestler too, you know?'
'Probably why he's so good.'

Then there was Chris Benoit. He was billed at five-ten but was nearer five eight. What he lacked in height, he made up for in densely packed muscle and intensity. He was my favourite wrestler. He tagged-in to confront 'Scotty Too Hotty', a breakdancing master who was a carefree fan favourite and wrestled in the usual pro wrestling style. But Benoit was his own genre. Every chop, kick, or suplex was done with maximum intensity.

I felt my gut brace when I watched him.

Everything he did felt real. His conviction was real. The way he carried himself. If everybody wrestled more like him, nobody would call wrestling fake then: they would respect it for what it was.

I didn't care about good guys vs bad guys, I cared about real guys vs fake guys. And Benoit hit hard and sold with a snap. It was exhilarating. He was small, fierce, intense. The Rabid Wolverine. I wanted to be just like him, even more so than Dad, I wanted to let my anger pour through my performance; what would be real was my emotions.

I could hear laughter from Mum's bedroom. It sounded as if they were tumbling about, giggles muffled.

I turned up the volume.

'Do you know Benoit trained at The Dungeon?' I said.
'Really?'
'Like Dad.'
'Wow.'

There was pride and disbelief in my brother's answer. Stu Hart and The Dungeon were regularly name-dropped on WWE programming. It was still regarded as the best school out there and much of the elite talent in wrestling at the time had been trained there.

Another shriek. Salma.

'I wish Dad still lived here,' Cal said.

'Me too,' I answered.

I did think so. Or if he didn't, at least Mum should have found a better girlfriend. I had no objection to Mum being gay. But I didn't tell anybody about it, much in the same way I didn't tell anybody where Dad lived or who he lived with. The details of my life were kept to myself. These things didn't matter so much if people didn't know. Kids at school would notice Mum hanging around with Salma and I would deny she was anything other than a friend and she definitely didn't live with us.

Last year I had seen a friend of mine, Dorothy, who was a skater and came from a bohemian lower-middle-class family in Headingley and unafraid to admit her dad was gay, break down in tears in class when the other kids dug her about it.

Your dad's gay!

That's *disgusting*.

He sticks his dick up other guy's arses?

He sucks other guys' dicks?

I felt bad for her but did nothing. This made me feel worse, but I didn't want any suspicion falling on me.

An operatic scream.

We had our own dungeon.

Salma ran through her slow diminuendo.

*

By the summer of 1999 I was thirteen; Dad turned up in the latest vehicle he had procured: a hard-edged, silver-coloured Ford that looked like a vision from the seventies. Inside, it had mustard-coloured décor, sellotaped windows and a radio we could pick up Leeds United matches on while we spent weekends driving around council estates, parking up somewhere and seeing the onrush of people coming to stare at the range of knocked-off music tapes in the boot, while me and my brother sat there, not knowing where to look.

We got in the car. Cal in the back, me in the passenger seat. 'My boys,' Dad said.

'Why do you always say that?' I asked.

'Sorry!' He laughed, 'You get more like your mother every day.'

We drove out past Kirkstall, up the long steep valley and toward Bramley Fall Park where the grass would be long enough and secluded enough for us to take some bumps.

Today, we were going to a field to learn how to fall.

We had tried to hire a leisure centre, buy judo mats and searched for wrestling gyms near us. I had been in touch with a wrestling school in Buckinghamshire also. It was called Bulldog's. The place where my hero, Bruce Logan, had trained. The latest edition of PowerSlam magazine featured a centrefold pull-out with him draped in the Union Jack, championship slung over his shoulder. I had also emailed Stu Hart's son, Bruce Hart, who was now running Stampede Wrestling in Calgary and the plan was to learn the basics and then complete my training in 'The Dungeon'.

From there?

I had an idea that I would travel to Japan and wrestle a Strong Style, hard chops and German suplexes, which was a sort of Heimlich manoeuvre except you pull somebody backwards and slam them directly on their upper back. My lack of size or character wouldn't be a problem there; like Chris Benoit, I would be a wrestler's wrestler, admired not for a gimmick but for my technique.

How real I would make it.

We got out of the car. Cal ran along to the sparser grass. I followed and swept the woodland floor for branches and twigs. Dad hobbled toward us in the distance.

With his left knee fused, his leg didn't bend or straighten, and he stuck it out to drive himself forward like a gondolier.

'Ooh ah,' he growled. 'If I was a horse, they would have shot me!'

'Why would you be shot for being a horse?' I asked.

'Because when you're too old and knackered to be a racehorse, they put you down.'

'Good job you're not a horse,' I said.

Dad told us to warm up with a few hundred squats and push-ups and followed it up with a sequence of rolls: over the shoulder to the left, over the shoulder to the right, forward roll to forward roll, backward to standing, then forward again. The idea, he said, was to improve co-ordination and ring awareness.

Was this what WWE guys did?

I'd never seen a wrestler roll on TV.

When Dad had finished critiquing our scruffy efforts, he told me to quarter-squat, fall backward and throw my arms out like a cross.

I did, but not everything happened at the same time.

Falling backward was unnatural enough; what was nearly impossible was landing with your palms and soles all at the same time. It was like letting yourself fall backward into somebody's arms, except knowing nobody was there.

'You look like a scarecrow falling out of an aeroplane,' he said.

He told Cal to crouch on his hands and knees, then instructed me to squat down deep, chin on my chest, and pushed me hard enough for me to fall over my brother.

I threw my arms out like a cross at the last second.

Bang.

All the wiry connections of my body landed with a thud, elbows shooting a tingling pain.

'Was that any better?' I said dusting mud from my funny bone.

'Again,' he said.

I squatted and he pushed me.

This was repeated. Dad never got angry. He just said *again*.

Who is this guy? I thought, dusting myself off for about the thirtieth time, looking up at his bulk in a black T-shirt.

I was incapable of bumping correctly and he wouldn't tolerate a nearly-bump or a good try. Yet he didn't seem to be frustrated or enjoying himself at any point. He had stone-killer eyes.

'I'm bored,' Cal said, but we did this for most of the day. My brother was obsessed with wrestling, but not as much as I was. I don't think anybody loved wrestling as much as I did. Cal played the video games, had the action figures, watched the shows, as did I, but for me it was more than an obsession. It was everything I cared about and contained all the meaning in the world for me. To be in the business, to be like Dad, was all I wanted.

By now, hours in, my body was bruised and cut. Cal was wandering around the high grasses thrashing a stick against the chaff. It hurt to throw myself against the ground, and already the wind had been knocked out of me two or three times. Inwardly I longed to learn *moves* and sequences. The sun beat down. Even holds and technical wrestling. But this wouldn't happen until I could bump. The first thing a wrestler learned was how to fall. Dad was quite clear on that. And while it was boring and painful, it was still *wrestling*. I was being trained to wrestle by Earl Black in the way that he had learned to wrestle and the wrestlers before him had learned to wrestle; this was a tradition that connected me to the mythic realm of men.

I rolled back onto my feet after about the fiftieth and bent over, panting.

'What were the rings like, that you trained in?' I asked.

'Depends,' he said chewing something barely visible with his false teeth. 'Some of those old British ones were boxing rings. Back then, if you were a wrestler, you needed the same fighting licence as a boxer. Queensbury rules.'

'When did you hurt your back?' Cal asked.

'I was wrestling the 'Indian Rubber Man' Johnny Walker. He suplexed me, and the beam under the ring broke, which smashed two more discs in my back. I was thrown from the ring and realised that I couldn't move. When the crowd noticed, they started kicking me. The only person to come to my rescue was one of the wrestler's wives, Kay Noble,' he was laughing now, barely able to finish.

'She was also a wrestler,' he said, eyes smiling, a roar of laughter. 'And knocked out four guys before dragging me to safety.'

After a while, the pain had begun to persuade me that throwing myself at the grass wasn't a good idea, but this story inspired me. My ribs were aching and my joints stiff. The ridge of my hips, the bony curve I didn't know I had, slammed and slammed again, feeling *bone*-like. As we laughed the aches disappeared, I was taking bumps like Dad had taken bumps in North America, Europe, Singapore, Malaysia, Australia, Japan, and I understood how that life was taken away from him by his broken back and I thought about his time as a bouncer in Sydney, how the police had forced him out of Australia and he moved to England to go cold turkey. To Leeds, where he kidnapped and re-trained attack dogs, and where he would eventually meet and break up with Mum and live in a skyrise, subletting his council flat to scumbags to pay for smack.

Again, he'd say.

Never angry. Never losing patience.

Again.

We did this for hours.

Then days.

Again.

Then weeks.

Again.

Until I knew how a wrestler falls.

*

I picked myself off the mat at the Dojo. It had been thirteen years since I took bumps in the field with Dad. He retired at the age of twenty-seven and now I was beginning my career at the same age. There felt a symmetry to this. I was continuing where he had left off.

Snap.

I threw myself at the canvas. The force, the motion, the fall was all the same but padded by the machinery of the ring.

It was more forgiving than a grass field but the first thing you realise when you get in the ring is the physicality of it. How much everything in it hurts. The turnbuckle pads feel like a boxing glove against your face. The ropes like cheese wire across your back. The canvas burns and the boards beneath it are solid. Watching wrestling on TV didn't give a sense of what it felt like every time you hit the mat. I was already thinking differently about every wrestling match I had ever watched, all the bumps I had never felt.

Even bumping *the right way* was a violence on the body and had more impact in the ring than I realised, even with the padding; it would be nigh on impossible without.

The bumps still felt the same. It didn't matter how long apart they were, like an echo, stretched across time.

I got to my feet, kidneys bruised, feeling the air knocked from me. Even though this was make-believe, it was more real than whatever my life was before. It made me feel alive.

Trev wiped his feet on the apron before stepping through the ropes while we watched ringside.

'Respect the ring,' he said. 'You always wipe your feet before you get in. You wouldn't just walk into somebody's house, would you? It's about respect but also hygiene. Nobody wants to bump in your shit.'

We nodded.

I sensed a bond growing between us, but nobody spoke. It was written into the code of the place. We were starting on the bottom rung and it didn't matter what we said.

Trev snapped himself backward. The ring crashed. Girder and board snapping and brimming with the impact. We practiced on crash mats first, then Trev called us up onto the ring apron and one by one, we entered the squared circle, ready to throw ourselves at the mat.

'If you fear the bump, it will hurt you,' Trev said. 'You need to attack it.'

Hulkamania was first in, quarter-squatted, pursed his lips and... nothing.

He just stood there like he was about to shit himself.

'Attack it,' Trev said. 'Attack!'

The tension of the wait and the fear in his eye were palpable. I exchanged glances with Adem.

Hulkamania got set, threw up his arms and collapsed in a pile.

This happened about thirty times. Each time he looked more and more like he was having a seizure, the bumps were twisted and ugly, and the falls were ugly like they killed him inside.

'I'm sorry,' Hulkamania said this time struggling to relieve himself from his deep squat position. 'I just can't go on.'

There was a twinkle in Trev's eye.

'You sure?' he said. 'Non-refundable?'

Trev gave him a hand and leaned back to pull him to his feet.

Hulkamania nodded, accepted his dream was over and, as his head dropped, I felt the enormous relief he felt as he walked over to grab his stuff and returned to the outside world.

Nothing was said in the aftermath. Tim and then Adem had a go, both better than what had come before but lacked the snap of Trev's back bump. When it was my turn, still bruised from Marilyn, I wanted to prove myself. In the summer before I went to college Dad took me out to a field near my house and taught me how to fall.

We did it over and over.

Until my elbows felt broken, and my ribs were aching, I was slammed and slammed again.

I got so good at bumping I would take big flips at school. Have some idiots throw me up over their head, tuck and roll into a perfect flat pack bump on the common room floor.

I quarter-squatted, snapped back, exploded into the mat. Soon as I hit, I recoiled and turned toward Trev.

He raised his eyebrow and said, 'You sure you've not done that before?'

I shrugged.

'Beginner's luck,' I said.

He touched his chin.

'Did you say you were a lecturer?'

'Well, sort of,' I said.

'Do it again,' he said. 'This time harder.'

I steadied myself for another and turned look at Trev while he and Owen carried on talking.

'He's called Wes Brown, isn't it?' Owen said. 'He could have a gimmick where he's Rampage Brown's *mini-me*.'

They laughed.

I ran my tongue around my mouth. Something ached in my hip. My knees were burned.

'Say that again in six months,' I said.

And hit the mat.

*

The next day I squatted next to Trev on the mats beside the ring.

'What's Marilyn's problem?' I asked.

He cracked a smile.

'Marilyn is Marilyn,' he said.

'I mean, does he think it makes him look hard or what?'

'Marilyn trains people the way he was trained. When he started, the business was on its arse after World of Sport was cancelled. Most shows were tributes to the WWE in front of ten people in a village hall with people dressed up as The Undertaker and stuff like that.'

I laughed.

'So, he thinks we have it easy?'

'You do,' he said. 'Wrestling schools didn't really exist then. They only opened as a way to keep the business alive, and they made it tough, especially when you were like Marilyn and just some skinny fifteen-year-old. They beat the shit out of him.'

When Adem counted his ten it was my turn, and I counted my ten and took us to four hundred.

We were only a couple of weeks in but already feeling close as a group.

I didn't even realise Owen had been listening until I heard him pipe up from behind, squatting away.

'I heard he scurfed The Dude at training last night.'

'Is he alright?' Trev asked, face expressionless, but enough in his response to suggest he wasn't happy.

'I think so. Marilyn roughed him up pretty hard, but not too bad.'

'What for?' I asked.

'I don't know,' Owen said. 'One of the guys who was there said it was to teach him a lesson. He was getting too comfortable.'

'For fuck's sake,' I sighed.

Trev had a hard look in his eye, still saying nothing; I knew he wouldn't because we were all scared it would happen to us. What would you do if you came out against somebody like Marilyn? Let's say you beat him up, what then? He'd make your life hell. He went back years with every promoter and knew all the boys.

He would never try it with me though, I thought. Not in a million years. I just had that aura about me, I guessed, that let him know if he ever touched me, I'd batter him.

'Is Marilyn actually hard?' I asked.

'The thing with Marilyn is,' Trev laughed, 'even if you could beat him up, he's one of the toughest, craziest motherfuckers out there. He'd probably enjoy it. I've seen him take a pasting. He puts on this front, but really he's had a hard time, and got bullied really bad when he started out. He had a hard childhood.

I think his dad was a drinker and used to beat him up. He got bullied. And when he started training, schools were new and wouldn't break kayfabe. They beat the fuck out of him. But whatever you did to him, to his credit he's a psycho, he'd come back with weapons and God knows what. He's legit nuts.'

At the end of the session, we climbed around the apron and two guys at a time rolled in the ring and the rest of us watched. Adem went with Trev and Trev showed his quality, transitioning from one hold to another, always a step or two ahead. Even though this was still *working*, it had a competitive element, like a hip hop dance battle. They grappled back and forth, Trev coming out on top, flipping him with an arm drag and both of them rose on guard. It was time to move on. Owen was standing there. Adem walked toward me and stretched out his hand. I let it wait there for a moment, making Owen sweat he tagged in on the other side. I vaulted over the top rope and felt my feet moving beneath me. We circled, cagey at first, before locking up with a collar-and-elbow and I felt him trying to grab a hold as soon as he could, trying to take control.

He threw my left arm up, ducked beneath it and took me down with a waistlock. I scrambled, correcting my position to gain the advantage. Squeezing his back close to my chest and looking for a headlock but he grabbed one of his own. I worked my way back to my feet. Headlock clamped; I knew how to escape. The reversals Dad had taught me were fifty years old in some cases and impressive in their own right. Stuff nobody had seen before. Manoeuvres straight out of lore.

I swivelled, turning his forearm in on itself and seizing a top wristlock before transitioning it into a headlock using my arm like a lasso around his head. As soon as it was on, I reached round with my other arm, switched it into another headlock and then reached round for a hammerlock, bending his arm behind his back.

'Slow down.' Owen said. 'Make it mean something.'

I held the hammerlock.

'That was cool,' Trev said. 'Owen's right. Don't give it all away so soon. But you sure you've never wrestled before?'

I shrugged.

*

While Trevor had taken most of my training sessions, Jack Tanner sometimes filled in, but being on the intensive beginning course meant I was allowed to go to other sessions through the week. Marilyn Draven ran 'psychology' classes on a Tuesday night which were supposed to be about narrative logic and, after a few weeks of training, I felt it was time to see what he could teach me and maybe win him round.

The session had gone on ten minutes and I was already regretting it.

'Who trained you?' he shouted. 'Who fucking trained you?' he screamed.

Marilyn knew who trained me.

'Trevor and JT.'

'Trevor and JT are your friends. I'm not your friend. I fucking hate you. Get out of the ring.'

I got out of the ring.

As soon as I was out, he called me back in for a guy called Jay to work a *heat* on me. His job was to look dominant, own the ring while he beat me up. My job was to react as if his strikes were real, to gain sympathy from an imaginary audience.

With Jay dominant, he g-walked around me monologuing to the archway walls covered in asbestos-looking funk. In a match situation, this would be where I make my comeback but Marilyn yelled, 'Stop.'

We were motionless while he addressed Jay, 'Your movement is awful. You look like a fucking robot.'

Jay took it with a sad dignity because the thing about Marilyn was he's always right.

'You,' Marilyn said to me. 'Work a heat.'

I worked the most generic sort of heat, circling and stomping, like some sort of violent vulture. The ring squeaked and bounced with stomps and strikes. There was the action itself and then the melodrama of the movement. Everything needed to be big. He *sold* theatrically over to the ropes and I used them to strangle him. Then I gave him a suplex.

'Stop,' Marilyn yelled. 'Why did you do that?'

'I don't know.'

'Why don't you know?'

'I just did it.'

'The more moves you do the less they mean,' he said. 'Who's he, fucking superman?'

'No.'

'Well he must be if he can kick out of all of this.' He flicked the tail of his undercut. 'Either that, or your moves are shit.'

*

I knew it would be tough but I never expected this. While Trev was gentle and taught me a lot, Marilyn was brutal and would tell you exactly where you were going wrong. There was nowhere to hide without the crowds and the costumes. Stripped of the theatre, this was just two guys wearing sportswear play-fighting in an archway while another guy screamed at them. I rubbed my elbow. My knees burned. Something in my back ached.

Marilyn said we had five minutes to plan a match. Jamal is a European powerlifting champion. He was six feet tall and fourteen stone. This would be small by Wrestle World standards, but he was on the larger side for British wrestling. His gimmick was that he's a powerlifter, and he called himself 'Jay Langston'. He was going to wear his medals to the ring. His entrance music was going to be 'Black Skinhead' by Kanye West.

I got in with Jay. He was babyface, I was heel. So I acted all cowardly and sheepish about facing him. Nobody liked a chicken-shit. I always dreamed of being a bad guy. The role seemed like a persona I could pour all my aggression, frustration, and existential angst into that came from the dark shadows within me, in the aspects of my personality I had chosen to reject and wear it like a mask.

I wanted to be hated. To take pleasure in disgrace. It was the family business.

So when he tried to lock up, I backed off. He tried to lock up again and I poked my body through the ropes, out of bounds. When we finally locked up, collar-and-elbow, he heaved me off and I took a back bump and shook my head in disgust.

'Stop,' Marilyn said. 'Both of you, stop.'

'What am I going to say?' Marilyn asked.

'I don't know,' I answered.

'Why are you bumping around for him like that?'

'Because he's a powerlifter.'

'Yeah, but he's not Andre the fucking Giant, is he? Look at him. You're roughly the same size. He might be stronger than you but it wouldn't be obvious on a show and you wouldn't fall about like that, would you?'

Marilyn talked us through the choreography of a headlock sequence.

He called it to us step-by-step.

We locked up and Jay powered me into the corner to demonstrate his strength. The same thing happened again. The third time, he backed away sportingly and released his grip. But I snatched a headlock and wouldn't let go.

There's a lot more to the sequence that I still can't remember. We got every step wrong. Marilyn screamed at us and we started again. This happened about thirty times.

I felt like I was melting but also took a perverted joy in pretending to not be affected. It would make a good story. Marilyn screamed at us for nearly three hours. Until we ran out of time.

We sat down before we got changed and Marilyn asked, 'What is wrestling?'

'It's a spectacle,' I said, thinking of Roland Barthes. *The virtue of all-in wrestling is that it is the spectacle of excess. The grandiloquent truth of gestures.*

'That's the WWE answer,' he said correctly.

'It's sports entertainment,' Jay said.

'What does that fucking mean?' Marilyn asked.

We didn't know.

'Wrestling is storytelling' he said. 'We tell stories.'

Marilyn wasn't finished.

'Why do you wrestle?' he asked.

'To win,' Jay said.

'And what does your character get if you win?'

More silence.

'He gets paid more,' Marilyn said. 'At its most basic level, that's your motivation. Every wrestler wants to get paid. You get the winner's purse.'

We nodded.

The winner's purse was a kayfabe idea. Wrestlers don't actually get more money for winning than losing. They have an agreed rate like any freelancer.

Marilyn asked me, 'Who's your character? Why does he wrestle?'

'Dirk Dresden.'

'Who the fuck is Dirk fucking Dresden?'

'He's a Judge Dredd-style guy, maybe from the near future.'

'The near future?'

'Yeah.'

He replied high-pitched in disbelief, 'How the fuck can he be from the future?'

'I don't know...Because, *wrestling*?'

He quivered with rage.

'If he was from the future, why the fuck would he wrestle?'

'No idea.'

'You're supposed to be intelligent, a fucking writer, and you're telling me you're going to be a law enforcement official from the fucking future? If that were true, why the fuck would he wrestle?'

Part of me had already left my body and was on the Tube home. But I was still here engaged in a dialogue with a sociopathic Socrates, my sense of self punished by rhetorical questions. I could take the bumps. The stomps. The physical abuse. It's the questions that hurt. Marilyn finds a weakness, a vulnerability, and attacks it. I told myself I don't want to be a wrestler. But wrestling was my history. Growing up, the days in the field, Dad's scrapbooks. Poses and action shots. Old sepia. Earl Black.

Sometimes I was still the teenage boy who dreamed of lacing up his boots and getting in the ring. Take bumps on the bare floorboards. Cut my own forehead with a pencil sharpener blade just to be like Dad.

'Why do you wrestle?' he demanded in his Gravesend scream, 'Not your fucking character. *You.*'

'Because my dad was a wrestler.'

'What was he called?'

'Earl Black.'

'There you go,' he said. 'You're Earl Black Jr.'

*

A few days later the Leeds sky was a deep mauve when I got to Akbar's. A bus stopped a few feet ahead of me and Dad hobbled off it and down the street. Having seen me he moved like a speed-walker in slow motion, a crazy grin on his face, eyes full of charisma.

'Hello, young man,' he smiled.

'Dad.'

We went inside and ordered lagers and poppadoms, which Dad sat breaking up in plate-like, arthritic hands. The light glared from above and shone into the welt-mark compressions across his skull. Then he looked up. His tortoise head and eyes, the lines furrowed across his red-skinned forehead relaxed.

'It's like looking in a mirror,' he smiled.

'A crazy mirror.'

He laughed, as he did before telling any joke. 'You're just like your mother.'

The table rocked with his roar. The more miffed I looked the more he laughed. People stared, I touched my palm to the side of my face.

Behind him was a vast white column and palm trees and glowing orange walls filled with people eating at tables with shield-like naans and talking in Leeds accents. It was grey and wet outside, getting dark. It was home.

'What's wrong?' he said, eyes wet with laughter, voice cracking, 'You're not embarrassed of your dad are you?'

I shrugged. 'No,' I said.

'You look at me with such disdain!' He smiled. 'You've always told me off. Even when you were a kid. I like how you summed me up a few years ago: *a wolverine of confusion, obfuscation, and forgetfulness, voluntarily divorced from conventional reality.*'

I laughed. 'Pretty sure I never said that.'

'Oh well,' he sighed. 'I have an unconventional grasp of reality.'

That he did.

'When you started training,' I asked. 'Did they give you a hard time? I've heard stories about guys protecting the business and not wanting to break kayfabe, like how they broke Hulk Hogan's leg.'

He paused, monstered a popadom dribbled in mango chutney, and drank half his pint.

'When I started wrestling in 1965, I worked for Hal Morgan, an ex-wrestler who promoted in Sydney. There were hundreds of servicemen's clubs, surf clubs, sailing clubs, rugby league clubs, soccer clubs, which had wrestling every week. The wrestlers were wrestling every night, sometimes twice a night, dashing from one venue to another. This is how we gained the experience.'

'What did they teach you?'

'Just the basics, how to fall, holds, a few strikes. Then you'd work with somebody more experienced than you and learn that way. Wrestling in a gym isn't like wrestling in front of a crowd. The psychology and timing which is so important for a good match can only be learned in the ring.'

I raised my pint to my lips.

'Did you learn the structure?'

'The what?'

Poppadom shards had fallen around his neck. He paused again. Tuned into the past.

'You know?' I explained as he looked back at me in confusion. 'The set-up, shine, heat, comeback, big heat, comeback, finish.'

'We never did any of that. Some guys liked to plan the finish, but we just called it all out there. The Briscoe's finishes were so long you had to start at the beginning of the bloody match, I could never remember them.'

Calling it out there, or on the fly, was the improvised style I thought all wrestlers used, before I started at the Dojo.

'So you didn't plan anything?' I asked.

'Wrestling was simpler back then. You didn't have everybody killing themselves, jumping around everywhere, trying to be acrobats. I could get them up just working a headlock. You worked every night and you just knew one another's stuff.'

'You can't get away with working a headlock for that long these days.'

'Why not?'

'The fans are smart to it. They have higher expectations.'

'Only because you give them too much. It's down to wrestlers to educate the fans, not the other way round. There's a lot of psychology in wrestling, you know?'

'It's the storytelling that interests me.'

'In life,' he said. 'If you punched someone in the head twenty times, he would not start doing somersaults.'

'Was realism ever a consideration for you?' I asked.

'I tried to keep it as real as possible.'

'What did you say when people said it wasn't real?' I asked.

'When people used to tell me it was fixed... I'd say, how do you fix a match with a bear or an alligator?'

We laughed; I slapped my hand on the table. Dad's eyes watered.

When the waiter came, I ordered for the both of us because he said he couldn't see the menu.

'Did I tell you about the riot in Singapore?' he said, eager to share, even if I had spent a lifetime listening to these stories.

Revitalised by each re-telling.

'It was raining bricks and bottles,' he said. 'An uprooted rambutan tree landed in the ring. The wrestlers tried to take refuge under the ring, but it was set on fire, and we were fighting for our lives. We spent the night in a broom cupboard.'

I smiled. 'It's not like that now,' I said.

He broke the rest of his poppadoms into pieces and ate them like crisps.

The stories Dad told me were based on fact, but fictionalised just by his perception of things. It was the same with experiences I had shared with him, people we knew: they weren't fabulations, but they were heightened by his crazy way of seeing things. These stories were proof of who he was. Sat there in the deflated bodysuit of his former glory.

The drooping face that mine would one day become.

When our meals arrived, I watched him dip a naan into a balti bowl, absorbed with innocent intent.

It was getting dark.

'Where you staying tonight?' he asked.

'At Mum's.'

'You can always stay at mine. I have weights, steak, anything you want.'

'Your place is bizarre,' I said. The walls were painted brown and now he had put a bed in his living room for people to stay, but they never did. Bugs ran around in his cutlery drawer. His towels were musky. Yet he seemed surprised.

'How is my darling?' he asked.

'Not well.'

'How come?'

'You know why.'

'I don't.'

I stared at him in disbelief.

'You know she's in full-time care?' I said.

'No.'

'You do,' I said. 'I told you.'

He looked blank. 'I must have forgot.'

'How do you forget something like that?' I stared across the table. 'What the fuck's the matter with you?'

He tried to stand up, rocking for momentum, the table almost tipping. I reached out my hand for ballast.

'Do you want some help?'

'No,' he grumbled. 'I'm fine.'

'Are you sure?'

'Strange I'd forget that,' he said and roared with laughter. 'Must've been hit by too many chairs.'

I walked him to the bus stop, the night like a dream in the façade of the buildings across the road.

He pulled a cigarette from his inside pocket.

'I thought you'd stopped?'

'It's therapeutic,' he said. 'The stress of living with your mother.'

'You haven't lived with her for fifteen years.'

'I know. I'm still getting over it.'

We made it halfway and sat down on a wall.

'Are you still writing?' he asked.

'Not really.'

'You ought to write something about wrestling,' he said. 'You could even do something about a crazy old man like me!'

I smiled.

'There's no novel that could contain you,' I said.

He laughed.

I moved away from the bus stop bench to ruminate and stretch my legs and I could see him look me up and down.

'You're getting skinny.'

'I'm not, I'm like twelve stone.'

'What are you doing?'

'My carbs are 200g a day. I do four days strength training and cardio three or four times a week.'

He puffed a smokeball. 'And wrestling?'

'Yeah.'

'That's too much. You'll fade away to a wisp.'

I glanced at our profiles mirrored in a window: the same face divided by time.

'I remember watching wrestling with you and Mum when I was a kid,' I said. 'Why didn't you ever break kayfabe?'

His eyes lit up.

'It's like a magician's trick,' he grinned. 'There's no fun if you know how it works.'

*

NU BLOOD was the Renegade trainee show that happened every two months at The Queen's Head in South London, and the try-outs were only a few weeks away. There would be about ten spaces on the card with only half for heels, which means I'm competing with a hundred other people at one of the best training schools in the country for a spot on the show. When they arrived everybody shook hands softly, in the way that it was customary for wrestlers. Nobody wanted to work with somebody stiff.

Joe didn't banter, preferring to keep a professional distance; he was almost always humourless, which was funny for a former comedy promoter, other than when he let his guard down and the jokes came spilling out and he opened himself up for reactions he couldn't control.

One Thursday night when I got back from Leeds, Joe popped in see how things were going and pulled up a chair at ringside while I worked a 'trap' spot on The Preacher.

The sequence itself was simple enough and taught as one of the standards. Known as the 'trap spot', the hero is 'trapped' in a chinlock and fights out of the hold, runs off and is knocked back down with a clothesline. The second time, the hero ducks the clothesline but gets caught by an elbow. Having learned to evade the clotheslines and back elbow, the hero ducks the third and hits his own move and makes a comeback.

The first time I saw a trap spot as a teenager I bought it wholesale. Saw a bleach-blond vampire Gangrel choking the life out of a stoner martial arts dude and willed him to escape the hold.

'If you just run in straight lines,' The Preacher said. 'I'll get you. You don't need to think about what I'm going to do. Just be open and ready to take something, right?'

'Right.'

The Preacher was the standout trainee, Marilyn's protégé. He had already worked some of the best wrestlers in the world on trainee shows. But that didn't mean Marilyn went any easier on him. Being Marilyn's trainee meant even more pressure.

The Preacher was popular with the fans and his great strength was in painting himself a portrait of suffering. When a villain put the heat on him, he gazed out into the crowd like a messiah, a body recoiling in pain, as expressive as the subject of a Baroque painting, all flowing black hair and contorted muscle under duress.

A trainee called Gregory, who was about six foot five, with man boobs and skin as white as milk, tapped me on the shoulder and boomed in a deep, knowledgeable voice, 'What you want to do is, open your chest out. Give him a target.'

I nodded, 'Thanks, Greg, Will do,' I said.

Who did he think he was? Everything he did was lumbering and implausible; even his gimmick was insane. Which was something like he was born into money, but then won the lottery anyway, just to rub it in. It made no sense, totally mental. Ha! I loved it. Another idea he had was *Stealth*, in which he was an assassin sent by a secret conspirator who would turn out to be Gregory himself.

Gregory had never had a match.

We ran the spot again and I ran past without hitting him. I heard a cackle of laughter.

'What the fucking hell was that?" I looked over at the shutter and Marilyn standing there.

I shrugged.

'I just keep getting my feet wrong,' I said.

'I can fucking see that. And you, Patrick, what the fuck are you letting him run past without hitting him for? Next time he misses, you tag him for real, got it?'

The Preacher sighed.

'He's just a strawb, Marilyn,' he said.

'Is he?' Marilyn answered. 'Well, if he wants to be on shows and he wants to get it all given for him on a fucking plate, he can pay his fucking dues.'

All I could feel was Marilyn's gaze on me, critiquing each movement; the knot in the stomach at waiting for the next blast of feedback, knowing my best wasn't good enough.

Trev held his face in his hands.

*

I walked to Oval Tube station with The Preacher, matched him stride for stride, him a few inches taller, awkward outside the setting of the Dojo, more prominently muscular across the chest and shoulders in a short-sleeved Hawaiian shirt, pink chinos and a straw hat. He spoke into the ground, eyes darting beneath his bushy eyebrows.

'So, Wesley brother,' he said. 'What are your ambitions in this fine sport of manly entertainment?'

I told him my story.

Told him how Dad was a wrestler, how he wrestled across the world as 'Sailor' Earl Black, that I was going to train at The Dungeon before I became a writer instead, how I was drinking too much after the publication of my first novel. Told him a less intense version of the truth, which was that I had dreamed about remaking myself as some kind of contrarian bourgeois intellectual and when the book was published, it was a mess, unproofed, in need of more work, and I bottled it on stage at events, too afraid to say what I really thought.

I appeared at literary festivals and bookstores, dressed up like an author, hair side-parted, and sounding like one with all the correct portentousness and writerly import to my voice, but I knew inside I was a coward, an imposter, and hated myself.

I had believed in the transcendental power of language to reveal truth and the fullness of the self, but I was a fake and I had lost faith in novelly novels. In their fake plots, fake events, fake characters. I lost myself in drink and drugs and had the deal for my second book cancelled, which was a relief given how cartoonish it felt, though now I was in danger of losing my hourly-paid position teaching at the university, but I didn't feel like I deserved that anyway.

He smiled and explained that he was a recovering alcoholic having done time for assault. Wrestling gave him the buzz he needed and becoming The Preacher had given him a second chance.

I puffed my chest out to walk beside him, feeling as if I also belonged like him in the mythic realm of wrestling. The changing lights. The passing cars. The people on the other side of the street were unaware of who and what we were. None of them knew about *our world*, we were like Bill & Ted travelling from another time on our excellent adventure, being crazy in our own way and wild on nights out, but were basically invisible to the people who walked among us. We could literally do as we pleased and nobody seemed to care. I was falling in love with this kayfabe world where anything was permitted and the man I was I within it, this world where people played their characters inside and outside the ring, living like geniuses, punk libertine maniacs devoted wholly to the artistry of pro wrestling.

No matter what Marilyn said, Dad had been there fifty years before him, he *made* the business, had worked legends like Dory Funk Jr and Anthony Inoki and didn't look like some skinny glam rocker from Margate in a trench coat. Jack Tanner had said that Marilyn didn't even get beaten up when he was training at Bulldog's, I had no idea what to believe.

All the hurt usually started up on the walk back to my flat, the climb up the staircase, then the hardening of the body through the night as it came back to feel more like its natural state after the white glow of adrenaline had made me feel supernaturally alive and strongman-invincible.

The ache in your bones, red-hot muscle under duress, the thrill of feeling alive after so many years depressed, drunk and living in bad faith. In this world, I wasn't judged on regimented ideological positions like in academia: they saw the quirks of my character and I had preferred who I was in this world, somebody more like the proletarian I once was without pretention or self-regard, we just were who we were, becoming ourselves in an unassuming way. Nietzsche believed that civilisation caged the animal within us. This cult of wrestling existed beyond the ordinary, coming alive as figments of the imagination acted out under archways, in the ring and recorded on screens, but these immersive fictions had no fourth wall and were enacted through fake names, social media avatars, in bodies we stylised as props and characters that were ascribed roles in a world of make-believe.

All-In wrestling was the first style of pro wrestling to gain popularity in the UK, but the high demand created a shortfall in quality workers and shows were derided as 'fake'. To combat this, wrestlers began to resort to increasingly *hardcore* acts of violence like using chairs as weapons, leading pro wrestling to be banned in the UK. In an attempt to give the impression of a respectable sport, Admiral-Lord Mountevans formed a committee to create a set of unified rules, and they were adopted by nearly all promotions by the 1950s. The result was a more gentlemanly iteration of the 'sport' which was based on grappling and wrestlers using their wits to escape submission holds. After British wrestling stopped appearing as part of World of Sport on ITV in the mid 1980s, the business fell out of the spotlight and smaller indies eventually facilitated a revival, but with no wrestlers under contract, no training schools really following any regulations, no paramedics at shows, promoters without licences or public liability insurance.

The whole system was policed by the old boys, a caste system of hierarchy, basically an honour culture based on the fictions of their personas. The only way to break in was to pay your dues and earn the respect of the veterans.

On the one hand, what veterans often said or did seem arbitrary and silly – it was only wrestling for God's sake – but on the other, I was desperate to be a wrestler and craved their respect. But then there was the madness of it, these carnival people living in their version of reality, each like some little kingdom with its own mad king.

Wrestling brought us closer to a state of nature, playful, free and relishing the power of make-believe and the possibility of being a child again.

I would show them that wrestling was the blood in my veins.

The next day I woke up feeling broken. But it was better than a comedown. The self-defeat of a hangover. Those long mornings that became days hiding in my bedroom. Then weeks of avoiding people for things I had done or said. Only to catch up with them again, pretend nothing had happened and feel things were okay if they went along with it.

I turned over and when I straightened my back it ached like a bump.

The burned skin on my knees and elbows scuffed against the bedsheets. The light was bright. I was sleeping in the front room, which was a large space overlooking the railway tracks near Finsbury Park. My curtains were semi-transparent, white and yellow in the blasts of cool spring sunshine. I tried to stretch awake, rolling around in bed. My cat, Lucy, sidled in, took one look at me and left. I was getting used to waking up to the generalised pain of being a wrestler. A train roared past and strained the subsidence a little more. I was getting used to the light that howled toward the house at night. This room cost more than my entire two-bedroom flat in Leeds, yet there was damp over the walls like an old map, the furniture looked reclaimed from the seventies and the windows were single-glazed.

Eventually, the house would fall into itself.

Brittle, like the joints of Terry Funk, I remember from the documentary *Beyond The Mat*, who could barely haul himself out of bed in his opening shot, after taking thirty-two years of bumps doctors said would give him chronic pain if he was lucky, but was unable to retire.

Unlike a hangover, I wear these leopard-print bruises, the cramp of my lower back and tender wingnuts of the spine with pride. I rolled out of bed, staggered over to my desktop on a workbench by the window, opened out my hands as if I was cuffed and took pictures of my bruises to send to Dad.

He replied a few minutes later, 'Now you know what a wrestler feels like.'

I smiled.

Somewhere, in Leeds, Dad would be shuffling about, growling at the next person he saw that his boy was a wrestler.

I put on my kit and stood in front of the full-length mirror I had borrowed from my flatmate Lauren's room the week before.

I have been going to the gym four days a week on top of training at the Dojo three or four nights a week. I've been living on a 'clean' diet of brown rice, lean meat and vegetables for weeks but it's difficult to gain size and remain lean, or stay lean and gain size, without the help of chemical assistance. Given my history with drugs and alcohol I was wary of going down that road.

I don't ever do anything by halves: my mind works in absolutes and if I started on the gear, I'd probably end up a freakish cartoon, body dysmorphic and rapid Incredible Hulk style muscle sprouting out everywhere.

I started out on Hollywood celebrity workouts before I realised they were using the same drugs that bodybuilders and athletes were.

Similar to the way that female body image has been defined by plastic surgery, augmentation and photoshop, the male body is now subject to a kind of kayfabe, where bodies that are chemically enhanced, photoshopped and synthetically pumped up are presented as the natural result of puritanism. I spent six minutes on a tanning bed the other day, but I was still as white as an ordinary guy and not chestnut orange like a wrestler. I was down to twelve stone and about twenty-percent body fat. Neither jacked nor ripped. Again, ordinary.

I had a few ideas for what my entrance music might be. One song I coveted was Linkin Park's 'One Step Closer' as it was what I used as a teenager, walking into my bedroom to it and dreaming of being a wrestler, but I had settled on 'Mayday' by the indie electronic band Unkle whose album *War Stories* I used as a soundtrack to write my first novel.

I pressed Play, ran out of the room, waited the twenty-four seconds for the beat to drop before I strutted back through the door, face in character, staring at the wall. There was a stomping metallic bassline between war-like drum loops and a jangling sense of threat. Yes, I thought, raising my arms as if I was on the stage entrance heading toward the ring, this was perfect.

When my kit arrived a few days later I stood in front of the full-length mirror. I had wrestling ankle shoes, MMA grappling shorts and a mouthguard.

I had floated the idea of my MMA gimmick, but it didn't get over. Notwithstanding the fact that I had never done MMA, apparently I was one of any number of trainees who turned up, each thinking they could re-invent the business and were just marks for themselves, in long shorts and kick pads. Owen thought the idea idiotic, especially since he fancied himself as something of a shooter and had done MMA at least once more than me.

In Dad's era, the most respected wrestlers were also legitimate submission fighters known as 'shooters'. These were guys like Billy Robinson, a master of catch-as-catch-can he learned in the Wigan Snake Pit. This was a semi-defunct British version of *jiu jitsu* based on holds called 'hooks' which originated in funfairs and evolved from ancient styles like Cumberland, Indian *pehlwani* and Irish collar-and-elbow.

In the age of kayfabe, before the secrets of the business were openly known, a wrestler had to be able to protect the business.

All the wrestlers I admired growing up, like William Regal, had learned hooks fighting in wrestling booths on Blackpool Pier in the old carnival way, or Bret Hart who was 'stretched' by his father Stu in The Hart Dungeon, where his trainees' screams could be heard throughout the house. Kurt Angle was an Olympic gold medallist in freestyle wrestling.

In each of these, it was the realism I admired. I respected the lineage, but I wasn't a real fighter.

When wrestling was performed in the carnivals, some bouts were thrown for money. This was the origin of the form. Promoters found out they could put on better shows and make more money if they staged it. When an over-enthusiastic fan turned up who looked like they thought it was real and could be scammed, a mark was drawn on his back using chalk. Even though most fans are smart to the business now, they were still getting worked and *marks* in their own way, just like me, believing I was something I was not.

The other trainees who had made it onto shows had outlandish gimmicks. This was largely down to the influence of Marilyn, who believed that nobody wanted to watch trainees wrestle, so they may as well be entertaining.

There was 'The Preacher', who was originally intended to be a part angel, part demon figure like from the graphic novels of the same name but was turned into a fan favourite by people shouting wisecracks about his resemblance to Jesus.

The Dude, a stoner surfer guy, who had shaggy bleached blonde hair and came out to 'Sell Out' by Reel Big Fish. Rikimaru was some kind of ninja assassin. Jezebel a bitchy supermodel. Queen Boudica a Game of Thrones-style warrior queen. Even Marilyn Draven was King of the Goths and wore a muzzle and a dark cloak to the ring, sometimes dripping with blood that was probably fake but you never knew.

I had no ideas for a character. Dirk Dresden was out. What else? The only character I wanted to play was a version of myself, something like the way Kurt Angle or Chris Benoit did. They didn't have *gimmicks* as such, they were just themselves. Angle emphasises his dorkiness but could go in the ring. While Benoit was a machine. He just kicked the shit out of people. Why couldn't that be me?

Among the old boys, even Trevor, the idea that wrestlers wore kickpads and had MMA gimmicks was an in-joke because every *strawb* who walked into training wanted to do that; it was an ego move to say I don't need a gimmick, I'm just going to be a wrestler's wrestler.

I thought about maybe Earl Black Jr being a Tory or a contrarian, but these didn't stick. Earl Black Jr made sense, but I didn't want to hang off the back of Dad's achievements, I wanted to be my own man.

But who else could I be?

It was the only thing that stuck. Marilyn was right.

I pressed Play again, ran out of the room and waited for the beat to drop before strutting back through the door, face in character, staring into the fourth wall. But something wasn't right, no matter how much I prepared for it and imaged how things would be I wouldn't know until I did it for real, had the eyes of bona fide fans on me reacting to my character in a way that was organic and would determine the authenticity of my performance. What if it all went wrong? What if people didn't buy into me? What if I became paralysed by fear, like the first time I performed at a poetry festival when I was sixteen and so nervous I felt like I had floated outside of my body and was reciting the verses from the ceiling?

All of those things could happen, of course, but I had done a lot of things since then and I knew, deep down, when called upon there was a monster inside of me that would take over when I entered the stage, and for those moments I would be confident and determined and full of showmanship. I would tap into my emotional memory like an actor and recall something real and apply it to the moment, everything was going to be as real as possible. All the sadness, the anger, the despair, all of whatever it was that felt so dark and empty inside, the feelings of insecurity and exhaustion that led me to drink or fight or behave self-destructively, all of this would pour out into my character in a wave of artistic violence that would feel like a fight.

I knocked on Lauren's door.

'You good?' I asked.

'Yeah. Come in.'

I went inside and found my flatmate Lauren sitting on her two-seater sofa, smoking.

'Everything hurts,' I said.

She took a closer look at me in my MMA shorts, green vest and ankle boots.

'Oh my god,' she said. 'Are you meant to be *that* bruised?'

'I guess so. Trevor says your body gets used to it.'

I rubbed a new canvas burn I had found on the back of my elbow.

'Have you got a gimmick yet?' she asked.

'I just want to be really legit. Like just wear MMA shorts and have a really realistic style.'

'Like Brock Lesnar?'

'Yeah.'

'The Rock was my favourite wrestler. I prefer characters really.'

She took a small drag of her roach-end.

'Most people do.'

'So you're not going to do an MMA gimmick?' she asked.

'No,' I said, looking at the collage of bruises that were dotted around my arms and chest.

'Wrestling reminds me of a bit of stuff I've read about ballet,' she said. 'They sometimes call it making or building a work *on* the body. *The story comes from inside the body*.'

I went back into the living room, answered some emails, wrote a few hundred words of nothing writing, looked through the online orders of the poetry magazine I was working for and sorted out the different issues to send from the various boxes which were now in permanent residence alongside the cat litter tray in the box room upstairs.

In the afternoon I played *War Stories* on my earphones and headed down the street like Earl Black Jr. His movements were more definite than mine, he was surer of himself. There was more purpose in his stride and a steely glint in his eye. I climbed the stairs to the gym, nodded to a jacked personal trainer on my way in without feeling like he could read my thoughts, swiped through the turnstile already ready to go and headed across the free-weights area, where the big guys grunted the loudest and the smaller guys watched in near silence.

On Mondays, I worked my posterior chain, the muscles on the backside of your body from your head all the way down to your heels: neck, upper back, lower back, hamstrings and calves.

Whereas Monday revolved around overhead pressing and the shoulders, Thursday was bench press and chest, and Friday was squats and thighs with a focus on core strength. These workouts were based around powerlifting to build functional strength and then I did rowing or sprinting for cardio as well as the conditioning sessions at the Dojo. I may have only been 5'9 and a bit, a little over thirteen stone, but this programme gave me the strength to throw around guys who were two or three times the size of me.

I warmed up with some rowing and then worked up to a few heavy sets of deadlifts. Each week was on a different cycle for my main movement for the day. Today I was on sets of five, but next week would be triples, and the next week singles before a deload.

I liked to deadlift hungover, feeling drenched with sweat and a lager headache and body cramps, full of latent carbs, the re-rejuvenation of my body as I busted out the heavy sets and sweat poured from my head listening to Marilyn Manson's cover of 'Sweet Dreams (Are Made of This)'. I warmed up with just the bar, then single plates, then doubles, until eventually the bar was stacked, and the weights sounded like a sledgehammer coming to blows with metalwork on the gym floor, and the other guys craned their neck round to see what kind of load I was working with.

That's right baby, I thought, pulling four hundred pounds to my waist.

Nobody did deadlifts because they were functional, rather than aesthetic. They required technique and good form, something I hadn't quite mastered. I knew my back rolled on the heavy sets and could feel the cramp and pinch of the downward force on my lower back.

For the last sets, I pulled out a bottle of liquid chalk, wiped it around my hand, waited for the white lather to dry, miraculously, within a few seconds into a powder paint on my palms and pulled the last few reps.

I stared into the mirror between sets. Every rep and every set were a chance to re-make me and find definition in the white mass that had been created by a legacy of a thousand nights out, takeaways and lots of drugs.

The body was a canvas that could be carved and modelled, re-purposed as a weapon, a low-slung broadness and thick neck girdle which was about to withstand public displays of suffering. A depiction of the self that could be illustrated by mime, choreography and symbolic gestures that were enacted in the ring, but also registered in the day-to-day performances of everyday life where, even off-stage, a pro wrestler was often still a pro wrestler, fulfilling the impression of what a pro wrestler might be like, consciously and often unconsciously, carefully managing the presentation of their masculinity. I enjoyed being introduced as a wrestler, people thinking I was a tough guy, wearing my crewcut and close-fitting T-shirts, the jokes about 'not messing around with *him*, because he's a pro wrestler'. It was infinitely better and more interesting than trying to explain what you did as a freelancer in the literature sector, something which felt surly, bourgeois and a dead end conversationally. Wrestlers, on the other hand, were larger than life, and wrestling was a spectacle that fascinated people.

When I was done, I moved onto my secondary movement, which was several sets of pull-ups, before sets of rows and curls and then rounds of high intensity sprints on a rowing machine, until my T-shirt was puddled with sweat and I could barely breathe.

My heart breakdanced against my chest.

A vein pulsed on the side of my forehead. I was dizzy, caught my breath, and then I went again, harder, faster until I was losing my sense of who I was, enveloped in a black shadow while I felt like a full-body hard-on, a throb, and I pushed through the pain and beyond myself until my muscles failed and I was on my knees, awash with sweat on the gym floor, an inferno of burning calories and swollen muscle.

I caught my breath and, smiling inwardly, strutted across the gym floor and into the changing room where I took off my shirt to reveal my pumped-up body. A guy who was talcing his bollocks looked up and smiled: 'Getting there, dude.'

Getting there?

That couldn't be right. I *was* there.

Obviously not according to this guy.

I looked in the mirror and saw what he saw: a work in progress, a first draft of white muscle, and a pot belly, despite my dieting and cardio. I headed back out onto the gym floor and repeated my workout again. This time even harder. When I showered, tears merged with spume in the downward rush.

*

The next Sunday I walked across Holloway Road to the Renegade show, sweating out a hangover in the sun, thinking about how I got so drunk the previous night that I lost control and upset a girl who was the friend of a friend.

It was the doubt that terrified me, the black space, filled with speculation.

When I was drunk I knew no bounds.

I remembered dancing on a speaker, shirtless; I whispered something into her ear before she disappeared, and somebody moved me away.

Before doors, the crowd lined up all the way down the street in a parade of blue hair, plaid, baseball caps and wrestling T-shirts. I stood there in a bomber jacket, sweating, the hangover clinging to me like smoke, skin itching.

On the way in, one of the trainees was taking tickets; he tore mine and directed me to my seat without recognising me.

I was in the silver section a few rows from the ring and stood looking for a chair in the dark.

Somebody called my name.

I looked left and right and struggled to work out where the voice was coming from in the noise.

'Wes!'

Oh shit. It was Owen waving at me, straight ahead. He had a girlfriend with him who looked equally young and credulous. I craned my head around, pretending to look elsewhere but it was too late.

The little shit had seen me.

'Hey man,' I smiled. 'Of all the wrestling shows in all the world.'

He shook my hand in the weak way wrestlers did.

'You got a seat? Come and sit with us.'

He gestured over at some empty seats. I paused before faking a smile.

'That'd be great,' I said.

As we took our seats we talked about the main event between 'The Bone Collector' Bruce Logan and Fergus Devine. For fifteen years he had dragged British wrestling from the doldrums after the cancellation of World of Sport on ITV to a few WWE tribute acts wrestling in front of fifteen people in a leisure centre, before it exploded and became the hottest scene in world wrestling.

Bruce had a background in *jiu jitsu* and was called 'The Bone Collector' due to the limbs he had broken, which was all *kayfabe*, obviously, as in reality he had a reputation for being a very safe worker in the ring.

'I'm looking forward to Bruce Logan,' I said. 'Be amazing to see him in the flesh.'

'Oh it is. I've trained with him.'

Of course he had.

I bet he had, and that was why Trev told me in his last match he put on a rest hold in the middle of a babyface comeback and killed the fire, ha! Was it?

His girlfriend didn't say much but smiled in the background.

'Sorry if I was snappy in training the other week,' I said, deciding to give him the benefit of the doubt and make sure

I didn't get any heat. 'I've had a lot on at work. I just thought grappling should be done fast, like catch wrestling.'

'Hey man, it's cool. Was just something I wanted to share with you that helped me. I've been fortunate to train with the best.'

'I'd love to learn some hooking and do a bit of MMA at some point,' I said.

'You won't find true catch anymore. Doing a form of submission wrestling will get you to the closest mind set.'

I crossed my arms and looked to the ring.

It was steeped in a red-purple glow which made it seem enlarged, before 'The Imperial March' from *Star Wars* blasted out and fans flooded from the bar to their chairs; others stood by the ring with their arms folded, having solemn-looking discussions about story arcs and performances of the wrestlers.

The ropes were white in the blood-red dark, the corner pads and apron were black with white Roman eagle symbols on them, and all the while fake smoke rose like incense.

I stood up along with Owen and joined seven hundred fans as they clapped and chanted *Renegade!*

The pre-fight atmosphere buzzed with nervous energy.

When the bell rang and the music hit for the first wrestler, a burly dude with a black beard made his way to the ring. My stomach churned, nervous at the thought of one day coming down the aisle with such immense expectations on me.

Then I was nervous again as Trevor made his way out to oppose him. Some pride too, as he stood on the turnbuckle and raised a cheer from the crowd. The other guy was about three times the size of Trevor, and they told a David and Goliath story, with Trev utilising his speed, quick wittedness, and technique against the power of his giant opponent. In the end, despite Trevor's valiant efforts, he wound up being turned upside down and pile-driven headfirst into the mat.

When the match started with a hard collar-and-elbow lock up, the two wrestlers tussled back and forth, and the crowd went along with the show. I couldn't get Mum calling it fake out of my head. Rather than enjoy it on its own terms, all I could do was see it from the perspective of somebody who thought it was fake. Wasn't it all just seeing fake punches and fake men having fake fights? How could anybody buy into the fakery of it all? But wasn't it really that so much of life is equally silly, we had just become inured to it? At some point, you had to let go and embrace it as a ceremony like the coronation of a monarch, a rock band taking possession of a crowd with a fascist fervour, or a judge in robes in the theatre of a courtroom.

Everyday life is full of performances – roles we play, in costumes, partaking in rituals.

Power is constituted through acts, symbols and gestures. To open Parliament, the monarch has a golden carriage and a tradition of Black Rod knocking on the door, not somebody turning up in a taxi and sending a text, or an announcement at the back of a newspaper. No, the way people mediate and understand power is through theatrics, dress-up and make-believe.

In *Mythologies,* Roland Barthes describes pro wrestling as a spectacle of excess, displaying the grandiloquence of gestures which belong to ancient theatre.

Could I see myself in there? The venue held about 1,500 people, all squashed together in a sea of limbs and roaring faces, packing out various levels facing down on the ring that looked like a bearpit. The atmosphere was something between the Extreme Championship Wrestling arena atmosphere of Philadelphia in the mid-1990s, with a grungy, adult wildness, and the fervent devotion and chanting of a Premier League football match.

The fans were mostly hipsters and rockers or nerds, highly knowledgeable about the workings of the business, and connoisseurs and critics in equal measure. Could I see myself walking out on stage here? Could I perform for these people and satisfy them in a place like this? Would they actually pay to come here and see me, a better, more jacked, *over* version of me and invest in me the way they did with other wrestlers?

What a thought!

I didn't need to go to America or Japan. This would be insane enough, and right now, this bearpit and the British independent scene was at the centre of the wrestling universe and had eyes on it across the world.

Although I had begun watching the show in a more analytical mode, too self-aware to properly engage with it and not sure if I should be pretending to be a fan or whether people were just genuinely caught up in the kayfabe, as the show progressed, I felt myself think less and less and the sensory impact of the moment grew stronger. I was aware of being a body belonging to a sea of bodies, something like the 'mystical bodies' that congregants form in a church.

I found myself immersed in the stories. Oh, it was brilliant!

At times, I caught Owen's eye and we smiled with excitement at what was happening in front of us. I knew I'd shame myself for it later, but right now it felt splendid.

A highly choreographed four-way elimination tag-team match played out with all the thrills and spills of an action movie; then the danger and risk of a ladder match, in which the competitors fought to ascend a ladder and claim a championship belt dangling from the ceiling, and then the Japanese strong-style realism of Bruce Logan vs Fergus Devine.

Bruce Logan entered the ring, all eighteen stone of him, thick muscle and six feet of height, body hair doused in baby oil and looking every inch a real pro wrestler.

A cloud of white smoke billowed under him as he climbed up on the turnbuckle to look out into the crowd. His body, his movements, his eyes were dedicated to the performance.

Bruce slammed his opponent to the mat and signalled that he was going to the top rope, and we cheered him on as he threw his ageing body through the air, for it to ripple and crank upon landing, for our entertainment.

He was stomped in the head and rolled around the ring, withing in agony. The more pain he endured, the more we cheered; the performance had elevated him to something beyond himself.

Bruce was knocked to the mat. He was thrown across the ring but he reversed the whip and began his comeback.

When he hit his Rolling Tiger Suplex finisher, which was basically a Full Nelson version of a German suplex, the ref counted to three and I leapt to my feet and cheered with the rest of them in a fury of pure pleasure.

*

On the day of the try-out I arrived at the Dojo on a bright autumn afternoon. The whole roster of the school was here getting changed into their sportswear. Between the snatches of conversations between the more experienced trainees, there was silence and nervous energy. Most training sessions I had been to since the intensive course disbanded were made up of five or ten guys who were already on shows and I was way behind. I was just the latest strawb. It was all right in-ring, when we had something to do, but in the water breaks and the times around the sessions, I was still invisible.

I did the rounds and shook hands with Trev, The Dude, The Preacher and the rest I didn't know so well. We warmed up as a group, smashing through a few hundred squats and push-ups, stretching off before Joe and the trainers put a card together.

One by one the matches were announced by Joe, who had been in consultation with Trev and Marilyn at ringside and the workers began brokering their routines.

I knew that on the final card there was likely to be at least one women's match, a tag match and this would narrow down the available heel spots for singles matches down to about four.

Everybody was going to get two matches in scenarios Joe was considering for the card. A few minutes later, I sat cross-legged when they called out the first matchups.

I was to get two attempts. First up, I was up against 'Hercules' Alex Zeff, a strength coach and strongman who was sixteen stone of solid, lean muscle with a big bald head; he had a reputation for hurting people.

'Anything you want to do?' he asked.

I had an idea for what would make me stand out from the rest of the guys here, who were all modern indie wrestlers and liked to get their shit in. That meant, unlike on the highly produced televised American shows where wrestlers were on contracts, worked several nights a week and didn't mind not showing every single thing they could do, these shows were structured in a way that no match should ever be better than the main event; the levels of risk and excitement in each match would be curated by an agent beforehand and the choreography of the shows as a whole tended to be more controlled. On the independent scene, however, wrestlers were freelancers and, while there was respect for the main event and your place on the card was respected to an extent, wrestlers tended to put on the best possible match they could, and most of them liked to do every possible sequence, move and near fall they could, to get over with the crowd and get booked again.

In this sense, it followed something like what had happened in cinema, with the wrestling from the 1970s being grittier, less choreographed, and arguably more realistic (although a lot of the strikes, especially in American wrestling, looked pretty *pony*). The independent wrestling style of recent years was something more like the big budget superhero movies, where there's such an excess of *everything*, explosion after explosion and CGI chaos that it becomes exhausting and renders things meaningless.

Where in Wrestlemania matches between The Undertaker and Shawn Michaels in the late 2000s were held up as examples of the best ever, they were battles between two of the greatest wrestlers at the grandest stage of them all and the many near falls and kick-outs of what would otherwise have been finishing manoeuvres was warranted. However, the template had been rolled out to almost every indie show you went to and had become predictable, unrealistic and senseless.

In the old days when the kayfabe was king, doing too complex or over-choreographed routines was seen as exposing the business. The veterans liked to claim they were above the indie demand for excess, but the way the business was heading it was difficult for anybody to resist. I wasn't saying I was even capable of some of the immense choreography and gymnastics some of the guys could do, but it wasn't my thing. I needed something rooted in character, pathos and believability.

Something that came close to resembling a fight but with all the aesthetics and theatricality of a story.

It wasn't so much that people believed it was real, but workers owed it to the fans to act as though it could be.

In the 1970s, Ric Flair, who Dad regarded as the greatest of all time, was the NWA World Champion and would travel the territories as Dad had. Most of the guys who he came up against were local heroes without much talent, but Flair would give them as much as he could, get them over and then snatch the match from them at the last minute. It was said that Flair could carry a broomstick to a three-star match. He was that good.

That's the kind of heel I wanted to be. In this day and age when fans wanted cool heels and big moves, I would be the butt of every joke and do as little as possible.

Everything I did was to get the babyface over.

I told my plan to Hercules, who went along with it. He was a strongman, double my width and with over-developed muscles that made him look like a sock full of snooker balls in his skin-tight stretch top, and, due to his size, I planned to get thrown around by him and then poke him in the eye like a weasel and start working his leg to keep him grounded.

The idea was to not do so much like the indie maniacs who would all be getting their shit in.

Instead, we would *let it breathe.*

That was the idea. About three minutes in, I had run through everything we had and held his leg in my hand, looking out at the wrestlers pretending to be fans.

I snarled.

'Why are you booing me?' I said.

'Nobody's booing you, you cunt!' Marilyn shouted. 'We just all want you to fucking die!'

*

Everybody wrestled twice and the next time round I was working The Dude and stuck to the script. No trying to be smart or realistic or do anything beyond what I was capable. Going to do the standard five stage match with all the silly, make-no-sense spots that the other trainees did and pull faces in the bits in between the sequences.

A grimace, a sneer, a howl, anything that registered the impact of the choreography into emotion. This was the only way an audience connected with anybody, and I knew I could pop the boys with some slapstick.

The Dude was a nursery care worker and student by day, long and gangly, with a stoner vibe, and I had dismissed him before I started at the Dojo for not looking like a wrestler in the videos I had watched, with his bleached blonde hair and, despite coming from Gloucester, a surfer drawl. He was just too skinny and his gimmick was ridiculous. It was guys like him who put me off indie wrestling because they made it look amateurish.

'So dude, we're working together?'

'Yeah,' I said.

'Cool.'

I felt a bit sorry for him but glad for me and we left the archway to get some space in front of the car mechanics' next door. He asked me what my moves did: suplexes mainly, I said, a sharpshooter. Did I have any signature spots, he asked; I had one or two, I said, and suggested a finish which he brushed off.

He ran the data through his head and a few minutes later had a match, all our bits fitting into the structure.

While I thought through the choreography, trying to remember it in chunks by rote, we stood at ringside and I watched Owen take part in a tag match. With his five feet fuck-all of height, his adolescent body and skin-tight Lycra T-shirt, even with his smooth technical wrestling, moving from one wrestling technique to another in a seemingly fluid chain, he didn't convince; there was nothing of a *shooter* about him. If anybody was going to be the shooter round here it was going to be me. Although, when I thought about it, I had nothing to substantiate that, no martial arts training or prowess beyond the fact that my dad was a wrestler and that somehow meant I could lay claim to a heritage that had nothing to do with me.

There was a lack of intensity in his work and when he ran in for the hot tag, the moment when the face team's fortunes are reversed in a match and the fresh partner storms in the ring to clean house and save the day, he ran in and took a waistlock, a rest hold, just hugging the guy in his arms.

The boys laughed.

This time it wasn't me shitting the bed.

I could see the opportunity on the card was opening up for me and now it was time to deliver.

Owen delivered a couple of snapmares, rolling my body head-first over his shoulder, but really it was another low-impact move that was better used at the beginning of a match or as a transition. He followed up with a wafty kick and then leapt from the top rope only to miss and fall in a pile, clasping his knee.

When we were up, I ignored everything in my head, the fact that all these critical eyes were on me, climbed into the ring and paced about, walking and talking, to get cheap heat from the crowd: *You and this reprobate stoner loser are denigrating the sport of pro wrestling! I am now going to demonstrate my superior in-ring skill and let that be a lesson to you!*

It was corny but established me as a heel.

The Dude, on the other hand, had a silly gimmick and enjoyed clowning around, running through the gestures and one-liners he had been crafting on live shows. He knew exactly how to get the crowd going and establish himself as the face, and I was the heel by default.

It was easier the other way round, usually: it's easier to find a reason to boo somebody than to cheer them, and a good antagonist should make the job of the babyface a case of turning up.

The Preacher took on the role of the referee and frisked us for foreign objects, pinging one of my bollocks in the process for a laugh. My eyes rolled around in my head.

Joe, the trainers and the wrestlers working on shows were sitting on the front seats. The grammar of my movements felt under scrutiny. The pinged testicle lingered in pain. The Preacher was still grinning as he tried to grab The Dude's bollocks. My mouth was tight. My face became a mask.

As the match began, we mimed our way through the story.

All the pain that lay in me was unleashed in a rabid intensity, chopping and kicking and suplexing with furious intent like my hero, The Rabid Wolverine.

This mask I had been wearing as myself had been truer than the one I wore these past few years as an aspiring author. Some kind of bourgeois contrarian intellectual too afraid to be himself.

Afterwards I shook hands with The Dude who, like me, was panting.

'Thanks dude,' he said.

I took my praise from the coaches and watched the rest of the card before we shook hands and went our separate ways. Owen limped over to me. Took my hand, patted me on the back and said I had done great. He had injured his knee during his match and would mostly likely be out for a year.

I was the last man standing.

When it was all over, I didn't want to spend another minute longer than I had to, forwent all the customary handshakes and snuck out in the melee, before walking off to the station, satisfied with what I had done.

I descended the escalator to the Tube and strutted onto the car which was nearly empty. In my tiredness, eyes having adjusted to the dark in my beaten-up haze, the world seemed full of starry light and swirling colours and a much better place than the one I usually experienced.

I felt like a man, I thought, and it was good.

But if I thought about it, the way I had changed my body, the character I played, the physical intensity and grit needed to survive were equally matched by a sixteen-year-old girl who trained with us, took the same bumps, did the same routines, pushed the same limits in herself.

In itself, what was actually *manly* about this?

I supposed feeling like a man meant to me feeling like Dad, or what Dad might have felt when he was travelling the world as Earl Black Sr.

I looked around. The Tube still wasn't moving. The doors opened and one of the trialists from the Dojo got on. It was too late, we had made eye contact and he was on his way to sit beside me.

I hated anything like this. After any kind of ordeal, I liked to sit alone and think through what had happened.

The guy was all right, though. I recognised him from a couple of training sessions we had both been to; his name was Gavin or something like that. He had no gimmick or character to speak of, but he was affable, whereas in the ring he wore face paint and screeched a lot.

'Hey,' he said. 'Do you mind?'

'Oh no, sit down.'

From what I remember, he had a day job installing broadband and had been training for two or three years.

He was still waiting for his first match.

'Wasn't at my best today,' he said.

'No?'

'It's the planning of the matches I find hardest, I always do too much or not enough.'

I nodded. 'Then you get heat no matter what you do.'

'At least I didn't get scurfed this time,' he said.

'What's that?'

'If you make a mistake, they give you a shot or two for real.'

'They do that?'

'Yeah.'

'Fucking hell.'

The Tube slowed as we made it to the next station. The doors opened and newspaper pages blustered about the carriage. Nobody got on.

'I thought it would be fun,' he said. 'But a lot of people just want to bury you.'

I nodded. 'I wanted to quit from the first session,' I said.

'Why didn't you?'

'I don't know. I suppose I just want to be a wrestler. Then there's not wanting them to win. You know?'

'I know what you mean.'

'I do want to be a wrester, anyway. Just to see what it would be like. I always thought I'd be really good, and then you turn up and realise you're total dogshit.'

He laughed.

'You're better than me,' he said.

I shook my head, but I knew he was as rotten as he said he was.

At the next stop we said our goodbyes and he got off.

On the empty seats were pages of newspapers that had fallen loose, fluttering near the doors as the Tube screamed through the dark. I was almost too pumped up to focus, but I took out a copy of Ric Flair's biography *To Be The Man* from my bag, and re-entered the world Dad had described: the mythos of pro wrestling that existed as a fantasy land like Narnia, which could be accessed from our world through the imagination. And now I was crossing the threshold into it.

That night I sat refreshing my inbox all night as I waited to hear from Joe Marsh. Lauren smoked beside me on the sofa watching TV.

How long would it take me to go from author to champion pro wrestler?

If it wasn't going to happen, there would be at least two months until the next try-out if I avoided injury and nobody new took my place.

I was thinking about the guy on the Tube, how he had shown up three or four nights a week for years and wasn't bad, but his face didn't fit, his gimmick didn't really make sense and he wasn't ever going to be on a show. I felt like I wasn't going to be like him, but how could I be so sure?

I might never get the chance.

I looked at the screen: Walter White explaining why he did what he did. He was good at it. And it made him feel alive.

However much I told myself it was fake, that I was above all this, and it didn't really matter, I couldn't bear another three months of moaning on the Tube home after training, with other trainees who weren't getting booked.

They existed in the lower orders of the hierarchy, putting up the ring and standing around in company polo shirts, doing crowd control and looking after the wrestlers' jackets during the shows, while the guys I trained with got to pretend to be who they really were, expressing themselves on the canvas.

The thought of not being a creative in some way made me feel sick. If I had never really made it as a writer, what if the same happened with wrestling too?

What would I have left?

I wouldn't be anything. Just a failure. Somebody who thought he could be things that he couldn't.

I refreshed the page, refreshed the page, nothing. What would it feel like, if written there was a match card with my name on?

And if it wasn't?

Just some loser, like the guy on the Tube, somebody who trained to be but never became a wrestler.

*

The moment I decided I wanted to train as a wrestler was a few nights after I had been around my friend Lachlan's house to do drugs and stream RAW on his desktop. We were drinking a slurpy red wine, had just got some supplies in and Lachlan began cutting the MDMA and ketamine on a footstool with a credit card until it was a powder fine enough to snort.

Then he wrapped them up in rolling paper bombs, passed one to me before carrying on his work of crushing the bleached MDMA crystals, which he tipped onto the top of the stool, chopped into lines, halved again, chopped some more and nudged them into a series of bumps, fattest in the middle.

'Hey, have you seen the pipebomb?' he asked.

'No,' I said. 'What's that?'

'I've only heard about it, but it sounds cool as fuck. CM Punk basically destroys the WWE.'

He scratched out five for him and five for me.

I looked at the screen.

CM Punk was sitting cross-legged on the stage with a mic in his hand. I had seen this guy a few times before, mostly at Lachlan's, when we watched wrestling after a few beers.

He had been leader of a faction called 'the straight edge society' and I had to ask Lachlan what straight edge meant. Apparently it was a subculture of punk, puritanical in its own way, a rebellion in self-control where adherents refrained from drink and drugs, and also promiscuous sex, meat and even caffeine.

I couldn't believe it; how could anybody *not drink*?

No hangover, shame, madness, but how was it possible to not drink or do drugs?

I had tried and failed several times and could barely last two or three weeks without getting completely hammered.

These guys were cool, moshing at gigs, covered in tattoos, but lived like Buddhist monks

There was a sadness in me I needed to drown out, even if for a few fleeting moments, an hour or two of pleasure before the hangover and the shame. The dread that often kept me in my room for two or three days at a time after a session before I pulled myself together and got back on it.

I swallowed the bomb with a gulp of beer and was immediately stung by acidity on the tender lining of my stomach.

CM Punk directed his ire at John Cena, the white meat babyface who kids still liked but the internet WWE fanbase hated.

Punk, on the other hand, was their darling.

'I don't hate you, John. I don't even dislike you,' he said. 'I do like you. I like you a hell of a lot more than I like most people in the back... You're as good at kissing Vince's ass as Hulk Hogan was. I don't know if you're as good as Dwayne though. He's a pretty good ass kisser. Always was and still is.'

He paused and the crowd gasped.

'Whoops! I'm breaking the fourth wall!' he said and waved into the camera like he was coming out of the screen, that he was on a level only we could understand, I'd never seen anybody kayfabe with such irony before.

Who was this guy?

He continued his promo in much the same way, an open mic shooting on the unscripted honesty which may or may not have been entirely approved of. I chatted with Lachlan, was he getting heat for this backstage? Yes, he said. This was the fault line between reality and fiction that was so interesting. Nobody cared about the real in itself. That was boring. It was the guessing at what was real and what was only the appearance of the real, and the deliberate blurring was tantalising. Promos were usually authored and approved by creative and here he was, speaking his own mind, or what seemed like it; there was reality in it, even if it was kayfabe.

'I'm gonna train as a wrestler,' I said to Lachlan.

He was blissed out on the floor.

'Cool,' he said.

'I'm gonna do it,' I laughed. 'No fucking about.'

I bent over the stool with a rolled-up banknote and sniffed the short lines one after another.

'One of the guys on a writing programme I'm on saw the pics from Liverpool and says he'll pay the fees if I write something about it,' I said.

'You gonna?'

'I don't know,' I squeezed my limbs together like a little crab, all the drugs flowing through me and feeling the k-cramp. 'I was thinking about going to Canada at some point, but this could work. I don't give a shit about writing; it just seems like a good thing to do.'

By the fourth, my nostril was clogging up with crystals in the rug of my nose hair, began to fizz and buzz, and I could feel the beginning of the uplift in feeling. I switched nostrils, a crust forming above my lip as I sniffed up a line.

A buzzing sensation grew at first and then in waves that built on one another with more intensity, and I felt jerky, the ketamine and the MDMA working together to do strange things to my sense of things: I was buzzing, but also like I was underwater, the space between things in my perception of depth was flowing and somehow viscous. I looked over at Lachlan, who met my gaze and nodded to the rhythm. A grin cracked through his grizzly beard.

I took this to mean *it's okay, I'm with you too buddy. We're both going someplace different.*

'I love you, buddy,' he smiled.

'Yeah man,' I said. 'This is the fucking life.'

When we tried hanging out sober our conversation didn't flow. I could speak more openly when his girlfriend was around, though: maybe this was just the way some male friendships are. Two guys who don't need to talk. What did it matter? We had some similar interests, but mostly we just liked to get fucked up.

Whenever we bumped a few lines, the conversation would loosen up, Lachlan would put *Queen of Denmark* by John Grant on the record player and we'd speak more freely about our lives.

Lachlan was leaning back into his chair with his eyes closed.

'This is good shit,' he said.

I began to make involuntary machine noises.

'Yes,' I said like a Dalek.

'That shit's getting you up, buddy.' He laughed.

'Take your shirt off,' I said.

'What?'

'Do you mind if I take my shirt off?'

'Fill your boots.'

I pulled off my polo shirt and walked around the room like a robot. I looked in the mirror at the black buttons of my eyes, smiled and then began making robot noises again.

D-de-d-de-d-de-d-dee!

I was about sixteen stone now. Since I went freelance I had been going out three or four nights a week, drinking at home when I wasn't and eating nothing but pies and fried food. Drinking a bottle of whiskey a day at home. Heaviness had formed under my chin, giving my face a softer look, and I looked more like Mum than Dad. I was like a Mr Potato Head for that, a generic white guy: change my hair, add or subtract facial hair and glasses or earrings and I could look like anybody.

I took off my trousers and felt an even greater urgency to walk around the room like a robot. It gave me great pleasure to move my arms and legs in a stiff, mechanical way while I vocalised these strange noises. All the while a feeling of great satisfaction and love was filling up in me. I dreamed up ideas of how I could improve the lives of people I knew and how I could be a better son, brother, friend. A feeling of happiness rose up deep within me and soared over me in a dreamy way.

I could feel my heart pulse with each drum beat, leading me higher into some kind of nirvana-like delirium.

The liberation of suffering and pain into non-self.

My trousers were on the floor with my phone hanging out the pocket. I picked it up, started scrolling through my contacts for avatars I could share my love with, but every time I called them up all I could do was make robot noises. I went through every name, some professional contacts and people who Gmail had collated into my address book over the years. These were writers, editors, academics, family members, and I called them all and left messages in a robotic voice

If I got through and started making mechanical noises or telling them I loved them, they rang off.

I sent a text to Mum wishing her well and explained that from this point on, all messages would end, like this, with a kiss.

I looked at wrestling on screen as if the fourth wall was a membrane I could walk through. The boundary between here and there disappeared. If I reached out, I was sure I could touch the ropes around the ring, I could slam the body of a wrestler, the crowd a panorama.

I looked to my left and Lachlan had taken off his shirt and trousers and was sitting on the floor with his back against my chair.

'I'm coming in buddy,' I said.

'Come on down,' he said.

I rested my head in his chest hair and we held one another like the wrestlers running through their routines.

In the night I opened the front door to get some air and found the house had been uprooted from the ground and was hurtling through space. Outside was a blanket of starry blackness.

Shit.

I had to tell Lachlan.

'Lachlan,' I shouted. 'The fucking house is in space!'

Where was he?

I moon-walked upstairs and saw him lying on the other side of his bed. When I jumped on it, the white sheets turned into an Antarctic expanse of snowy landscape. It was difficult to move. I began the expedition across the bed, though in my mind I was an explorer crossing a lost continent.

Half an hour later, I made it across the other side.

I went downstairs and was struck by a sudden feeling that the house was moving.

I opened the door to the night.

'Lachlan,' I said. 'We're heading to Mars.'

'Sure are, buddy,' he smiled.

I looked at the stars and the planets in their orbit and thought *shit, I better close the door.*

What else?

D-de-d-de-d-de-d-dee!

I moseyed on over to a cupboard door looking for some company. Inside a conference was taking place and I had just arrived on stage.

'Oh wow,' I said. 'I wasn't expecting so many people.'

A guy hosting ushered me to sit beside him. The audience was mostly made of grey-haired old women with corduroy skin, button eyes and cottony hair.

'We've been looking forward to your address,' the host said.

'I must say, it is quite an honour.'

'We're ready when you are.'

I began what felt like an hour of a lecture to the old women about literature and discussed a number of issues facing the industry until my focus became clear, my eyes widened, and I saw that I had been speaking to a load of blazers on a hanging rail.

Lachlan was still lying on the rug with his chest hair out, watching TV. I looked at the screen and The Undertaker was making his way to the ring. Fans held their phones aloft like flares. He was the dead man, a seven-foot-tall wrestler in his fifties wearing a wide-brimmed hat, mascara-dark eyes and leather trench coat.

His entrance music was a funereal piano theme and as he got to the ring post, he raised his open palms and the arena filled with light.

I sat down, bombed the last of the ketamine, then waited to fall into a looping of realities.

I had completely lost sense of who or where I was and lived lives that seemed every bit as real and lifelong as the one I had previously lived.

When one life ended, I was reincarnated into some other life that pulsed and danced into the walls of perception which narrowed like the heartbeat of another world and I was alive in it.

If it felt real, then what was wrong with living life this way? It was my day-to-day life that was fake, lacking meaning and I could drink whisky all day through the week and then on a weekend, come down here and do ketamine, cocaine and MDMA until I was in a world that made more sense, beaming with synthetic contentment I knew was only the illusion of happiness but was good enough, even if I was already becoming apprehensive of the dread I would feel on the comedown, the fear that would keep me in bed for days.

When I came back into a sphere of reality I took to be the usual one, if a little underwatery, I looked up and saw Lachlan.

'Hey buddy,' he said. 'Another bump?'

'Yeah,' I said in slow motion.

The size and dimensions of the living room re-focused. Big, then small, everything with a greener tint.

Oh, this felt good.

As he lined up the powder, I breathed hard through my nose, loosened some crusts of powdery snot that had formed in my nose and sniffed each of the torpedo-shaped bumps. When the music stopped, Lachlan put on *The Rip Tide* by Beirut and I drifted away on the melancholy notes of the accordion, horns and organs that swept me along in their psychedelia that sounded like sadness, a strange melancholy I had been feeling, beautiful and surreal in its own way, dissipating all around us.

*

As I came to, the ketamine haze had taken over and I was swimming back through memories. Lachlan lay giggling to himself, and I looked up at the framed gig artwork he had done for Unkle.

'This is moreish,' Lachlan said. 'Shall I see if I can get some more in?'

'I've got money,' I said.

We bumped the last of the MDMA and, sitting cross-legged in my pants, I was riding a wave of love and started thumping through my phone again. When I got to Mum, I stopped and sent her another message. 'From now on, I'm going to end messages like this with a x.'

Soon the drugs arrived and we marched off in our dark coats, came back and devoured the rest like a pair of fiends. The next day I woke up and pulled my face from the Chesterfield and knew I had to get out of there.

What happened?

Drugs.

Lots of drugs.

It had been good to a point, being able to just feel something *real*, a release from the day-to-day suffering but always I wanted more, had to take it to the next level and knew even in these moments of intoxication that there would be a price to pay when I woke up in the netherworld of a comedown.

When I did, I peeled my face from the slobber and leather sofa. My eyes were shot, my brain ached as if had been microwaved and only death animated my body like a zombified corpse, burnt out from the insides and stuffed with my ashes.

Why was I like this?

I picked up a copy of the novel I had published a few weeks before. It was black and with a grey colour palette that was too dark. It had been published in US trade paperback size to save money but wasn't long enough and was slimline like a pamphlet. Inside the book was full of typos and plotting that went nowhere, bad writing and then my name across the front.

Since I had given up on being a wrestler, I had transferred all my ambition into being a writer, a star, a real person.

But instead of being the big performer I dreamed of being, I bottled it. Too many things were going on in my life to comprehend; the narrative identity I had created for myself had begun to fall apart. Since those days wrestling in the field, I had put all my determination into becoming an author and I would finally let everybody know who I was inside, I wasn't a nobody, I was a *somebody*. But things hadn't worked out that way. I was afraid to state my opinions. My novel was full of typos, barely made sense as a story and looked like a graphic novel. When I went on stage at literature festivals, the crowd, who were mostly my friends anyway, *kayfabed* me, allowed me to pretend I was an author when, really, I knew they were only being kind and the publication wasn't the sensation I had dreamed of and we all knew I was a fake.

When the drugs coursed through me, everything seemed so clear. It felt so good to be alive. Life, existence, the universe, all of it seemed to begin, even beautiful now, and I could see how everything fitted together with such clarity. All I needed to do was take all the warmth that was filling me up with joy, skin clammy to the touch and heart-rate racing, yes, this, this certainty, this assurance, this conviction in my inner being, all I needed to do was bring this into my ordinary daily life and it would start tomorrow, from the very moment I woke up.

No, I thought, back to the phone calls, the hugging, taking off my clothes and talking non-stop bollocks. All the time without anxiety that being off my head brought, would have to be paid back. A blast of dread sank through my body.

Oh, please.

I knew I needed to get out of there and when I opened the door, this time was not in space but instead a blast of pale grey haze of the same sky I had grown under and become sick of, which my eyes struggled to adjust to.

I went out, squinting like a mole into the pale bright day.

I walked around the streets like a convict, an outsider having committed an atrocious crime. I was somebody living on the edge of things, while Pakistani men set stalls up on the main road selling fruit and vegetables; women hauled children along the road by their hands.

There was a street I liked to cut up through in the middle of the many terraced streets which dipped and then rose at the entrance to a park.

I liked it here, it was inexplicable, it looked like a huge chunk from the side of a moor had been cut out and terraformed in the middle of a city. I walked uphill steadily, until I saw a guy in the distance in orange robes doing ninja stuff.

What the fuck?

Was I still hallucinating?

Seeing him there, like a Buddhist monk, with his shaved head, cutting artful shapes through the air, terrified me.

I had to get home

That was that.

I began to run, then stopped a few seconds later to catch my breath, then started up again, until my shins were splinting, and I kept trying to thrust forward before the pain got too much and I had to bend over, panting.

When I got home, I opened the door, climbed the stairs as if not to be heard, listened out for my flatmate and waited for the march of his footsteps to diminish. I turned the key in the door, slowly, closed the door, and snuck across the corridor to my bedroom without being seen or heard.

Thank God, I was safe.

I should turn myself in. Get myself to the nuthouse. All of this had to end somewhere, didn't it?

I often thought this, but never did anything about it, never would. I closed the curtains, got into bed and slept.

It was dark when I woke up and I checked my phone. Eleven o'clock. God, that's all I needed.

I felt even weirder, turned over and went back to sleep.

The day after, I wanted to stay in bed but had to get up for a piss and was caught by Matt on my way out.

'Didn't know you were in,' he said. 'When did you get back?'

'Yesterday.'

'Yesterday?'

I avoided making eye contact.

'I've just been in bed,' I said. 'The whole time.'

'You been to Lachlan's house?'

'Yeah.'

'Oh dear,' he laughed. *'Lachlan's house.'*

I asked him what he was doing today, and he said he was going to work soon, so I watched the build-up to the football, then three football matches, and at about five o'clock we went up to the petrol station at the top of the road, bought a bottle of Brut and some cigarettes. I had some beers in the fridge and when I got home I ordered a chilli balti, put on a pair of sunglasses some girl had left here during one of our many house parties and got warmed up for the night ahead.

At about seven o'clock I got a message from Lachlan.

'Partying?'

Too right I was.

Lachlan was in Nation of Shopkeepers. I dusted off the Brut, drank a few bottles of beer, put on my coat – which was now missing four of its toggles, one for each of the four fights I had been in lately – and set off.

There were some hipster people I barely knew. We struggled for conversation in the noise of the crowded bar, and I struggled to know what to say to these guys anyway. They had a set of interests that seemed so niche and beyond my day-to-day comprehension of the world: bands I hadn't heard of, people I didn't know.

I was just here for the drink really, to not feel so alone.

I had a member's card, ordered pint after pint at a discount rate and then moved onto shots and keyed lines of cocaine in the bathroom. Several hours later, I walked out to a blast of cold air that braced me, having been kicked out for sleeping despite being convinced I wasn't asleep, and saw a pair of bouncers asking some guys to leave.

There were three or four of them, sandy-haired rugby toffs from the home counties. I had seen their type before: clever enough to get into Leeds but not one of the elite universities, people who treated my home like a holiday destination. St Anger wasn't having any of it.

I waited for them around the corner. Such disrespectful bastards. How could the bouncers let them get away with it!

Fuck it.

I clenched my fists. No doubt about it, I'd teach them a lesson in how to be a man.

So pissed, adamantium claws might have sprung from my knuckles.

I was an avenger, *St Anger* wandering around dishing up violent justice to the ignoramuses and bourgeois Neanderthals.

Dad would have laid them all out by now. He had dirty tricks. Steel toe-caps. Knuckle-dusters. One kick and a guy would be brought to his knees where Dad would finish them off with a right hand. Or, when somebody got in his face, he held his hands on his belly and he asked them *what did you say?* Their jaws agape and easier to break, he knocked them out with a single punch.

I couldn't think of a time I had lost a fight where it was one on one.

I rubbed my knuckles, waiting for the posh boys to finish up and come my way.

I poked my head around the corner.

Here they came.

One turned and shouted *nobhead* to the bouncer. They sniggered like public school boys.

Twats, I thought.

That laughter cut right through me, rife with condescension, as if it was aimed directly at me to keep me in my place.

Well, I was shit-faced but I didn't care.

I was the son of Frank.

A real man.

I put my game face on when I heard them coming toward me, jumped out from round the corner and shouted in my Batman voice, 'IF YOU WANT SOMEBODY TO FIGHT, FIGHT ME!'

I smashed a few in the face, leading with my chin, throwing wild punches as if I couldn't be hurt until – bang.

One blindsided me.

Blackout.

*

At about eleven-thirty, after hours of constantly refreshing, a pop-up flashed on screen, 'Yo. You're in for 2nd Nov show. Reckon you can have your gear ready in time? The deal is twenty in Renegade dollars which you can use for training/ merch. Cool?'

I sighed with relief and a stab of joy and satisfaction ran through me.

I couldn't believe it. I had to check the words again – I could see them but not read them. I was going to make my debut. Yes, it was there. I knew it, but somehow had doubted it, but here it was in black and white, I was going to become a wrestler.

'Cheers Joe, absolutely!' I wrote. 'I can get some stuff together for the 2nd and be working toward getting some more expensive boots before too long. Was thinking all black with taped wrists. Enjoyed today and felt the gimmick come together when I was beating down The Dude in training. Earl Black Jr. A Strong Style wrestler from Yorkshire who is very aggressive and outraged by Renegade woke politics. Total reactionary bastard.'

'Perfect.'

Dad would be so proud. I rang him up and he said one of his magic 8-ball phrases, *Today London, tomorrow the world!* or something like that, but I could tell he was made up. My match was announced a few days later on social media. The print of The Dude on one side in a Hawaiian vest and orange bandana with his tongue sticking out, eyes smiling, then there's me staring earnestly, arms folded, hair side-parted like a librarian. Earl Brown Jr.

I forwarded the graphic and sent Dad a message.

'They've got my name wrong. I'm Earl BLACK Jr, but...'

The green dot appeared on Dad's avatar and *Frank Earl is typing* appeared on screen.

'I will have to change my name to Earl Brown.... Lol,' he replied.

'They're changing it. The promoter is on holiday and the co-owner mixed up the surnames.'

'The photo looks good anyway. Looks like an old-time shooter.'

'Yeah, I look a bit psychotic too. In the eyes.'

'You are psychotic... Ha.'

'Renegade just tweeted the SLAM! Article about you.'

The article was a retrospective on Dad entitled, 'Earl Black: A career cut short' about how he toured the world as a pro wrestler from 1966 to 1973, before breaking his back in the ring.

'That's nice,' he said.

I copied and pasted the promo from the Renegade website.

NU BLOOD MATCH NEWS!
On November 2nd at NU BLOOD the ever-popular 'DUDE' will be in action against a young man making his NU BLOOD debut: 'EARL BLACK JR'. Of course, you all know happy-go-lucky, fun-loving The Dude. While Black Jr is a second-generation

talent. His father – Earl Black Sr – is a noted pro wrestler who was trained at the legendary Hart Family Dungeon. Black Jr is technically gifted with a vicious streak – something that he usually reserves for opponents that he sees as morally deficient to himself. This will be a good one!

'I guess you didn't quite 'train' in the dungeon but it's near enough,' I said.

'Trained in the dungeon? I suppose it sounds good. I had been pro for four years before I went to Calgary.'

'Did you do any training there?'

'Not really. At least it gets you over.'

Getting over meant getting acceptance from the fans mostly. But you also had to get over with the boys and promoters. It basically meant you were credible. I wanted to get over with Dad.

'Everybody knows the dungeon through WWE, more so than even Stampede,' I replied.

'Never let the truth get in the way of a good story.'

*

In mid-October, I arrived at King's Cross to meet Grace, stepping out of the Tube station onto the plaza in the dark. It was a cold and clear night. I walked up to a hotdog and coffee kiosk with a hat-shaped roof. I was wearing my long black coat with the toggles still missing from various fights, and the ones remaining looking out of place. I had left my glasses at home and struggled to make out much detail in the scene. Fumes billowed from the sides of the kiosk with a theatrical bluster and the smell of burnt onions, sizzle and coffee; some people sat around on granite benches a few yards away, while others came in and out of the station doors.

I sent her a message months ago. Her profile said she was a teacher from Kent who liked philosophy, jazz clubs, and football, by the looks of it, as I flicked through the pics of her at an Arsenal game at the Emirates. Another showed her lying on a field wearing round glasses, smiling, with a little blond boy behind her. The main profile pic was one of her in a cellar bar, beautiful, dark hair and dark eyes in the way I liked, raising a glass across a table, a slight tilt to her head, as she grinned furtively. Her eyes were dark, almond-shaped and one was half-concealed in shadow.

There was so much mystery in it, the way she seemed open but letting you in only so far; the dark and moody, slightly racoon-like look she had was cuter. She was exactly the kind of girl I would go for. I had in fact messaged her months ago, she replied, then nothing came of it. When she had replied again, I paid forty quid to reply.

I had drunk a bottle of wine before I came out, but it was already wearing off. I had been on so many dates lately, most of them had gone badly and, given that nobody could keep up with me, I found that I could still get a decent night out of it if I turned up half-pissed.

What if she was nothing like her profile?

I could feel the buoyancy and disregard giving way to anxiety and self-absorption as the alcohol began to leave my body.

The sky above was suddenly blue: a hazy aurora was projected onto the clouds, and I remembered a poster I had seen on the Tube for a Festival of Light. A girl came toward me in a purple coat and a beanie hat.

This was her.

'Wes?' she asked.

'Yeah,' I said and smiled. She smiled back.

She looked nothing like her picture but seemed nice enough, very friendly and more nervous than I thought she might have been.

How should we greet?

I hesitated, gave her a half-hearted hug and she reciprocated.

God, I was so awkward.

'Anywhere you'd like to go?' I asked.

'I don't really know London very well. I'm happy to go anywhere we can get a drink.'

I smiled.

'Well, that's narrowed things down to about five thousand bars.'

She laughed and her eyes brightened. In the streetlight, I could better make out her face, her smile, the shape of her mouth.

'I know a place, it's about a five-minute walk but I quite like it.'

We walked across the concourse, under the shifting blue light to the other side of Granary Square.

'I thought you might have known London, being from down here,' I said.

'I don't come into London that much,' she was looking down at the floor, eyes smiling. 'Did you say you were from Leeds?'

'Yeah. I spent a lot of time down here before I moved though, too.'

'You don't really have an accent.'

I laughed.

'I'm not sure that's true,' I said. 'If I do it's because I work with too many middle-class people.'

At the end of the plaza, we took a left and headed down York Way. The side of the station building was lined with arch-shaped windows, surrounded by creamy brick, and the bars and restaurants on the other side of the road were busy. So far, so good. I felt good in her presence, like the person she thought I was.

When we arrived at the pub, I pulled open the door and followed her in. The atmosphere was thick with heat, people talking over one another and mad laughter.

We were out four people deep from the bar.

'What do you want?' I asked.

'Hmmm. Is it cocktails?'

'Yeah.'

'I don't really drink cocktails. I'll have what you're having.'
I smiled, raising an eyebrow.
'What do you drink then?'
'Wine, usually. Or beer.'
'Beer?
'Yeah.'
'I can get you a beer if you want?'
'No, I want to try something different.'
'Do you want to try an Old Fashioned?'
'What is it?'
'Bourbon, orange peel, and a cherry.'
'That sounds good.'

We waited at the bar, I ordered, and when we got our drinks we went round into the back room and found somewhere to sit at the far end of a long table.

We cramped into the corner.

'It's a bit busy,' I said.

She nodded. 'Saturday night.'

'I prefer drinking midweek, really.'

'I'm not much of a drinker. I just feel sick after three or four drinks.'

'I'm the same,' I said.

The bar extended to this side of the room and it was lined with people waiting for drinks.

The far end of the room was lined with gaudy rose-flowered wallpaper, whereas the rest of the walls were a deep dark green, with various plush red leather chairs, brown leather panels on the bar, and gilded mirrors, all in the warm light offered by the copper helmet lampshades on barely visible cord that seemed to float above our heads. It had all the vulgar inviting splendour of a private members club, but tempered by eclectic hipster bric-a-brac and carefree attitude.

Some girls directly in front of us were dancing; a group of guys stood drinking nearby, occasionally bent double with howling laughter.

Grace leaned over her drink, staring down into it, stirring the cherry with a cocktail stick.

I liked the way she held herself, in her long-sleeved purple dress with overlapping straps at the neck. She had a fine-boned poise, arms folded in at her elbows. Her brown hair was centre-parted, twirling at the sides, and her lips were red and her nose had a slight bend just as mine did, except hers was from fighting with her brother and she looked good.

I sank the last of my drink. 'See that guy over there?'

She looked over. 'You mean the moron nearly falling over?'

'Yeah.'

'I bet he does this every week. He's called George or Eric and has an important job in the city but his dream is to one day to not be a massive nonce.'

She laughed.

'No. He looks more like somebody I've probably taught.'

I could see her loosening up, we laughed, talked some more about how she was the acting Head of Sixth Form; she taught philosophy and history, but was really an RE teacher, her favourite philosopher was Kant and philosophy of mind was her favourite area.

She had finger-puppets of the great philosophers and so did I.

What a coincidence. What else did we have in common?

I said that I liked Nietzsche and existentialism, how I was teaching creative writing but only one module, the rest of the time I was doing arts admin for literature organisations and mostly wrestling. I had grown tired of the literary world and had supposedly got into wrestling to write a book about it but had no plans for that just yet.

Things were going well, I snuck out under the table to get more drinks, three or four times, and we laughed and chatted until a solemn look came over her face.

Her eyebrows arched. 'You know that I have a son, right?'

I nodded, but in reality had forgotten.

Did this mean I could be a stepdad if things went well?

I swallowed my drink, the tang of orange on my tongue and thought that it sounded like a good life. How would I tell my family? *Hello, I have a stepson.* Things were moving suddenly very fast.

I nodded. 'Yeah. I remember you saying.'

Her look became more authoritative, and I could see the schoolteacher coming out in her.

'He's disabled. This isn't going to be a problem for you?'

In the picture I had seen of him there was nothing visibly disabled about him, though even if there was, what did it matter? I wasn't an animal.

'What does he have?' I asked.

'Speech and language delay, dyspraxia, he's a little bit deaf.' She looked at me with a sad smile. 'Not everybody finds it easy, that's all.'

I nodded. 'No. Not at all.'

'He can be hard work. Last week he threw his shoes at his headteacher!'

I laughed loud and hearty, then backtracked realising how crazy I sounded, checking to see if Grace saw the funny side too and she did.

'I mean it's not funny,' Grace said. 'But you have to laugh.'

'Sometimes people say I have a schoolboy's sense of humour, but I say what's wrong with that? Schoolboys are really funny.'

She laughed.

'They're not so funny when you work in a school full of them,' she said. 'But yeah, even then, they do make you laugh.'

I placed a finger on my lip, rubbed the stubble on my chin, all the while gazing into the dreamy look in her eyes.

'You okay with me being a wrestler?' I asked.

'I wondered when you were going to talk about that. What kind of wrestler are you? Like WWE stuff?'

I nodded. 'Well, I'm training to be.'

'I used to watch it with my brothers in the nineties. I loved The Rock.'

'You know my dad wrestled his grandad?'

'Wait,' she said, eyebrows furrowed, 'your dad was a wrestler too?'

'Oh, wait until you meet him,' I said, laughing like something had been released from her.

'How do you get a match then? Sorry, I have no idea how any of it works.'

'No problem. Why would you? I do actually, you should come.'

She pursed her lips, then dimples formed in her cheeks and she took a second to look away.

I needed a piss. With the table blocked off by the others, I climbed under again and scrambled across the floor and got a funny look from a woman at the other end, I apologised and pulled a face at Grace who was watching with amusement.

When I got back, I climbed in the same way, popped up beside her and her body was open toward mine. I slid my knee inside her thigh. She held her glass to her lips.

'I've only ever been on three dates,' she said.

'Three?'

'This is my third.'

'Bloody hell,' I said. 'I've been on too many.'

'How's this one going?'

'Pretty good,' I said.

I noticed her hand in my hand. She looked up at me, eyes fierce in the dark. I leaned forward and kissed her.

*

On the way back to the station, as we walked hand in hand, I had the sense this was going somewhere. Clouds of strobe light ghosted above the surface of the crowd like electric jellyfish. I asked her to stay at my place or kiss some more down by the canal, but she laughed and said I would have to wait. We went to eat at Nando's where I ordered a butterflied whole chicken and eight beers. Afterwards, we kissed again before she boarded the train. By Wednesday, I was on the same train myself, drinking a Pinot Noir before dinner at her place and by the weekend I was joining her on a work night out with her teacher friends. Three weeks later I met Eliot, made cookies with him and played shopkeeper with him, while I caught Grace at the door, eyes wet with tears. All of this was moving so fast I was scared, but the sense of momentum and knowing it was right bypassed any doubts I had. I was staying at her place four or five nights a week, coming back to London to train at the Dojo or give a lecture on a Friday afternoon about the writing industry at UEL, but for the morning of the show, I woke up to a brief moment of clarity in my own bed, having spent most of the night awake, staring at the stars and thinking of all the wrestlers who had come before me, I had enjoyed a brief moment of not being me before consciousness returned and the strange seriousness of this monumental day hit me.

I wanted to pick up my phone and call up my past self, the gawky teenager dreaming himself out of his life through wrestling and say *hey buddy, you'll never guess what, we only fucking did it.*

I could barely eat my porridge, had a coffee run riot through me, packed my bag with my kit, said bye to Lauren and marched to the Tube station where I took the Victoria line across town and changed at Stockwell for Balham, feeling like a spy, somebody operating on a level beyond the other civilians, who stared back at me with their glum faces.

I got outside the venue but had to stop to scratch my freshly shaved chest and armpits which were prickled into a kind of pre-pubescent, boiled chicken look of too-smooth pale skin and razor burn.

I walked around the block, without music, just focused on going over the choreography from the match I had against The Dude at the try-out. I had been watching videos of his matches, picking up his sequences and pre-empting whatever he might have me do. When I got to the venue, I bent over, heaved and roared, but I hadn't eaten enough to produce anything other than bile.

Grugughghg, another load of bile. My eyes were watering. I spat out a glob that hung off the bottom of my lip. My eyes were raw.

Cars passed. People waited at the lights. Life went on all around me. Then there was me, some lunatic with a crew cut retching outside a pub because he was about to have a pretend fight with somebody, which would somehow help me become real.

I took a look around at the junction outside the pub. It was a grey, overcast day that I knew would never forget, whatever the outcome may be.

Did I have it in me?

Yes, I did.

Somehow, I knew that when I hit the ring, something ancestral and pumping in my blood would take over. Beyond the anxiety, I was looking forward to taking my steps into the ring and then the pub after. It wasn't unusual for me to volunteer myself for something, become sick with nerves, smash it and think about the next big challenge. For all the doubt I had, there was also a lot of belief and entitlement, with nervous drama seeming to be the price of ambition.

I ran my hand through my crew cut and across smooth cheeks. I figured that Earl Black Jr wasn't the sort to have a beard and had shaved my face too. I was as hairless and hardbody as I was as a teenager.

I dry-heaved; this time nothing came out.

I had been here before as ring crew, the first rung on the ladder, helping to assemble and dismantle the ring. Carrying jackets, like I had once done for Bruce Logan's black sleeveless robe when I crewed shows, emblazoned with the Union Jack and Japanese emblems from his tourneys around the world, and then got heat for when he found it bundled in the back because somebody had knocked it off from where I left it.

The young boys did whatever menial jobs were going. This could be tightening the turnbuckles. Sweeping debris from the canvas. Mopping blood from the floor. Buying drinks for the pros.

Their reasoning for this was that they had done this once and it was about respect.

I walked past the main entrance and down a side street round the back to find the van, ten or so trainees hauling parts of the ring from the van. I greeted them with weak handshakes, some that were yanked into hugs, depending on the closeness of the bond or how jealous they were, and got in line. A big man in a vest and gloves, Aaron, wiped sweat from his forehead and handed out the parts.

Ten-foot-long ring posts, boards, judo mats, ropes, a coil spring, underlay.

One guy who had been training for two years but was yet to have a match, like most trainees from the Dojo, patted me on the back and wished me well.

Some just ignored me.

People were waiting for me to make a mistake. Then I'd be gone. We made a conveyor belt of lifters and carriers coming in and out the building.

But all I could think about while I was carrying the materials was the match. I heard a story once of a guy who got so scared he ran out of the venue, and nobody booked him for five years.

With the ring up, the veterans arrived and brokered their matches with the strawbs, walking through spots at a half-pace, all expression in their faces, with sound effects. Stepping and moving with balletic grace.

I looked around.

The back of the pub was used as a comedy venue and had a balcony running around the ring like the Globe theatre.

The fans would be right on top of you.

'Hey man, how you doing?'

I turned around to see The Dude.

'Good,' I answered. 'Shitting myself, but good.'

'Ah, you'll be fine.'

I took the keys, phone and wallet from my trousers, slipped shoes off and left them in a pile on the ring apron.

I climbed into the ring, which was busy with wrestlers walking through their matches, people bouncing off the ropes, ducking strikes, running lines across the canvas. The noise of the ring was immense. Awkward and ever-shifting creaks of girder and board, like an old ship.

We locked up, toe to toe, like a ballroom dance. Dad would hate this.

Before Randy 'Macho Man' Savage and Ricky 'The Dragon' Steamboat at WrestleMania 3 in the '80s everything was called on the fly.

This match changed the game.

And here I was, fifty years after Dad's last match, walking through every step of the fight.

Joe told us to get out of the ring and take all bags and belongings upstairs. The doors were open.

The fans were coming.

I got my stuff and swallowed a nervous ball of energy that wrenched in my gut as I climbed the staircase overlooking the ring. The upper floor was a private bar and looked like a gentleman's club, all dark mahogany and leather, it was easy to imagine plumes of cigar smoke and insider goings-on.

I sat in my corner.

There were comings and goings in the haze of Lynx Africa and Tiger Balm, all clove oil and teenage boy.

One guy was helicoptering his dick around, to everybody's dismay. There were sequin jackets, spandex leotards, and Mexican-style masks as everybody got changed and had very serious conversations about the routines they had put together, like drag queens about to kick off before showtime. I slouched against the wall biting my thumb. I would not be a wrestler until I walked through that door, crossed the threshold, performed my routine in front of the gaze of the crowd.

I got up. Paced about. Sat back down. Checked my phone. Sat back down in my corner.

What if I forgot everything? What if I died in front of the crowd? What if I got dropped on my head like Darren Drozdov, the former All-State Athlete who become a quadriplegic after a powerbomb went wrong? What if I did that to somebody else?

I got up and paced again.

The place was full of drunken wrestling geeks. I could hear them the other side of the double doors. Banging on the barriers. Stomping their feet. Soon I would be fed to them. Sacrificed to the roar.

I had friends who had come but not Dad. Grace would be here. Somewhere in the crowd with Lauren. The stakes too high to fail. But then there was the fear of the unknown: this wasn't training; I had never been out there in front of a crowd and anything could happen.

The first matches were soon up and the partnerships stood by the door, styling mimes of their key sequences in repetitions with last-minute emphasis.

In the bar wrestlers were in their full gear. All the early 90s-style gimmicks. Marilyn Draven in his trench coat and cannibal mask. The Preacher with his bible. A far-right campaigner called James Hardcastle, a bald nut in a cheap suit and tie who was going to interfere in my match to get one over on the hippy, The Dude.

The doors bucked open and one wrestler lunged into the bar. Panting. Another not far behind as if they had both been transported from a battle in another time-space. Red with slap marks and awash with sweat. When they were both through the other side of the curtain, they embraced, bodies alight with heat.

I stepped aside as they walked past.

One full of energy, while the veteran catechised parts that could have gone better.

A hand on my shoulder.

The Dude was standing behind me.

'You ready to talk it through, brother?'

I nodded.

I recited the match. The Intro. The Shine. The Heat. The Comeback. The Finish.

'Cool,' The Dude said. 'But remember you throw a gut punch the second time I go to the top rope. Yeah?'

'Yeah,' I said. 'Then you do the Russian Leg Sweep?'

'Sweet.'

The matches ran through the first half of the card, each wrestler calm and steely-eyed beforehand and then returning hot and sweaty afterward, depending on the outcome of the performance angry or elated, all of them seeming like they had seen their life flash before their eyes. The interval came and I followed a couple of the others to the supermarket across the road, bought some chicken breast, fruit salad and an energy drink, and waited. Anxiety ran through me to a point where I felt like the atoms of my body were getting ready to split.

I felt faint, pale-faced and light-headed.

Oh, this wasn't good.

I found a corner to get changed, pulled out my wrestling attire and cotton sports tape in a rigid roll, pulled down my trousers and slid into my black trunks. The terror subsided for a moment into a kind of spectacular excitement: today was the day I was going to become a wrestler!

Once I got all of this out the way, the feeling was going to be fantastic.

There was muscle developing across my chest and shoulders but as one trainee had said, I looked like a guy who used to be fat and had got in shape, I wore the residue of a softer, more feminine body. I was pale, pockets of fat beneath my pecs and a small round belly.

Jack said that nobody normal becomes a wrestler. Everybody has a mental health problem. And so do most of the people who come to these shows. Issues with self-esteem. A void they were trying to fill. What was it they were trying to find in a wrestling ring?

I told myself how stupid all of this was. It was fake, a *fake* match, a *fake* fight, which meant this must be fake *fear*, fake *feelings*, fake *me*.

But it didn't stop it from being real. During The Attitude Era the WWE ran a promo that opened with a defensive sounding, *I know what you're thinking, I'm not a real athlete, just a wrestler* followed by montages of wrestlers posing in a warehouse cut with clips of injuries in the ring. Voiceovers played. *I'm six foot ten, three hundred and twenty-eight pounds. I won boxing's golden gloves three years in a row. I was a national champion at the University of Miami. My jersey was retired at Florida state. I was the Ultimate Fighting Champion. When you step through those ropes bad things do happen. Had over two hundred stitches. I've suffered a dozen concussions. I've broken bones. I've separated shoulders. Damn near broke my neck. I've blown out knees. But I still got up. This is who I am. This is what I do. I'm not really an athlete? This isn't real? Try lacing my boots.* When it was time, I walked out through to the balcony, pumped out some air squats in good rhythm, wound my arms in circles and paced about like I was about to go and kill somebody.

The Dude came up alongside me, we hugged and whispered *stay safe* in one another's ears.

I waited for *Mayday* to hit and the beat to drop to make my entrance. Just as I was about to go out, I pounded myself in the chest and let out a scream.

Laughter.

Marilyn Draven was standing behind me.

'Jesus,' he said. 'Could you be any more of a strawb?'

I pulled open the door and stepped out into the crowd.

All eyes on me, I sucked in my gut and strutted past the fans, eyeballing some on my way with my meanest face.

Some made wisecracks about my nipple. I looked down to see a red circle had formed around it from where I pounded it before coming out. My movements were like stop-motion, too adrenalized, and when I climbed up on the apron, slid into the ring and my feet sank into the soft heavy surface below the canvas, the whole thing felt underwater, my legs jellified with the spring of the ring. I climbed to the second rope, looked out and gave them the finger. When the bell rang, my sweaty pale torso was glistening under the spotlight. The Dude glowed in his orange tights and tie-dye bandana.

We circled.

Coming together for the lock up, I ducked under, scooped him up for a waistlock takedown like an amateur wrestler and rode him before he reversed into a wristlock, transitioned into a headlock and then a running spot which ended with him surfing on my back, before running hitting a double-knee attack and a series of kicks.

He wasn't wearing kick pads, so the laces of his leather boots cut my skin, and with every blow, I said to myself *this is real, this is happening,* like a voice in a dream.

I counted them, one, two, three, then chicken-shit like a heel, slide out of the ring and onto the next stage.

The Dude dived at me through the second rope and I clocked him with a forearm.

Waited for the heat.

Then moved onto the beatdown. I got back in, began kicking him into the corner with some piss-poor kicks, showed out to the crowd and heard nothing.

The adrenaline and the crowd had sapped my energy. My limbs were heavy. I was breathing hard.

The Dude sold anyway. The crowd were getting flat and somebody shouted, 'Default wrestler!'

'What?' I shouted.

'You look like the default wrestler on a video game!'
Everybody laughed.
Then a chant of *de-fault* broke out. I put my hands on my ears, as Dad had suggested. They got louder.

De-fault. De-fault. De-fault.

I went for The Sharpshooter, twisting his legs in a knot around my knee and was kicked off.

The Dude sprung back to his feet, somehow reborn and began his comeback, a step ahead of every move now. He booted me to the floor. Climbed to the top and leapt at me, I aimed a gut shot which he caught, transitioned into a Russian Leg Sweep and I bumped hard.

The crowd were dead.

The Dude hit another double-knee attack and, like Chekov's gun, having attempted his kick sequence earlier in the match now got to complete it during his comeback.

The crowd counted along to the kicks.

The blows came just as hard as before. As each one landed I heard an inner voice tell me the next step.

One kick and I crouched on one knee. Second kick and I got back to my feet. Third kick was a back kick bending me over. Fourth kick was a straight volley to the chest to stand me back up. Then it was time to throw a clothesline which he ducked, The Dude ducked it and knocked me down with a karate kick to the chin.

One. Two. No!

James Hardcastle is at ringside and has moved my foot to the rope without the referee seeing to break the count.

While The Dude remonstrated I stole a win with one of the slowest roll-ups from behind in the history of pro wrestling.

One. Two. Three.

Suddenly, forgetting to sell, I jumped up and down; genuine joy broke through the performance. I had survived, I had done it, it was over! I chopped my crotch and shouted *suck it!*

The bell rang, *Mayday* blared, and the announcer declared the winner of this match by submission was Earl Black Jr!

I slid out the ring, leaving The Dude dazed scratching his head, gave a little wave to the fans and climbed upstairs. Across the balcony, panting, sluice yellow with sweat in the lights, fans patted me on the back and shouted well done. I wiped their hands from me and told them to fuck off.

*

I was buzzing as I approached the door to cross to the other side of kayfabe. Normally it would take five or ten drinks and a few lines of coke to feel like myself, but all I had to do was pull on some spandex and pretend to fight somebody. I was thinking about how well things had gone and where I could be a few matches down the road when I could realise my potential as a technical wrestler, be *the next big thing* and when I pulled open the door, looked around one last time and sneered at the crowd. A chorus of boos rang out. The pop rippled through the audience. They fucking hated me. I was a heat machine.

Oh, I was a real wrestler!

I turned and walked through the door to find Marilyn waiting for me. Maybe he was gonna give up the bullshit and tell me I had done well?

I approached him.

'What the fuck was that?' he said.

My jaw hung. I was paralysed by fear and shame. What could I have done? I racked my mind as fast as I could. Nothing.

'Was it the match?' I asked.

'I couldn't even watch your shit fucking match,' he said, 'I had to stop watching when you gave the crowd the finger.'

'I was just trying to get heat,' I said.

I noticed my chest was red with slap marks. I wiped off the sweat and bent over to catch my breath.

'I give the crowd the finger. That's *my* thing.'

'Sorry. I had no idea.'

'No idea.'

'I'll get you a pint to make up.'

'I don't want your fucking pint. Don't you ever fucking do that again. Do you understand? You fucking cunt. I'm too angry to even talk to you.'

Was he for real?

I was second-guessing everything I did and felt stupid. I burned with indignation and shame. Did this fucking moron think he had somehow managed to trademark swearing? Stone Cold Steve Austin was flipping people the bird twenty years ago. Marilyn turned and walked away, It was over for now, I told myself I wouldn't let it get to me but I knew it would.

I put my hands on my hips and took it all in.

Was it me?

Was he genuinely pissed off because I had given somebody the finger? Was that a *thing*? That these wrestlers were so touchy, that even imitating them in any way was seen as some huge disrespect. Didn't they realise that we were only playing at being men in a pantomime?

I couldn't work out why they all had to take it all so seriously, other than the fact that their masculinities were so fragile because they were only parodying real tough guys.

Perhaps that was the point. Their masculinity was a fiction, a figment of their pathetic little imaginations and without their collective delusion, they were nobodies, nothing.

The best guess I had was that I had actually done quite well and in the absence of anything to truly get me on, Marilyn was making a big deal of me using the middle finger because that's the only thing he could nail me with. It was pathetic.

As if he was the first person to swear in wrestling?

Fuck him. Fuck all these motherfuckers.

Backstage, others were kinder, Trevor told me not to pay attention to Marilyn. I got changed, then tried to watch the remaining matches through the glass in the door and when the final bell rang for the main event, remembered my place in the circle of life, made my way to the floor and began putting the ring away as it came down, in all its puzzle pieces.

I carried a board at a right angle, ducked under the door and passed it to Aaron by the van.

One of the crew patted me on the back, 'Well done buddy!'

I smiled.

'Thanks!'

'You fucking smashed it!'

I went back inside, pulled up one side of the long girders and double-teamed it with another of the wrestlers who had been on the show.

Even though I was wearing my street clothes, the match was still on my body, I was shaking like I had been in a fight and my T-shirt clung to my body.

I walked back inside to find the bungees that held canvas on the ring.

I checked my phone and the friends were asking where we were headed. I told them I was on my way. When the last of the boards and girders were in the van, I made sure to shake every hand that needed shaking, took my Dojo dollars from Joe who passed me them in an envelope and said I had things to work on but had done well, and on my way out some big-hipped scenester with glasses and curly hair introduced himself.

'Great match,' he said. 'I really like the old-school gimmick.'

'Thanks,' I said.

'Have you got any promo shots done, if you don't mind me asking?'

'No.'

'Here's my card,' he said, pushing a business card into my hand.

'Thanks,' I said. 'I'll be in touch.'

'Cool. And your dad, was he a wrestler or is it all kayfabe?'

'No, he was.'

'Excellent,' he said. 'Maybe we can get you both down to my studio?'

'Why not?'

I smiled and headed off.

I had no idea if I had to pay for these or if he worked for the promotion, but I didn't care. It was all part of this transformation. I needed promo pics. The only ones I had were taken by Joe in the Dojo when I had the angry intellectual gimmick.

All those years I had stared into Dad's scrapbook poses and now I would have my own.

Earl Black Jr.

I made my way out of the front entrance into the dark night. The road was busy with traffic, I cut through the bustle, stopped off at a cashpoint to take out forty quid and had the match replaying in my head.

I could remember every part of it. Every echo, every pattern through the air, every blow that struck my body.

Funny how I could suddenly remember it all now, without hesitation, like a comic book frame of sequences.

What had I been thinking, though, with those crotch chops?

I don't know. It was because that's what wrestlers did in the nineties and what we did in the school playground.

As I approached the pub, I could see the veterans on a table nearest to the window. Marilyn Draven, Jack Tanner, Sarah Connor and their hangers-on and entourage who were higher up than me by dint of knowing them in some way, despite never having taken a bump for this business.

I opened the door, kept my head down and walked past them, eyes on the table ahead of me with Lauren, Lachlan, Grace and some of my other friends who had somehow intermingled with one another. Grace had already got over with everybody; she was shy but engaged with people and just how decent a person she was seemed to resonate with people. No jokes, tall tales or anything like that. She didn't have to dress up in Lycra to impress people or be liked.

I walked up to them.

A cheer rang out, but I kept my head down hoping the veterans weren't looking over. Nothing would be worse than them seeing me glorying at this moment when I had apparently insulted the business.

Everybody was thrilled to see me, and I remembered that, along with the buzz of the wrestling, they had also been drinking all day.

Grace came up to me first, pulled me toward her and we kissed.

'That was so good,' she smiled.

The others patted me on the back, hailing me like some kind of hero. We stood around a table. Lauren rhapsodised about this being more fun than my book launch. Lachlan gestured for me to bring it in, and as I snuggled my head into his chest he held me tight and said *that was real, brother*.

They were pissed as newts. I had to catch up.

I went to the bar and waited in a queue with many of the punters, suddenly changing the expression on my face to something more Earl Black Jr. Kayfabe lived on!

There was a tap on my shoulder, and I turned to see Marilyn Draven with Rhea O'Reilly standing beside me like a sidekick.

'You are a fucking cunt,' he said.

I nodded. 'Sorry Marilyn.'

He pointed at me and laughed.

'I'm not gonna say anything else before I get too fucking angry,' he said, then turned to Rhea. 'You would not believe this little cunt. Fuck me! If I'd have done that on a show when I was green I'd have had the shit kicked out of me.'

'I won't do it again,' I said.

Marilyn shook his head.

'There were elements of your match I liked. But you have a lot to learn,' Rhea added, in her thick Belfast accent.

'Okay,' I said, standing there with my mouth slightly open, knowing nothing I could say would satisfy them. It was a case of playing the idiot who was glad to have their attention.

Marilyn left shaking his head. Then Rhea stared a moment before turning away with the same look of disgust on her face.

All the boys were at the bar, I could hear the wrestle talk, the back-and-forth banter and waited in line, two deep all the way along the bar, and when it was my turn, I ordered a shot and a pint I tried to carefully manoeuvre the pint out through the crowd without spilling any.

I took a sip and Trev was standing in front of me.

'Well done buddy,' he said, pulling me in for a hug.

'Was it alright?'

'It was much better than my first match. Let's put it that way.'

'Marilyn keeps cunting me off for doing crotch chops and giving them the finger.'

'Didn't you call one fan a cunt too?' he chuckled.

'Ha,' I said, feeling my cheeks flush. 'I forgot about that.'

'Like I say, it's better to go too far, then you can rein it in. Rather than not go far enough and not make an impression.' He put his hand on my shoulder. 'Anyway, don't worry about it. Just make sure it doesn't happen again and I'll see you in training. Tomorrow?'

I took a minute to think about it.

This could have been it. I would have enough for something to write about. I could put all of this behind me. But there was something unfinished, this wasn't where things ended.

'Definitely,' I said. 'I've got so many ideas for where I might take things.'

Trev smiled.

This feeling was just too good to surrender. All these years of dreaming of being a wrestler, of drinking and being depressed, feeling like the world had fallen apart around me and here I was, beaming with joy, and I knew that whatever happened I wasn't going to end my story here. I had too much to prove. Nothing or nobody was going to stop me.

Somebody had handed me a pint without me noticing and I held the glass up to my eyes in awe.

'Maybe not tomorrow though,' I said letting out a cackle as all the excitement of the night rushed up in me as I downed another pint and then another. I drank and drank and drank until I was one of the boys and totally out of my mind and on the way home, alone, exploded vomit all over my shoes, eyes bursting, before falling in the darkness.

Part Two

Eight months later, I waited on the apron at the Dojo to leap in over the top rope, perform a sequence of shoulder, backward and tiger rolls before exiting the ring over the top rope in a single continuous motion. I had been on every NU BLOOD show since my first match and the ultra who came to every show, had seen my bland-as-sand wrestler body, black boots and trunks and recognised that I looked like the default setting of the create-a-wrestler function on the WWE video game, was my biggest fan.

The thing had caught on, and when I came to the ring, people chanted *de-fault* and shouted out things like KEEP PUSHING TAUNT AND THEN USE YOUR FINISHER.

I wasn't sure I wanted to be 'the default wrestler' or play a video game character but I affected some robotic quirks into my movements and otherwise used it as heat. The more I ignored it the more frenzied the shouts of *default* became and the more 'frustrated' I became in the ring and would eventually explode to give them a payoff for jeering me. Some fans had created a skin of me for others to download, and they played as me, the default wrestler on their video games just as I had done as a teenager, imagining who I might be one day.

It worked; heat, not the kind of good heat Marilyn got, but they had responded.

They thought I was a funny, a stooge, I was something different and cultish and happy to be for now. I was going to be the kind of heel that did nothing to get himself over.

Gave nobody reason to cheer me.

In some ways, I took this default thing as a compliment. I must have looked something like a wrestler, to be the *default* wrestler for God's sake, and I was getting a reaction, which was more than most trainees got, though I worried that Joe didn't see it as me being properly 'over', but these interactions were encouraging and made me feel like I was going some way in the right direction.

I had read somewhere that when the Olympic gold medallist freestyle wrestler joined WWE, his gimmick was that he was boring. I stole that and added a characteristic of my own: Earl Black Jr would move kind of stiff like a robot, a dangerous goon, a shit terminator. It wasn't the kind of thing that was going to make me a champion, which was my ambition now that my writing had all but completely dried up, but it was earning me a spot on the next two upcoming NU BLOOD shows, and I had shown what I could do in a singles, tag-team, eight-man and four-way match. I was versatile, in better shape and getting over.

Meanwhile, I was sleeping most nights at Grace's, had formed a good relationship with her son and took him to school and back every day, and the day after impressing during a four-way dance tag match with Grace in the audience and the match cues written in biro on my forearms, I went into training feeling like a champion, regaling them with a story of me completely pissed after the show seeing a guy trying to start a fight with a camp guy in a McDonald's queue before I stormed over and gave him some of what he was looking for, then went back with his mates and partied all night. When Trev asked me to step into his 'office' and we bowed under the corrugated door and I followed him along the next unit beside a car mechanics.

Shit, what had I done?

'How do you think things have been going lately?' Trevor asked. 'In training?'

I couldn't go more than a couple of weeks without upsetting somebody about something in wrestling.

'Alright,' I said. 'I feel like I'm getting better all the time. Getting in better shape. I know there's a lot to learn.'

'Good. It looks like you're enjoying yourself.'

'I am.'

A drill screamed fizzing yellow sparks as it touched a chassis.

'Please, don't tell anybody I told you. You know how things can change in wrestling. But Joe is really pleased with you. He wants to book you against Bruce Logan at the next NU BLOOD.'

I exhaled so hard my body felt empty.

Bruce Logan. This would be the match to get me over. Wrestling with the best technical wrestler in the world. The guy who was currently touring Japan and had a black belt in *jiu jitsu* and couldn't be more legitimate if he wanted to be.

'I can't believe it,' I said.

'Like I said. Don't say anything. But I thought I'd give you the heads up and you can get yourself prepared.'

'Yeah,' I said. 'What've we got? Six weeks? I'll give up drinking and try and train on a Saturday as well. I can't believe it.'

'You deserve it,' Trev placed his hand on my shoulder. 'Just don't fuck it up.'

*

I went back to Leeds a few weeks later, boarded a bus to Dad's that crept out of the traffic past warehouses and their corrugated iron roofs storing wood flooring and industrial goods. Some of the graffitied walls had been blacked out by darker spray. Further down some of the counter-graffiti had been graffitied again and formed a dialogue. Strangleweed, witch's hair, grew by the roadside.

This part of Leeds was directly across the river from where I was brought up in Burley. There was a large population of Polish men who drank cans of lager in the streets at night, people like my dad: retired, disabled, on benefits with the addicts, junkies, mutants and people who had lost their minds.

The clothes people wore were cheap, from no-name stores, that appeared flimsy and out of style. Where two tower blocks reigned at the end of the high street, a donkey lived on arable land. The hub of the community was a Cash Converters that had set up inside a brutalist hexagon at the foot of Town Street. When they were up, they could buy other people's possessions at knock-down prices. When things were bad, it was their stuff in the shop window.

Hidden behind contoured shrubbery was Armley jail with its castle-like entrance and high walls. When Dad did time here he called it the 'big house'. Once, when I was sixteen, I hadn't seen him for five or six weeks. I somehow knew where he had gone. It was the longest I had ever been without him. When a druggie in a tracksuit stopped me with my friends on our way home from football, I knew exactly why.

'Are you Frank's son?" he asked.

'Yeah,' I said.

He took me to one side.

'He's doing time but will be out soon.'

'What's he done?'

'Vehicular assault.'

It turned out that Dad had got into an argument with a butcher after he had been caught shoplifting. Rather than turn himself in, he tried to drive away and the butcher stopped him. Dad told him to get out of the way or he'd run him over. The butcher didn't move and so Dad ran him over. He was sent down for six months for vehicular assault and lost his licence.

This kind of thing didn't surprise or upset me. I just accepted it. I might have discussed this in passing with my brother but I would never tell anybody else, not even Mum. I could tolerate these kinds of things as long as nobody else knew.

When Dad was released I asked him what it had been like inside. He smiled and told me the place was full of pussy cats.

Life was tougher on the outside, he said.

I got off the bus, stopped at a shop for supplies and then walked up to the entrance to Dad's flat. Since he had moved here, he had cleaned up his act and there were no scumbags around. I buzzed the intercom and he came shuffling from his bottom floor flat, a dumb smile across his face, dressed in a black T-shirt with the sleeves cut off, black combat trousers and slippers that were battered flat, barely holding together.

'Evening,' he said and led me through the cabbage-smelling foyer by the lift shafts through a set of double doors and the metal grille he had on his front door. It was unseasonably warm yet the heating was on, and I was already boiling hot since I'd just run across the road from the bus stop against the flow of traffic.

I took off my jacket and placed it on the bed in the living room. He sat down in his armchair.

Even in his seventies he still carried some of his famous bulk. He had a smile that brightened his wrinkled face, soft from years of moisturising. He only ever wore black, he said because he always spills food down himself but I knew it was also because he thought it was slimming. He shaved his head to avoid the silvery greys.

'Do you want a coffee?' he asked.

I felt around for beers in my carrier bag.

'I've got beer?' I suggested.

'You're leading me astray,' he smiled. I eased open the ring pull in a gasp and passed one over.

He tapped the side of the can. 'Budweiser.'

'Yeah,' I said. 'Some people think it's bland and it sort of is. But I like that if you're drinking a lot.'

'We used to have what you call session ales, you know? It would be a lighter beer you could drink on the job.'

The diminished mastery in his fingers made him look like it had been slipped onto a mannequin, and as he raised and lowered it the same way every time due to the limited motion allowed by his wrists and shoulder, the movement looked mechanical and could easily have belonged to some kind of animatronic creature.

In his cut-off T-shirt, his muscles were visibly wasted and the grainy tattoos he recently had re-coloured were pearled like tapioca.

'Why are you standing up?' I asked.

'I was halfway through a workout,' he said. I followed him through to the kitchen where he had a bench and some free-weights setup. 'I can only lift light but I'm going for super sets. Get a pump.'

He squatted one-legged onto the base into a sitting position and then fell back onto the inclined upper portion of the padded bench, hunched over for his dumbbells and then began a furious set of chest flies, his chest expanded and his weighted arms beating like wings.

The dumbbells were very light but he treated the movement seriously with the correct breathing; despite the weight being small these were long-remembered motor patterns and he moved with the élan of a seasoned lifter. Sweat beads formed only on the upper reaches of his semi-bald eyebrows and he began grunting, grunting out awkward reps with his shot muscles.

'Looking good, Francis,' I said.

'You want to jump on?'

'No.'

'You were strong when you used to train. You were always stronger than me. I could never squat or deadlift. My body wouldn't have it.'

'Maybe another time,' I said.

'Got any matches coming up?' he asked. 'I've got my new hip. I should be able to able to sit long enough to get the coach.'

'Well, I should have Bruce Logan in a few months.'

'Bruce Logan?'

'Yeah.'

He smiled.

'From strength to strength,' he said. 'If they're gonna give you Bruce Logan now, they must like you.'

'Don't tell anybody.'

'I saw a match with him on TV. He's not a giant, but a very good technical wrestler. You'll have a good match with him.'

'Yeah.'

'Throw him around like a paper aeroplane!' he laughed.

I sat on the bed. Other than the time I had used it a few weeks ago when I had taken so many pills I was still awake at 6am knocking on his window, nobody had used it. He never noticed things like this. I could be off my head on crack and he wouldn't know. The walls were painted brown and all his furniture was from charity shops or was an invention of his. On the back of his armchair, he had gaffer-taped a heat lamp to keep his head warm and he had created a remote-control holder out of a stationery organiser. The chair itself was propped up on four stacks of books to make it easier for him to get in and out of.

I drank the last of my can and opened up another.

'Been up to anything, lately?' I asked.

'Not much. I've been sorting my will out.'

I nodded. 'But you don't have anything, do you?'

'I've left you my fridge and oven. And I want to be buried like a Viking, sailed out to sea on a burning boat,' he laughed.

'I don't need an oven and a fridge, to be honest Dad. I have those things.'

'Suit yourself.'

God knows how old they would be by the time I got them. At any rate, hauling them down the other end of the country wasn't going to do me any favours.

'Thanks anyway,' I said,

'What's the plan for tonight then?' he asked. 'I can't remember what you said.'

'A girl I know is having a Eurovision party.'

'Eurovision?' He repeated the word again in mock shock, 'Eurovision!'

'What's wrong with that?'

'My son, the intellectual, going to Eurovision Parties. You bohemians are all so strange.'

He lifted the can again to his lips in his mechanical way.

'I'm not gonna sit around pontificating my whole life, am I?' I said.

Both his hands cupped the can, his lips pursed, and his eyes gazed far ahead into the distance.

'When I left Calgary with Angus to go to Kansas City, I did not tell anyone where I was going, which hotel, or when we would get there,' he said. 'Despite this, a welcoming party of blondes was waiting for us at the hotel. Angus gave them an earful and they left. The girls who follow wrestlers have a 'bush telegraph' to send information around the world. They know who is appearing and who is wrestling under another name in another territory, even Japan.'

'I have a girlfriend,' I said.

'Just one?'

His eyes widened.

'One's enough for me,' I said.

'You always were vanilla.'

The wall beside him was covered in framed photographs of me, my brother and then a selection of his favourites from his scrapbook. Only thirty or so images remained from his career and here they were, on the wall for him to look at every day.

'You've got a pump,' I said looking at the pulse of his mottled old arm.

He flexed and used his free hand to push the muscle up. 'I'm on Atkins, working out three or four times a week. I'm feeling good.'

I looked up at the picture where we looked most alike, posing in his fighting stance in trunks, black gelled hair, I shared the same shaped pecs, belly length and muscle build except his body was tattooed and more muscular, inscribed with his style of manhood.

Except he would sleep with women without feeling anything. And what's more, they went along with it.

'Sometimes when I look at you,' he said. 'It's like looking in a mirror.'

*

As soon as I got back home I watched videos of 'The Bone Collector' Bruce Logan, thinking how crazy it was I would be wrestling a figure from the TV who himself had wrestled Ric Flair, CM Punk and Kurt Angle.

These are people I wrestled in my dreams and going toe to toe with Bruce would connect me to the mythic tradition of pro wrestling, part of the folklore which emerged from rigged sporting contests of the carnivals.

When I was a kid, I had pretended to be him or pretended I was wrestling him, and now I would be doing it for real. What were the chances?

I was nervous but also proud too. What would everybody think when I wrestled the great Bruce Logan? The way I imagined it was, we would meet up before the match and he would sense the respect I had for him, he would appreciate the old-school approach I had and my lineage, then we would work in the ring, only partly choreographed and the rest called on the fly.

We wouldn't need to plan too much because we were *workers*, everybody would see how formulaic their approach was, how tiresome it was coming up with these elaborate routines when what was needed was two *workers*, two guys who could listen to the crowd and tell a story with their bodies and wits alone.

It would be just like the old days.

I had followed his career since the late nineties. Dad would buy me copies of PowerSlam magazine and I read it cover to cover. It introduced a view of the business I never had, especially since Dad didn't break kayfabe. Even when he was training us, he tried to tell us that taking a bump was about 'going with' the momentum of a throw to minimise impact and not land funny. PowerSlam wasn't like the 'Apter Mags' the WWE put out which never broke kayfabe, no, it featured articles that considered the quality of booking decisions, the work rate of wrestlers and who did and didn't deserve a push. At the time, British wrestling was still suffering from the end of World of

Sport on ITV: shows consisted of WWE tribute acts or a few guys in a sports hall, nearly killing themselves for the benefit of about ten people. Bruce Logan had flown the flag for British wrestling. His style was a mix of traditional Mountevans rules and high-impact, American-style TV wrestling. He had been in the business for over thirty years and his accomplishments far exceeded my dad's. I watched one of his TV matches in the US, trying to imagine me in the ring there with him. Grappling across the canvas, me in my black trunks and white body, him with his densely packed steroid muscle, the missing-tooth grin of a middle-aged tough guy.

To work him was an honour not afforded to many people.

Even on training shows, the standard was so high now that I didn't want to be the guy who fucked up. It made me over-cautious and perform within myself. I turned down spots or moves in planning to make sure I didn't have too much to remember.

But when had I ever messed up?

I never did.

Everything so far had been smooth, nothing had gone wrong, it was time to bring it.

Why was I even wrestling otherwise?

I sat on my sofa watching highlight reels of his top moves, Logan thinking up counter-holds and reversals, how I might duck his penalty kick and snatch a German suplex or roll through his Jim Break's armbar into a Sharpshooter. His attempt at a Rolling Tiger could be reversed into rolling Germans of my own. We could trade European uppercuts. He could hit his straight jacket neckbreaker. Yes! This would be money.

I imagined the crowd, how I would rise up to make this my best performance, show the other wrestlers and Joe what I could really do, and I wanted Dad there. I had been nervous to send Dad footage of the first match. I copied the link and pasted it into a message to Dad, finger hovering above the return for a few seconds key before I clicked send. When Dad had seen it he said he liked it and that I would settle into my own style after a couple of matches.

I was ready for him to see me wrestle:

WES BROWN

Tickets are on sale for Renegade.

You probably want a front row seat.

And they can put you somewhere safe

so you don't get jumped on.

FRANK EARL

Ok.

Will apply tomorrow.

That will be for the 21st of June?

WES BROWN

Yeah.

Tickets selling well and not even a match announced yet.

FRANK EARL

From strength to strength.

Later, sudden spasms of activity on my phone and notifications from my Twitter, a feeling of excitement rushed through me and as I swiped onto the stream, saw the match announced was Earl Black Jr vs Buzz Barratt.

Wait, what about Bruce Logan?

I thought it must be a mistake and then the shock subsided into resignation. Of course, this was too good to be true, wasn't it? Of course, I wasn't getting Bruce Logan.

My heart sank.

Joe had either lost his bottle or been talked out of it by the other promoters or wrestlers. Maybe Marilyn vetoed it? Somebody behind the scenes had pulled the plug. One of the other two owners, Jim or Glen?

Yes. It had to be.

There I was, pulling a shit pose like a strawb with gaffer-taped fists, my sour grin, the generic short side-parting and my pasty white body standing beside the bald head of Barratt whose gimmick was that he had a big beard, was a scenester came to the ring eating a bowl of Lucky Charms. Really? It was the sort of thing that might work on kid's shows but would struggle with an adult crowd. The promotional announcement on the Facebook page read:

> NED BARRATT made a big noise at Glastonbury last week and caught the eye with his daredevil antics; this Sunday he takes on the imperious EARL BLACK JR in a battle of the best of the new generation!

Maybe this wasn't so bad? It was a good sign that I was even being considered after only having five matches and only one of them was a singles.

Yes, this would have been a step too big for me anyway. My time would come.

The post had twenty-one likes. Of all the wrestlers in the Dojo, Barratt was somebody I had good chemistry with and could have the best possible match. If I couldn't have Bruce Logan, I was gonna steal the show.

After eating, I went on the search for my Ric Flair T-shirt. Shorts and ankle boots, put my headphones on and re-entered memories of last night at the Dojo, Mayday by UNKLE playing in my ears.

In the afternoon I lifted heavy, pulled a four-hundred-pound deadlift through the sweaty turmoil of a hangover, pumped up my back, biceps and neck; then smashed one-hundred-metre sprints on the rower. I was exhausted by the end, gasping for breath, pumped enough to not give a shit if anybody saw me and pulled up my T-shirt in the wall mirror to see the strained outline of a six-pack appearing beneath the pale excess.

A little more pain, I thought, that's all it would take. A little more pain and this asceticism would reveal the *me* inside the hideous body and big round face, I would be admired, women would be interested in me, I would become my own hero and this beastly version of me I had kept inside could emerge, thick-armed and heavy eyebrowed.

Soon I would parade around in tight T-shirts and a crewcut and people would see machismo exuding from me like aftershave.

When I was finished I went to the supermarket to buy protein, brown rice and veg, and called into a Turkish barbers. I sat down, gown covering my upper shoulders, only my head above like a cameo.

'What do you want, boss?' The boss man said.

'I want like a crew cut,' I said. 'Zero on the back and sides. One on top.'

'That's gonna be short!'

'Yeah, mate.' I nearly whispered. 'That's fine.'

The barber rubbed my fingers with ointment that had the odour of wet hair, cracked my knuckles, massaged my neck like they were trying to snap it in half, set cotton buds aflame which had been dipped in liquor, then dabbed my ear lobes until the hairs in my inner ear had been singed.

The clippers zoomed over my head.

The side-parting fell, almost intact on the floor like a large moustache. Flecks of grey, the minor hair loss around the back of my head, the respectability had all gone. With the body fat gone and this haircut, my face looked squarer and gave me a military look.

When I got home, Lauren wasn't in which gave me a chance to sneak into her room and stare into her full-length mirror. I cut a promo in character. Monologued on how I was wrestling royalty, the best technical wrestler in the UK today and how I would suplex people skull-first into the canvas.

I was born into the business and wrestling was in my blood.

When an hour or so had passed, I ate another meal of chicken breast, boiled rice and green beans, and went out, got the Tube, hurtled through the underground darkness to Brixton and ascended to the surface. In that archway it didn't matter what politics I had, or anything like that, I was taken on my own terms, one of the guys.

*

I caught one of the javelin trains on the high-speed line to Kent. Within an hour, I was walking up the road to Grace's house and I cooked dinner. A bottle of Pinot Noir. Steak. Risotto.

'Where did you learn to cook?' she asked, stirring the rice wildly while steak sizzled in the pan.

'I didn't,' I said.

I sidestepped across the kitchen and kissed her. I knocked back some more wine, we were in a stage of the relationship where everything was good, and our bodies hadn't become familiar.

'Seems like a posh meal,' she said, grinning.

'I don't understand why you think I'm sophisticated. I'm a yob.'

'You think you're a yob?' she said, wrapping her arms around me, pulling my face to hers.

We kissed.

'I'm just a thug from the streets,' I said.

She rolled her eyes.

'Hmmm,' she said. 'I'm not sure about that.'

The rice began to stick. I pulled from her arms, leaning over her shoulder for the spoon and blamed her distracting me. She laughed.

I told her about what happened with the Bruce Logan match, and she agreed Barratt would be a good fit anyway, even if she wasn't able to come that day. We ate in the backroom, drank wine, listened to Blondie and by next morning Grace had left early for work and I walked Eliot to school. He missed the first sound from words and could only really use single syllables. Things he couldn't say he gestured, a mime artist with endless patience. He looked nothing like Grace. His hair was blonde, his eyes were big and round, and his lips were small and pouty. This Germanic sort of look must have been what his dad looked like, though Grace didn't mention him much, and I was glad to keep things that way. I didn't want to think of him as *somebody else's* child. As we walked hand in hand down the road, I wasn't a pretend dad, I *was* his dad, Or at least another kind of dad. One who performed the role of a dad rather than biologically. But biology mattered too, and there would always be some way in which I would only ever be the 'fake' one, no matter how much you believed otherwise.

Then again, maybe authenticity wasn't measured by a 'true' nature and the roles we played counted for something more.

Maybe the only things that were real were fake.

For the rest of the day, I answered emails and updated websites, mostly thinking about what was next for Earl Black Jr, small tweaks to my move set and different ways into the Sharpshooter. Soon enough, it was time to collect Eliot. I put on my hoodie and sneakers and headed out the door.

I followed through the crescents of semi-detached houses and out onto the street to Eliot's school which was called Arethusa Road, named after the training ship Dad sailed as a boy. The dockyard had long since dried up. There was a retail outlet, a cinema, a Nando's we sometimes went to, while the Dockyard itself contained Georgian and Victorian buildings that were used as sets for film production companies.

Chatham reminded me of Leeds. Semi-deindustrialised, migrant communities living alongside often angry white working-class people. Terraces, failed attempts at regeneration, soulless shopping parks.

Where the men of Chatham would once build warships they have turned their attention inward and sculpt their bodies in the gym on Pier 5, where I join them, still lifting, still trying to make myself a man.

I carried on down the road deeper into the suburbs and semi-detached houses, each looking like exactly the same sort of housing across the country. It brought out a hint of sadness in me to see the uniformity of outward appearances, replica retail parks, hangars for manufactured pleasure, the repetition of small lives.

By three-fifteen, all the parents were piling into the school gates. The same people who, in their tracksuits, faded highlights and vests, ignored me in the morning, ignored me in the afternoon. One guy I called flathead had a flat back to his skull which I gazed at every day before the kids were released.

Is this what my parents looked like to other people when I was growing up?

Did I?

I dressed like a wrestler now, black skinny jeans, muscle T-shirts and sneakers.

Footballers dressed the same, tech entrepreneurs, I could have lived on an estate or been a multimillionaire. Who knew?

These people couldn't know me and I couldn't know them. In so many ways I had changed over the past few years. Like an imposter to begin with, I wore the novelty of being a wrestler and enjoyed the attention it gave me. Everybody was interested. It sounded like a crazy idea and everybody wanted to know what I was going to do, how I would get in shape, would I be able to do it? Then as time went by, people began to introduce me as a wrestler. Eventually, I was an imposter and became the person I was pretending to be.

I posted the match graphics and action shots on social media, was getting booked regularly, people called me Earl and I responded to it if as it was my name. At parties, no more was I some freelance literature professional, whatever that was, I was a pro wrestler. Some people sniggered at me not being six-foot-eight and three-hundred pounds, but most didn't. A wrestler was what I was.

I had transformed my appearance to a point where people didn't really question it and made jokes about not getting into a fight with me, as if no line existed between me and where my character ended.

Soon I was going to be a champion, what would I do then?

Push things as far as I could go.

See where the limit was.

The matches were already becoming too complicated for me to remember, I was always doing somebody else's stuff, intricate spots and sequences that the babyfaces knew inside out because it was *their* stuff and that meant nothing to me because they were just choreography. There was nothing real in it. Whereas if a spot made sense, it had a logic to it, something you would use to harm your opponent, I could remember it, no problem.

The door opened to the school and Eliot's teacher, a small woman in her sixties with crease-lines in her smile brought Eliot out by hand.

They stopped. The teacher pointed ahead and Eliot looked around until he clapped his eyes on me. He came running toward me.

'Me got sticker Wes!' he said. 'Me got sticker!'

'Wow!'

'You proud me?'

'Of course I am,' I said. 'You must have had a really good day.'

We hugged. He held my hand as we started to make our way out of the playground.

'You champ?' he asked.

'Ha!' I said. 'Maybe one day, one day I'll be a champion like my dad.'

*

On the Saturday before the match against Barratt, Dad came down and I met him at Finsbury Park station.

'Hello young man,' he said smiling.

His stomach had been shrunk by a gastric bypass in order to lose weight for replacement hip surgery. Vertebrae in his back were welded together. One knee had a ceramic cap. The other was fused. His shoulder was titanium. Now he hobbled towards me, completely bald, half his usual size and wearing his aviator reading glasses and a coat that covered him like a gown.

'How you doing?' I said.

He moved toward me like a Greco-Roman wrestler going in for a clinch, shoulder height in a square stance, and embraced me.

'Looking big,' he said.

'How was your journey?'

'Not bad. The Megabus came down quick but there was no space for my fucking leg.'

I carried his bag feeling like Bret Hart when he was a young boy. With Dad, however much he had shrunk into his monkish appearance, no longer standing eye to eye, I would always be his young boy, carrying his bag.

We walked down Stroud Green Road past the greasy spoons, off-licences, chicken shacks and wig shops.

I slowed my pace to a creep so Dad could keep up.

'Are you hungry? There's a Vietnamese restaurant down the road I thought you might like.'

He was breathing hard.

'Yeah,' he grunted. 'Won't be as good as the ones in Saigon though.'

'Well?'

'The food is incredible there. Fruit you've never seen. All the ingredients come in fresh that day. In Ho Chi Minh City they call it now and all the shellfish are fresh from the Mekong Delta.'

'Okay,' I said. 'It might not be as good as Saigon. But I thought you might like it.'

'I'll have to take you out there one day. You'd love it.'

'I would like to. But there are other places I'd like to go to. We do have different tastes though like how you're always going on about Singapore. It sounds like a police state to me. Whereas I've been wandering around East London lately, and I like places like that.'

'What the hell for?' He paused for breath.

'I don't know,' I said. 'It's all under-developed. A wasteland. Almost entirely owned by global capital. All these monuments to future capital.'

'What a strange fellow you are,' he said, back on his feet laughing, sweat filmed across his forehead. 'How far to go?'

'Just across the road down here.'

'I'm fucked.'

'We'll get you in there and get sat down. We'll get a taxi home.'

He pulled out a cigarette and put it in his mouth.

'Singapore isn't a bad place,' he said. 'No crime there. No litter.'

'No freedom.'

'Not to break the law, no.'

'Haven't you spent your life breaking the law?' I asked.

'Don't be facetious,' he grinned.

He leaned his back against a railing that backed onto the road and smoked in small wisps. He barely took a drag. He used to say he smoked because of the stress of living with my mother. Fifteen years later, he was still smoking, still insisting it was the stress of living with my mother.

When Dad flicked his butt across the road, spilling cinders, we met Lauren outside the restaurant and sat by the window.

'Hi, Frank. How are you doing?' Lauren asked.

'Fine now I've seen you,' he said.

'You're too kind.'

'So then, have you got a boyfriend, *Laurel*?'

'Not at the moment.'

'Criminal,' he smiled. 'You must be too picky. Have you ever been to Vietnam?'

'No. I'd like to, though.'

A glint of light caught his outgrown grey eyebrow.

'I don't know why everybody is hanging around here. When I was your age, I was out seeing the world.'

He pulled out a smartphone and, with a pursing of his lips, dragged his finger across the screen until he found his stash of holiday photos from Saigon. He pushed the phone across the table to where Lauren and I were sitting and she swiped through hundreds of photos of noodle soups, Ho Chi Minh street scenes, random pics of pornstars and models and Dad in his shorts, military vest and a palm-leaf hat.

When the Vietnamese waiter came over, Dad tried to order in *tiếng Việt* but they were at cross purposes.

'Can't really be Vietnamese,' he said.

*

In the evening we went back to the flat and watched a documentary about Ric Flair who many, like Dad, regarded as the greatest of all time. He was a selfless heel who could get a good match out of anybody. The film told the story of how he developed a heel persona on the two greats from the early era of the popularised pro wrestling in the fifties: Gorgeous George and 'Nature Boy' Buddy Rogers. Flair adopted his look, nickname and figure-four leg hold. While Gorgeous George was one of the first great heels of the television era in the 40s and 50s, a character of Wildean excesses who wore a dazzling sequined robe, a blond quiff coiffed with bobby bins who refused to enter the ring before his attentive male valet perfumed the canvas.

Bob Dylan said meeting George changed his life. Crossing paths with the Gorgeous one gave him all the recognition he would need for years to come. Muhammed Ali went on to borrow mannerisms from George, a trend that can be seen in boxers and MMA fighters since the 1960s.

This kind of excessive and effete masculinity ran against the grain of the white-collar spartan macho values of fans who came to the shows. One of the biggest stars of the era was 'Nature Boy' Buddy Rogers, six foot tall and ramrod straight, an athletic-looking German American who, despite his bleached blond hair, had a sturdy wholesome look and the stare of John Wayne. By the seventies, Flair was *the man* and had styled himself in custom Armani suits, Rolex watches, alligator shoes, and re-invented what it was to be a villain. He toured the world in a private jet, dated Playboy models and would tell anybody who was listening he was Ric Flair! The Stylin', profilin', limousine riding, jet flying, kiss-stealing, wheelin' and dealin' son of a gun! In the days before the WWE, the NWA was the international governing body for pro wrestling which recognised one world champion and facilitated agreements and represented state territories at Board of Directors meetings.

Flair's persona and in-ring ability carried the belt from territory to territory; a generous heel, he would allow any babyface in the area to dominate him and convince fans that their guy was going to be *the man,* only to beg, cheat or steal his way out of the way.

Dad was sat on the end of my bed because the sofa was too low for him to get up from.

'Was he as good as people say?' I asked.

He lit a cigarette, inhaled, rolled his tongue and said, 'He was better. The guy could have a match with a broomstick and make it look good. They'd line up every no-good babyface in the territory and build him up to make them think he could beat the champ when he was in town.'

I looked at the screen and Flair doing one of his signature spots. A babyface began a comeback on him, a couple of stiff shots to the head, whip him off and Flair would flip vertically into the turnbuckle pads, spill over to the ring apron, where he would land on his feet, then fiendishly try to run across to the other turnbuckle where he would be outsmarted and knocked down by a babyface who was always one step ahead.

I wanted to extend this kind of generosity to the babyfaces in my matches. I would do whatever it took to make Earl Black Jr look shit and get the babyface over.

'I'm going to steal that,' I said.

'Another good one you can do is stand on the apron and let the baby throw you into the ring with a headlock. Then when he tries it again, lay back with your arms outstretched so he could not reach your head. Then he pulls the top rope, and slingshots you over the top rope and into the ring.'

Dad was smiling as he said this and the laughed at the punchline as if it was outrageous. I loved these old spots. These were things that would make me stand out but it also went deeper than that. It was wrestling heritage, I was connecting to a time before me, folklore in the mythic realm of men.

I got up and pulled a tub of natural T-Matrix from my drawer and put it in Dad's hands. He strained to read the label.

'What's this?' he said.

'It's a testosterone booster.'

'I suppose it won't do you any harm. You could do with a shot of human growth hormone.'

'Yeah,' I said. 'That's what I'm thinking.'

'Let me know if you want some. The protein shop near me sells all sorts. They don't do you any harm if you just have a couple of weeks on and come off.'

He passed the tub and I put it back. Its promise of higher testosterone from fenugreek and micro-nutrients seemed a bit feeble. There wasn't anybody, athlete or actor, who wasn't on gear.

'What about Dianabol?' I asked.

'You can't get that. They stopped making it years ago.'

'I thought it was the most popular oral steroid?'

'That's not Dianabol, it's some formula that's very similar to it. Stacking it with Deca will give you quick results. I'll have a chat with the bodybuilder I know who runs the shop.'

'Yeah, might be worth getting some soon. Want to build some lean muscle and trim down in time for a big run of matches.'

'You can get steroids which only cut you up. But all steroids cut you up.'

'I just want a basic one, something you can take orally. I'm not stabbing my arse with anything.'

*

The next morning I woke up in the room with the poetry magazines and the cat shit. I had put newspaper down on the floor around the tray but even then she found a way to shit through it. The curtains remained from the previous occupants: a dark rag separated the bright cold sunlight from this dingy, catshit room. I walked down the half-flight of stairs across the hallway and into my room, where I found Dad hanging his clothes with no pants on.

'What are you doing?' I asked.

'I didn't make it in time,' he grunted, moving as he did in stiff alternations between unbending legs.

'Fucking hell,' I said smelling a foul whiff of shit. 'Don't you have any spare clothes?'

'I travel light.'

Even amid the wrinkled hoods of eyes and studied forehead, there was a childlike quality to him, something blameless and inescapable.

'There's travelling light and just not fucking bringing anything,' I said. 'You can't go to the show smelling of shit. Can't you pop into Sports Direct on the way? There's one round the corner.'

'I've washed them now. They need to dry.'

'Fuck,' I said. 'I have to go very soon. Are you going to be alright getting there?'

'Laurel's coming isn't she?'

'Yeah.'

'Most of this stuff has cleaned off,' he said. 'It's this gastric bypass.'

I opened a window, went into the bathroom and shaved my face, armpits and chest with a beard trimmer. The skin on my body was still red from yesterday's sunbed and I imagined if I got into a hot shower the water would somehow deepen into a darker brown. I knew I should eat but I already had butterflies, nausea and the gnawing pain in my stomach.

Earl Black Jr versus 'The Scenester' Ned Barratt. *A battle between two of the Dojo's brightest stars.*

The match was going to be broadcast live on social media and a finish had been booked where Trev would turn heel by putting me over in a mic segment before attacking Barratt. I yelled bye to Dad, put on a pair of sports briefs, black slacks, grey T-shirt, tan brogues, checked my kit was all there in my rucksack, took a deep breath and set off.

Doors were 3pm. First bell was 4pm. This meant getting to the venue for about 11am in time to put the chairs out, the ring steps up, the ring posts in position and for the carousel of people coming back and forth with girders, beams, panels, ropes, boards, pads, boards, foam, mats, ring skirt, pulleys, canvas. I set off about 10am and sat alone drinking a coffee at a café on Highbury Corner before walking round the bend through the stage door to the semi-darkness of The Garage.

I took the hands of the workers, promoters, trainees and merchandisers in mine with weak handshakes.

The extension of a floppy palm was now second nature, and then I joined in with the assembly line of the ring, going out through the exit to the van where Aaron had a sweat on, hauling pieces of the ring out with his gripper gloves on and armpit hair curling under the neck of his string vest. Planks were passed sideways, deposited on the upper shoulder and neck of the next guy, who crab-walked them into the venue.

To get the corner through the door I slung the board slantwise across my neck.

Barratt was on the other side, 'Y'alright mate?'

'Yeah buddy,' he said through the plank en route to the van.

He was about six five, bald with a pirate beard and in great shape. Unlike those of us who tanned, his skin stayed a natural white and his muscle looked like it was carved out of marble. But here he was in his street clothes, dungarees and a trucker hat, with the young boys who were always first to arrive. Barratt had been wrestling for seven years and was good, but there was always the chance of a botch with him and, because he wasn't interested in playing the game and did his own thing, it had allowed the other boys to bury him in the eyes of promoters and he had to perform on trainee shows like this to catch the eyes of RAGE bookers.

The veterans and pros came at later times, having earned the right to not put the ring up. I once made the mistake of not shaking the hand of a veteran, thinking he would find it an aggravation, only to find it had got Joe and Trevor some heat for not instilling respect. So whoever came in through the door, whatever their status, I would shuffle over to them with my polite face on, extend my hand and watch them as they barely made eye contact.

NU BLOOD had started out as a training show pitting rookies against pros, *because you only get bet better by wrestling people who are better,* though I had never really wrestled anybody other than trainees and the show outsold most other promotions in its own right. The Preacher leaned against the bar at the back of the room and shared a joke with Marilyn.

My heart sank. I thought he was at The Cockpit today for Revolution Pro. But here he was, in his hoodie under his leather jacket, beady eyes staring out at the ring being assembled before him.

'Who've you got today mate?' I turned and saw Paddy 'The Baddy' Malone and smiled, still grateful for the way he put me over at the last show. Fans didn't always rate his performances the way they should have done, and they didn't know what he contributed to the planning of a match and how inventive and generous he was.

'How you doing?' I said. 'I've got Barratt. You?'

'Wild Boar.'

'Oh yeah. You looking forward to it?'

'I'm going over mate.'

'Fucking hell.'

He ran his hand through his ginger beard, which was floss-like in the light, a grin on his lips.

He walked off, wheeling his suitcase into the bare brick stairwell of the pub as if he had arrived for WrestleMania.

All the boys who were regulars on shows had one, mainly because when wrestlers 'arrived' at arenas on WWE programming they did so wheeling their bags into the entrance as if they'd just turned up, and the fans reacted excitedly. The crowd popped. But the reality was they would have been there most of the day talking through their choreography, recording promos and having their matches agented by veterans who approved their routines.

We put the final boards in place, pulled over the canvas and I saw Bruce Logan come in through the exit door; everybody in the room moved toward him to shake hands.

I went to find Barratt and go through the match. We spoke earlier in the week about the structure and I had most of what he suggested down. We were going tell the story of a highflyer versus a wrestler.

He would have the advantage on me when we were vertical, he could outmanoeuvre and out-fly me, using the ring as his springboard for aerial attacks while I would ground him at every given opportunity, on the floor, alligator roll, it was like a Pokémon battle, one set of attributes set against another.

I found Barratt caressing an energy drink.

'You wanna go through it?' I asked.

'We'll walk it through in the ring,' he said. 'I've had a few more ideas, that alright?'

'Yeah,' I said.

I slipped out of my shoes, filled them with my wallet, keys and phone and climbed into the ring.

The match he had in mind was beyond anything I had done before. But it was all or nothing now. I performed well in my last match because I wrote the cues down on the palm of my hand. I couldn't do that now. This wasn't a set-piece four-way, it was a one-on-one and there was nowhere to hide.

I ran through the stages, was it hotshot *before* or *after* the Sharpshooter?

Was that my first or second attempt?

The sequences were all running into one another, half-remembered and in the wrong order.

I looked out over the top rope and saw Dad had shuffled his way in. He shook Marilyn's hand who was hunching and nodding a lot. They shared a joke. Dad laughed.

'I'll be back in a minute,' I said to Barratt.

I went over and hugged him. 'How did you get in?' I asked.

'Just walked in the door. Joe seemed to know me.'

'I had a seat reserved for you where you won't get bumped.'

I saw a hand stick out between us and The Dude was next to greet him. 'Hello Mr Black Sr,' he drawled.

On my way to the ring, I knew I didn't know the match, but stood on the stage, arms aloft, smiling through a black gumshield, manic eyes in the dark as I strutted to the ring and the chants of *default* rang out.

When Barratt made his entrance, the crowd cheered, I paced the canvas heavy beneath my feet while he ate his Lucky Charms and everybody laughed.

When the bell rang, we went at pace, me hitching him up from behind, high crotched him to the ground and rode him like an Olympic wrestler, while Barratt tried to bring it up to his level, exchanged wristlocks which I reversed into a headlock and took him over in a clumsy takeover.

He wrestled back up, tried to roll me with a snapmare.

I flipped to my feet, only for him to catch me with a running hurricanrana, an attack where both legs scissored around my neck before he flipped back on himself like a scorpion and flipped me to the mat.

He was one step ahead and I charged at him in the corner, he leapt to the outside, tried slingshotting himself at me with a corkscrew crossbody but slipped and missed by a few feet, not knowing how else to cover it. What do I do? I hesitated, feigning to move but planted on my feet. Then lurched forward and fell over as if he had made contact.

I knew it was the wrong choice as soon as I hit the ground. The crowd groaned. I knew it was awful.

Better get back on track, I thought, as I worked a heat with a bit more bite, laying in a couple of stiff ones and the crowd felt their way back into it. I threw him into the corner, chopping, kicking, laying the boot in. He grabbed me, called a spot I misheard and whipped me off, I planted my feet, grabbed him by the head, smashed him with a forearm and asked him what the call was again?

Take the buckle, move, he said.

When he whipped me across the ring I pirouetted round only then realising what he meant and then leprechaun-danced toward the corner.

He came in.

I moved. Ate an elbow.

Exploded out of the corner and I threw him over my head. I was blown and slapped on a chinlock to catch my breath. Barratt fought out, we ran through a couple of cat and mouse sequences before he fired up and bumped me about with a string of clotheslines. He hooked the inside of my leg, winched me above his head and crushed my back over his knee. He outstretched his arms to the crowd, eyes darted to them before backflipping onto me. I groaned as his weight splatted me and looked out through the middle ropes to see Dad's eyes on me, a nothing expression. What would he make of all this flippy shit?

I slipped out of the ring, passing him and shouted, Dad, help me!

This got some laughs before I turned and Barratt totalled me with a somersault over the top rope.

He rolled me into the ring. One. Two. No!

Up to the top rope he went, as he jumped I grabbed his legs mid-air, bumping him upon impact and synching on the sharpshooter.

Barratt fought across to the ropes to break the hold.

I pulled him back to the centre of the ring to try and synch it on again, he kicked me off, I fell backward into the ropes, then tumbled forward as he caught me around the neck with his legs, snapped backwards and rolled me up for a near fall.

I fed to the ropes, staggered up and as Barratt came to claim me, threw him throat-first onto the ropes and went for a brainbuster; as I held him vertically overhead he slipped over my shoulder and secured my head and arm for his Spanish Fly. My legs were so stunned with lactic acid I could barely jump; he backflipped which drove in a whirl to the mat.

Pro Wrestling was outwardly a show of excessive toughness, but inwardly, on the inside of the staged fight was tenderness. We protected one another, trusted one another with our bodies, moved to the same rhythm with the intimacy of a dancer and as we lay in a clinch, head to chest, we knew we had failed one another.

I lay there, defeated.

*

With a few matches having gone on before us the dressing rooms were already starting to clear with pros moving on to other shows or getting back to whatever part of the country they came from or getting a head start on the drinking and watching the show from the bar.

I sat against the wall, slimy with his sweat and unlaced my boots, everybody's eyes on me. I didn't need anybody to tell me I'd shit the bed. Everybody knew. The feeling of being humiliated and debased was rising through me. I could taste it on my mouth like a black tar. Oh I knew this feeling, it was always with me, in the shadows of my presence, ready to rise up and claim me as its own.

How could I get past this?

I had been lucky in my first matches. Nobody had noticed I was reading cues from off the back of my hand while I sold beside the ring between spots. But when it came to it, I wasn't up to it, I wasn't a wrestler. I could just leave, I thought. Hand on my forehead. Slumped into a position like one of Mum's thinking men sculptures. Get out of here. Never come back.

I didn't need to do this.

I could go at things my own way with literature. I had an idea that I would write some short stories based on my mythic Americana of when Dad wrestled, but given the added knowledge I had of what it felt like to move in a ring, to seek the toughness and tenderness of men that Thom Gunn found in the paradigm of the weeping wrestler, but in my heart, I knew this was me trying to intellectualise myself out of the mess I was in.

Almost as soon as the final bell had rung, the house lights came up and fans congregated around the ring while crew folded chairs behind them, the bungees came away from the canvas and the heavy boards and metal skeleton of the ring were dismantled and removed from the venue in a conveyor belt of synchronicity.

I had almost forgotten myself when Barratt came up and put his hand on my shoulder and said, 'Hey man.'

'That was shit, wasn't it?' I said.

'We got most of it down. Nothing ever goes completely to plan.'

'I'm sorry, mate.'

'This is your fifth or sixth match? You're doing well, mate. Nobody is good after five or six matches. The first spot was my botch and you recovered and then we had that clusterfuck in the corner but got past it.'

'I'm never gonna get booked again.'

'Joe likes you. I wouldn't worry about it.'

The rest of the ring came down in a reverse of the carousel that had got it up. The ropes and padding came off. The canvas was peeled back and folded a foot at a time and then rolled into a long tube. The ratchets under the ring loosened, the torsion slackened, and the ring posts collapsed inward. Then the boards and mats, corner posts and metal slats until just four cloths remained on the floor at each of the four corners of where the ring was. The last of the fans were on their way out. Somebody was sweeping away the muck at ringside. I went and joined the carousel, grabbing onto one end of a solid steel post, bore the weight in my arms with a shrug and kept my head down.

When enough of it had been put away to leave without getting any heat, I grabbed my bag and walked out of the venue, around the corner and across the road to The White Swan. RAGE fans in their black T-shirts were smoking outside. I hung my head as I entered. I could sense the stink coming from me, the way the punters evaded eye contact and conversations stopped as I approached.

Fuck me.

I could not hate myself more. Why was I such a moron? Why did I live in my dreams?

It was obvious that we had planned too much and had no chance of nailing it. No wonder they didn't put me on with Bruce Logan. Can you imagine?

I found Dad standing at a table with a woman who must have been in her late thirties, who seemed nice enough but had a reputation for blowing strawbs in the toilets.

I looked over at Dad who was slow to return my gaze, the look in his eyes was one I had never seen before. He was ashamed of me. His lips were downturned, his eyes didn't meet mine and he was rubbing the tops of his fingers.

'That could have gone better,' I said.

Dad looked up at me, 'I preferred your match with The Dude.'

'There was too much to remember.'

'You shouldn't plan so much. Why does a big guy like Barratt have to fly around everywhere? You'd never backflip somebody in a fight. I used to get them going wild with a headlock.'

'Times have changed,' I said.

'You have to educate them. They will buy what you sell.' He put a Polo in his mouth, 'I'm going for a smoke.'

'Fans won't buy a headlock anymore,'

'They don't buy acrobatics. I know that,' he said, cigarette in his mouth as he shrugged on his coat to walk away.

'Hang on a minute,' I said, pulling him back. 'You go on about how everything was back in your day, but you guys didn't have to do anything to pop a crowd.'

His eyes were defiant as mine probably were.

When he left, the older woman leaned in and took my hand and said, 'Your dad said the match was shit but I liked it.'

Her eyelashes fluttered.

'Did he?' I said.

'It's not as bad as people are making out.'

I loosened her hand from mine, went to the bar and ordered a pint with a Jägerbomb.

The glasses clinked together as I downed the liquor. 'Can I have another?' I asked.

I looked around the pub and saw the wrestlers on two long tables at the back end of the room beneath the open-plan second floor. The first table was occupied by Marilyn and the veterans; the second was trainees and ring crew, and then other tables contained fans and hangers-on. After I downed a second Jägerbomb I was going to walk over there and get it over with. Somehow hearing how shit I was eased the pain.

It was a form of self-harm.

'What happened tonight?' I turned and saw Joe with his one glass of white wine.

'I don't know,' I said. 'Just trying to do too much.'

'It wasn't just the botches that were bad, and there were plenty of those, but the *match* was bad, it was like watching a video game. Maybe it was your dad being here, I don't know.'

'It started bad and got worse.'

Joe turned his back to me and joined another conversation between more experienced wrestlers behind me. Maybe this wasn't so bad? He had expressed disappointment but at least in showing disappointment it revealed some kind of investment in me. I couldn't be a lost cause, surely, if he cared.

Though it could just have easily been regret, maybe precisely because he had cared and had now given up on me?

Oh, the doubt rumbled through my guts.

Before the match went to shit I was getting a great reaction from the crowd, maybe the best heel heat from a male trainee at the Dojo. Oh bollocks, I remembered the match had been broadcast live online and couldn't bear to check the live stream or my social media and read the fan comments that would only confirm what I already knew.

I was the drizzling fucking shits.

I walked over to Marilyn and hovered around beside his table waiting for a break in conversation.

'What the fuck do you want?' he snapped.

'I wondered if you have any feedback on my match please, Marilyn,' I asked.

'To be honest, I didn't think you were that bad. Barratt should have known better than to plan so much stuff. He doesn't get it. Really, you shouldn't be on shows at all. You're too fucking green. Do you know how long it took me to wrestle in front of three hundred people? I spent years travelling across the country to wrestle in front of ten people in a sports hall. Trainees like you should be jobbers at this stage and just get used to being in front of a crowd. I'm not saying this to be a dick, I mean, I'd quite happily go on Wrestle World USA main shows and job. Do you know what I mean?'

'Yeah.'

'What did your old man make of it?'

'He thought it was shit,' I said.

'It was fucking shit. Look, if you forget something... I mean, I forget stuff all the time. Just throw the guy out of the ring. Use the ref to communicate spots between you. Ask him to ask the guy what the next spot is. If you mess something up, as the heel, take control and just work a hold until you remember what's next. And don't plan so fucking much. Do what you can do and say no if you need to. Just say, look, I'm green and I'd rather not do that than fuck it up.'

'Thanks Marilyn.'

'Oh and by the way,' he said.

'What?'

'You're still a fucking cunt.'

This made me smile and suddenly I didn't feel so bad about things. And Marilyn didn't really hate me as I had often suspected. Maybe this was all Barratt's fault? I was green. He didn't get it. We could have had a better match by doing less. I got a good reaction from the crowd. Botches happen. Bad matches happen. What did Joe expect? He had never been a wrestler, his background was as a comedy agent and his expectations were based on outcomes, not the practice of being in the ring and the wisdom that comes from it. How could he appreciate the difficulties?

I looked over my shoulder and saw Dad surrounded by a group of fans, all of them rapt as I had been as a kid to hear his stories. How much of them were exaggerated beyond any reasonable account of the truth was hard to say.

For the first time in my life, his nonsense was making me angry, and a fire burned inside of me.

Nothing I did could ever compare to his myth, the folklore of the business from the 1970s that lived in the imaginations of die-hard fans.

It was too heady, too intoxicating.

I, on the other hand, lived in the strip-lighting of a different era, one that rested less on legends and tales and more on video evidence and social media. I was too real, too familiar to be mythologised in the same way.

I walked over, drink in hand, to stand beside Paddy 'The Baddy' Malone, a friend from the Dojo and a good wrestler, even if he didn't look like one, with his pipe-cleaner arms and wild ginger beard, nearly always bleary-eyed. He had the look of an Irish traveller, a livewire bare-knuckle fighter, if a bit pale and sickly, the kind of look of somebody who might fight you for scraps in a dumpster.

'Well done today,' I said.

He squirmed to hear praise and only ever spoke out of the side of his mouth, 'I thought it could have gone smoother.'

'Mate, you opened the show with a pro and didn't look out of place.'

'The crowd didn't come up in the right places,' he said.

'Better than die like I did.'

Out of the corner of my eye, I saw the promoter at Slam Nation, Andrew Krupp, coming our way. He had a huge red beard and his head was bald, almost completely flat and the white of his lower gut protruded from beneath his T-shirt. I knew who he was but had never spoken to him. I saw him after the last show, completely pissed, windmilling his arms as he walked through the Highbury & Islington Tube station.

There were stories about him. He undercut the boys, had allowed a softcore gay porn company to record one show which was released without their consent called 'Lords of the Ring', would get pissed and put thousands of pounds behind the bar. He was a pro darts player, lived with his parents and was the opposite to Joe. One rumour about him was you could enter his inner circle and get bookings by drinking with him.

I knew enough about wrestling to show him the respect he didn't deserve.

'Hello Mr Krupp,' I said extending my hand. 'Pleased to meet you.'

His handshake dropped like a wet cloth.

'I wouldn't book either of you two,' Krupp said. 'Jack said you were looking for bookings, the pair of you. Not right now. I want to see more from you, and you'd have to come to my training.'

'We already train with Jack,' Paddy said.

'Do you know what I like?' Krupp replied.

'What Mr Krupp?' I said.

He took forty pounds from his wallet, showed it to us, then put it in his mouth and chewed it while he yanked his T-shirt over his head, exposing his belly for a minute before placing a pint on his head and walking off.

I turned to Paddy, 'What the fuck?'

'That's Andrew Krupp,' he laughed.

*

By the afternoon of the next weekend I was sitting across the room from Mum. All of her things seemed more pristine in her new flat; the cushions beside me were piled up with their price tags still on. It was even more like a show room than her last house but I felt at home in the stylised detachment of the place.

'What's with all the cushions?' I asked.

'Leave them. They're just to look at.'

'*To look at?*' I said.

She shuffled into the open-plan kitchen with half a grin on her face, opened the cupboard doo and took some tablets before returning the living room and lowering herself into an orange armchair.

'There's coffee and sugar in the kitchen if you want a coffee,' she said.

'Great. Thanks.'

'I'm sorry. I'm tired and I've got a headache coming on.'

She picked up a pair of glasses, rested them on top of her head and lifted her eyebrows, widening her eye enough to stare into her phone. Her eyebrows raised in a fixed state of concentration. She didn't bother to hide the squint of her missing eye anymore with the contact lens that had been made for her, hand-painted to match her grey-coloured eye.

'Cal's on his way,' she said. 'He's bringing Elsie.'

I nodded. 'Good.'

'So,' she said. 'Anything to tell me?'

'Not really. Things are going pretty well. I'm not as skint as I was. Been trying to get the flat decorated.'

'That's nice. How's Lauren?'

'Fine.'

She rested her hands together on her lap with her feet up. Her arms were short and thick, busting at the seams, and her forearms were cross-hatched in scars that had softened into a lighter shade of pink.

'Are you still wrestling?' she asked.

'Yeah.'

'What for?'

She looked up at me, glasses on top of her head.

Things had always been this way.

The first time I had watched wrestling, it had been amazing, the moment after the lines of cable had been laid in under the paving stones and terraced houses in the endless summer of

1996, cradled on the serpent's tail tattooed on Dad's arm while Mum pressed an iron across another T-shirt. Mum had her eye on the TV. One wrestler rolled around on the floor, unprotected, while the other, a man standing six-foot-six in a gold pleather bodysuit stomped him hard with the soft sole of his foot, while his other stomped on the canvas for noise.

Dad said she wouldn't say that if she had been in the ring. *It's not the same on TV. You wouldn't say that if you were in the front row and you see the sweat fly off their backs.* Mum carried on ironing. Maybe it was real back in your day, Frank, but you can't tell me this is. No way. Her iron hissed. She wasn't having any of it. For her, the fakery of pro wrestling was something dishonest, tricking people into believing something that wasn't true.

It hurt for me to side with either of them, but who was right? I cuddled deeper into the serpent tattoo on Dad's arm. I knew what I believed.

I looked over at Mum presently, sitting down on her chair during this sunny afternoon, the clouds were slightly less steely than usual and the light coming in from the French windows behind her had a kind of angelic glow. Every time the clouds parted, a sheen of light appeared in beaming rays, before retreating again into the grey hard gloom.

Most people were excited by my wrestling. But she couldn't see anything worthwhile in something fake.

'I got in it to write a book about it really,' I said. 'But I'm quite good at it and it's something to do.'

'That's nice.'

'I'm wrestling for one of the top promotions in the UK.'

'And what does your dad make of it?'

'He likes it.'

'Do you win?'

My jaw hung.

I sat upright and wiped my mouth before answering. 'You know it doesn't matter if you win or lose?'

'That's no way to be.'

'No,' I said. 'It's predetermined, isn't it? It's a show, it's about how well you perform, not winning and losing.'

'Why don't you want to win? I didn't bring you up to finish second or third. Winning is all that counts.'

'Because it's *fake*,' I said, which itself was a sort of lie given how much winning meant to me. Fake or otherwise. Nobody wanted to lose.

She pulled her glasses off her forehead.

'Hang on,' she said. 'You mean to tell me that it's *fake*?'

'Yeah.'

'That's awful,' she said in a long sneer like it was some kind of con, a moral outrage to trick people into believing it was real.

I laughed. 'What do you mean?'

I couldn't stop laughing. She was playing dumb now for effect, a grin on her face but I knew she still didn't get it.

'Well, you're tricking people. Do the people know, the people who come to watch?'

'Yeah.'

She shook her head.

'I don't get it,' she said. 'It's not on. Your dad always told me it was real.'

I laughed.

'Well, it was fake when he wrestled, too.' I said. 'That's what makes it interesting. It's a *fake* sport.'

She shook her head.

'Bloody daft If you ask me,' she said.

When Cal and Elsie buzzed in a few minutes later, I budged up the sofa to let Elsie sit down and Cal held the room, cigarette in hand waiting to be smoked out in the yard.

'How you doing *ball*?' he said to Mum, patting her on the head. I laughed, she did look particularly small and round today.

'Fuck off,' she laughed.

'Hey, Cal,' she said. 'Can you have a look and see if you can put a patio down and how much it would cost?'

He was bobbing about, almost shadow boxing with her.

'Not gonna be cheap that, you know?'

'I know.'

I looked over at Elsie who smiled, huffing. Huge since the last time I saw her, only a few months ago.

I was leaner, more muscular and crossed my arms in a way that would bulge my biceps.

'You're looking slim,' Elsie said.

'Thanks.'

'Still wrestling?' Cal shouted from the yard.

'Yeah,' I said.

Elsie eyed me up and down.

'Are you sure you're big enough to be a wrestler?' she said. 'I don't know, just when I think of a wrestler I think of somebody like your dad or John Cena. Ooh, John Cena, he's lovely isn't he?'

'It's not the world's biggest man contest. It's about actually being a good wrestler too,' I said.

'Hey, have you won any matches lately, you big jobber?' Cal shouted in, laughing.

Smoke escaped into the air.

*

When I wasn't at the gym, training at the Dojo, or watching wrestling tapes, I had started my MA at Birkbeck and got on the javelin train twice a week to attend evening seminars.

This week was my submission and I glanced over at the opening again on the train on the way over:

> Let's get ready to rumble! – Crash! In the heat of the excitement, this fierce fakery, everybody talks American. This is awesome... The crowd chant. This is awesome... Nelson Vivas hits the El Matador, Andres Castrado with a quebrada moonsault, vaulting from the second rope and swan-diving backwards, mid-air, through shutter haze and stage

> lights casting a chiaroscuro across his three-hundred-pound torso, mists of sweat rising upon impact with the canvas. Chops! Chops to the body! Chops to the chest!

I was going for some kind of stream-of-consciousness that got the spectacle of pro wrestling in a high style. I thought the group would like it: it was unusual and energetic, and showed off my voice. But when it got to my turn in the seminar room, it was clear everybody hated it and it was as fake as pro wrestling. Some people thought it read like a cartoon, others that it was trying too hard to impress but that there was nothing there beneath the surface. All of this was delivered in a perfectly kind way, but it was this kindness, the pauses before they rephrased their criticisms and the euphemisms they used that hurt the most.

Basically, it was shit.

This is what they were saying and what I already I knew deep down.

At the end of the mauling, my classmates each handed me a print-out of the story daubed in red ink.

My blood boiled with shame.

I went home that night determined to put things right. It was time to stop messing around trying to over-write; whatever it was, I was always convinced I was never enough and always had to reach to be something else, something that wasn't me and that was the way to be successful and have the kind of glittering writing career I wanted.

The next morning I ripped up the draft and sat typing at a workbench. I had some ideas for a story called 'Kansas City' based on one of the tales Dad used to tell me. Instead of trying to impress and write in a literary way, I was just going to write in a flat, no-style kind of style, just focus on the moment, the story, and the characters.

On the train home it had seemed like I would never get over the humiliation, but I was already up on my feet, and they were right, I was glad to be told how bad my writing was.

What was it Rocky said?

It ain't about how hard you hit, it's about how hard you can get hit and keep moving forward.

When I was twenty-three and working in a bookshop, Dad had been invited to a wrestling seminar in Liverpool and on the train, we talked about the glory days. In between the usual stories, new ones sometimes emerged like the one about Terrible Ted, the wrestling bear, who he would drive around in the back of his pink Cadillac. I wasn't sure if a bear could fit in the back of a muscle car, but I had seen match reports and pictures of wrestling bears from the period.

'You have to get them as a pup,' he said. 'Before they open their eyes and then they'll find you're its mother.'

'What did you do with the claws?' I asked.

'They can be trimmed down, and you'd make sure they were well fed before you went out with them but bears love to wrestle.'

He smiled with longing for the bear, as if it were an old friend.

Once in a bar, he had shown his wrestling pictures to a barmaid on his smartphone. She was interested up until she saw the images of the bear and called out the animal cruelty and distress caused by removing the pup from its mother. Dad was hurt by the comments and reacted by reaffirming how much bears love to wrestle and how well cared for they were. Terrible Ted even had his own rider and demanded a bucket of cola before every match. He was a bigger attraction and better paid than most of the boys.

Dad believed this regardless of whether it was true or not.

We changed at Manchester and headed on for Liverpool where we caught a taxi at the station to the community centre where I could see boys hauling in parts of a wrestling ring through the fire doors from the back of a van.

Dad struggled out of the taxi, slipped a Polo in his mouth and lit a cigarette.

'I'll just have this and then we'll go in,' he said.

That's when he led the seminar but didn't really have anything to teach them beyond the basics. The kids didn't mind. Their usual trainer led them through some drills and I joined in, Dad had told them I was a good wrestler but I didn't know anything compared to them and struggled to get through a basic sequence. When I was on my knees, blowing for air, Dad took a picture and uploaded it to Facebook. That's where an editor saw the picture and was keen to pay for me to wrestle some more, but I declined, for years, until that cold night in Leeds where I ended up on my back, where it was either join a wrestling school or drink myself into a depressive stupor for the rest of my life.

It didn't matter that the kids didn't learn much in the ring. Dad told them enough legends to keep them happy and, once the session had finished, all the trainees sat cross-legged on the mats and invited Dad over to talk about how to make it as a wrestler and to take any questions. Dad told his favourite stories. After he had finished the boys formed a queue around the gym and took it, in turn, to shake his hand and thank him for coming.

I spent the rest of the day writing, like it was my labour, as if it was some kind of job. I had bought a pine workbench in the last months I spent in London and brought it to Grace's because I liked the association with carpentry – I liked everything about it, the idea of working minimally on a laptop on a slab of wood and that would be that. It seemed like some kind of *feng shui*, opening up a space for thought through uncluttered simplicity and it was a *workbench* - the two syllables sounded muscular, the sort of thing Steinbeck would like. I had to have things feel in some way masculine, like the way American authors talked about writing, boasting about calloused fingers and blunted pencils and paper all over the floor, the physical manifestation of labour. Digging at the workbench all day. Dulling pencils with their graft like labourers. Printing pages. Fingers blistered. No doubt people would see this as silly and showing off, but I had grown up with bricklayers, carpenters, masons, plumbers, painters, plasterers, decorators, and it was important for me, like them, to feel like a grafter.

Right now, my brother would have been out with my cousin in their van, about to graft in the gardens of people like me who live in inner-city suburbs. Heaving sod, cutting trees, digging.

I texted him about the book I was thinking of writing.

'I'm interrogating the idea that gender is a social construction,' I said.

'Uve lost me,' he replied with a crying emoji. 'I cut grass and dig for a living don't understand social construct.'

I laughed.

What bourgeois people could never understand was that when they were telling one another how vital stories are to their survival, that a poem with the wrong message could *damage* the world, was that nobody cared what they thought, and people mostly thought they were mental.

I wrote a draft of a story about Dad and a wrestling bear, some kind of story about fatherhood and knowing when to let go. Once I started I couldn't stop. It certainly felt better than what I had written before and while I believed in it, there was still a niggling sense it wasn't completely the literary equivalent of Strong Style I was looking for, but I liked it anyway:

There she was. Smokey the wrestling bear riding in the back of a pink Cadillac. De-clawed, de-fanged and drugged out of her mind. Earl Black pulled up at The Dreamland Motel, one thumbless hand on the wheel.

'Get in,' Earl stretched for the door. 'She ripped the truck apart. I had to belt her up in the back.'

Harley Cage was waiting on the sidewalk, wearing aviators and a leisure suit, hazy in the Cadillac gleam.

'Well, I'll be damned,' Harley said. 'She's happier than ol' Blue layin on the porch chewin a big old catfish head.'

Harley was one of the toughest guys in the business. His in-character and out-of-character voice sounded exactly the same. It was enough to make grown men quiver. He had beaten polio as child, shaken off cancer and survived several near-fatal car crashes he mostly caused. Nobody would ride with him. He got in the car.

Earl was wearing slacks and a T-shirt with a bear on the front.

'You're a kooky-ass guy, do you know that?' Harley said. 'Crazy as a pet coon.'

Smokey was famous. She had wrestled over three hundred matches. Most barely lasted a minute. She starred in films. Earl let her wrestle on set with film stars like Clint Eastwood and Lee Marvin. Football players like Rod Marinelli or Dick Butkus. Everybody wrestled Smokey. She was only six-two and three hundred but was regularly billed as eight five and six-fifty. This was wrestling. Showbusiness. Smokey was a special attraction and got Earl Black booked across the mid-South. But the act was getting old and the shows were drying up. Earl had sidelined himself. Everybody said so.

Harley growled at the bear, 'Who you looking at, beautiful?' Then he looked sadly at his flannel jacket and gold medallion. 'The boys keep ribbing my threads.'

'It's because you wear the same goddamn suit every day,' Earl answered. 'You look like Iceberg Slim.'

There was a bottle of dog shampoo on the creamily upholstered backseat above the sheets of bedding and Smokey snored, drool windswept from her snout.

'There's even a lizard on the circuit now,' Harley said. 'Some punk is wrestling 'gators in the Great Lakes.'

'Assholes.'

'You need to change up the act. Keep yourself fresh. Everybody's looking for the next big thing. One guy has a snake in North Carolina.'

'What do I do with Smokey?'

'Send her to a retirement home, a circus, a zoo. I don't know. Just let her go out the same way we all do, on top.'

'People love Smokey,' Earl responded angrily. 'People don't just see her as a bear, a special attraction, she's a character. A worker in her own right.'

'I'm not trying to ride you or nothing.'

Smokey sat up. The rear-view filled with the small black eyes, rounded ears and long snout of the three-hundred pounder he rescued from the roadside as a cub and called his daughter. They had a lot in common. Both had been orphaned. Both ate five thousand calories a day and they could share the same meals.

She wasn't the love of his life, but he wished she was.

They drove past El Dorado falls. There were ranches, hikers in the distance, and a waterfall. Before he was a wrestler, Earl was a merchant seaman. He sailed the world for five years. He was scouted in a gym in New Zealand and found work ever since. He went country to country, territory to territory.

Smokey fell asleep again, ramrod straight, still dozy. Paws rested on her grey-pink belly, racked with nipples. Earl was the son of a clergyman. Something about the sea, like the night sky, scared Earl and he liked it. The immensity. The sense of the infinite. The road felt the same way. The great pink ship of his Cadillac sailing down the highway, the sky stretched out before them. This was life on the road. On the long straights, the car streaked like a blur.

'Wichita was hot last night,' Harley said. 'Some hillbillies tried to invade the ring and we had to fight them back to the dressing room.'

'I had similar in Calgary but I got caught in the top rope. They're loose up there, you know? A woman wrestler laid out a lumberjack with one punch.'

Earl spoke in a low monotone staring at the road.

'Anyway, when I got back to the dressing room a pair of twins were waiting for me. Russians, I think and I made a real pig of myself,' Harley stroked his whiskers. 'How about you? Any luck?'

'Not lately.'

'You got to get yourself out there. I bet that thing is a pussy magnet.'

'She's been a good friend to me. That's for sure.'

Earl turned on the stereo, 'Wichita Lineman', and Smokey bellowed, paws waving.

'Please,' Harley groaned. 'I'm hungover.'

'You're always hungover.'

'That's because I'm always drinking,' he growled pulling his cap over his eyes. 'You should party, you know? I'm serious, I worry man.'

'Most music is just noise to me. This is a real song. Smokey likes country. It seems to keep her amused. Bears have a great sense of humour, you know? They like to play around.'

'I'll bet.'

'They *do*,' Earl's right eye shrunk into scrutiny as he said this.

'They also stink of shit. I think the bitch has shit herself.'

'Of course she has.'

'It's rotten. I might puke.'

'It's natural.'

'It naturally stinks of fucking shit, hombre.'

Smokey sat up hearing raised voices. The car rock and rolled. Her long-sloped snout, mouth half-open, grunted a moan. When her massive head moved it was animatronic and fabulous, night shade dark

Harley gagged and quivered.

'Let me out dude. I'm gonna retch.'

'We'll be there soon.'

'Let me out.'

'We don't have far.'

Harley pulled a snub-nosed Smith & Wesson from the glove box and pointed it at Earl's head.

'Jesus Christ, motherfucker,' he yelled. 'Stop the goddamn car.'

Earl slammed the brakes. The car drifted in a skid-marked half-moon, prairie dust rising.

'The fuck is wrong with you?' He bashed his fist on the dashboard. 'For godssake. You trying to get us killed?'

Harley doubled up; Smokey roared. Then he puked. They sat wordlessly in the spun-out vehicle. Brake pads scorched. Earl checked on Smokey and then walked into the flatland. What could he do? Harley was a veteran. He couldn't risk being kicked off the show. He had Smokey to feed. A luxury flat in Wichita with a swimming pool, floral wallpaper, a refrigerator, etc.

Bushes, loamy grasses, silt. The afternoon sunshine was overwhelming. He walked in the heat to cool his anger. The flies buzzed static. He stopped for a whiz by a wire fence where a wooden sign read Keep Grassland Free: No Government Acquisition painted with the kind of psychedelic styling, hand-lettered, like the placards of the peaceniks who protested outside shows, only to tell him what he already knew.

Animals are humans.

A shot fired. Greyish-brown topsoil spun. Another shot drilled past his trouser leg. Harley laughed, smoky-eyed. Then he fired again.

'You're an asshole!' Earl shouted. 'Do you know you're an asshole?'

At five forty-five they arrived at The Memorial Hall. Outside, fans crowded, trying to get closer to Smokey. Earl pushed past. The hippies were waiting with animal rights slogans on placards. The venue hosted Pink Floyd last night. Thursday was All-Star Wrestling. The first of the month was a television taping. The matches would play across the state on cable. There would be three and a half thousand people in the arena. A hundred thousand watching on TV. When they parked up, Earl chained Smokey's muzzle and walked them to the stage door.

Who would stop them?

Harley carried his bag in silence. Earl wheeled his luggage in a duffel bag, all black.

They hadn't spoken for nearly forty minutes. They had spats like this. It was part of riding with Harley. He was always getting them in trouble with promoters for being late because he got them into a scrap with truck drivers or rode around a hundred miles an hour.

He didn't have to be buzzed to go crazy.

'You're not still hot because I goosed ya?' Harley asked. 'It was a prank, for God's sake. You know I'm a good shot. I was aiming for your trouser leg.'

'What if you missed?'

'I've shot squirrels between the eyes as they jump tree to tree,' he laughed. 'I'm the best goddamn shot for twenty states.'

Earl scratched his head so he had a reason to not make eye contact.

'These slacks cost nearly fifty dollars.'

'You'll earn nine times that tonight.'

They entered the locker room making sure to shake everybody's hand, softly, almost not-touching. They were only practicing the illusion. A queue formed and the boys greeted Smokey like a dog. The promoter had ordered a bucket of meat and salad from a nearby diner. The room was large and bright and Earl began to undress and re-dress, pulling on his black tights and sitting down on a cantilever bench he laced up his knee-high black jackboots with a skull down the side.

Harley sat across the bench changing into his new red trunks. He had three-quarter boots and hockey socks pulled up to his shins. He rubbed baby oil into his grizzled body. He told Earl his theory that the soft slick would gleam right through the tube. Colour transmission changed everything.

'I don't believe it,' Harley spoke into his hand. 'I'm down to take a clean fall against The Coyote. Jesus, that guy is the shits.'

'Isn't he the promoter's nephew?'

'Damn right.'

Running order, match length, and results were taped to the door. Earl pointed at the card.

'He wants me to go ten with Smokey.'

The first bell had rung. The show was under way and the locker room looked as it would before a football game: a team of guys talking through high spots interspersed with wrestle talk, what was going on in other promotions, who they should look out for, who was getting over.

Trainees were running ring jackets back to the locker room. Stagehands. Now and then, the ring crashed with a slam. The crowd came in a crescendo and sounded like day-trippers going down a roller-coaster. Earl barked at one of the trainees to change the sheets on the backseat of the Cadillac. Smokey would shit about five times a day and constantly spray the upholstery with piss.

He sat there drinking a bottle of Coca-Cola.

Smokey was feeding, face-deep in the bucket.

Ted Walker, the promoter, introduced himself and they all shook hands. He had a white beard and uneven tan lines. Walker and his brothers had served in the Vietnam War. He was part of an underwater demolition team.

'Do you guys have everything you need?'

'Smokey likes a Coke after her match.'

'We can arrange for that.'

'Make sure it's in a bottle, please,' Earl said without eye contact. 'She can't drink out of a cup and things like that can make her cranky.'

Walker looked him in the eye.

'Anything else? What the hell. I can get her a bowl of porridge too if you want. I'll make sure it's just right.'

'She doesn't like porridge,' Earl said with no sense of irony. Walker glanced at Harley circling his finger around his temples.

'Have you got anything different?' Walker asked.

'I don't need anything,' Earl said.

Walker looked at the tattoo on Earl's arm reading 'Rebecca.' 'I don't understand why people get tattoos.' He spoke like a sergeant, 'Who is it? Some darling?'

'She was my daughter,' Earl said.

Then he spent a few minutes doing free squat and push-ups, working up a rhythm. Blood-flow.

When he got the call he led Smokey by the muzzle down the walkway. There were two tiers of fans already cheering her on. At ringside he asked for a mike. Then he told the crowd nobody was man enough to wrestle him. Earl Black was a specimen. All the women in the audience should go home and wash the dirt from their husband's fingernails because this is what a real man looks like. The crowd booed. He held his hands to his ears and squirmed. Boos, louder. Somebody threw a can of soda. It just missed his head. A smile shaped on his lips.

The referee kept his distance near the corners of the ring. Earl circled his opponent. They locked up in the middle of the ring. Smokey up on her hind legs, toe to toe. He grappled her with one arm over hers and the other slipping inside, trying to knock her down. He slid his forearm across her snout, wet nose streaking down his arm knowing one whip of her head could break a rib. Smokey knew how to do a flying mare and used it, multiple times pulling Earl by his neck. Earl rolled. The crowd cheered. Smokey clambered over him and he had a face-full of smooth-skinned belly. Her six nipples rubbed over his face. She was lightly-odoured, maybe even a little cat-like. She smelled like home. He swung his weight out from under her and took her head in a facelock, burying his face in her fur, the blue-black darkness. The chain was long enough to allow Smokey to manoeuvre about the twenty-foot-square ring but easily got tangled around Earl. This is how his thumb was pulled clean off. Without him having to look, Smokey swept his legs from beneath him and he tumbled to the mat. He grabbed the referee's legs, who fell over him and everybody laughed. Smokey lay her bulk across the Earl's chest and the referee made it back to a conscious footing to count the three. The crowd half cheered, half-sighed.

Smokey sat down, grunting, on her rump in the middle of the ring enjoying a Coca-Cola from a glass bottle, fizz on her cold wet nose.

Earl somehow knew then it was over.

That night they were headed back for Wichita. Earl had read in a guidebook that Kansas was named after the tribe meaning 'people of the wind'. He had tried to tell Walker but he pretended he already knew. Harley had been staying in The Dreamland Motel for three weeks and had six more left in Missouri. Before this, Harley worked Florida, Kentucky and Texas. He was always in demand. Earl had done the Missouri circuit for five years, since she died. Going round in circles. He led Smokey to the car and sat her down in the Kansas City dusk. The sky was a purplish dark, rivulets pinked in the clouds. A brown moth scattered across the bonnet.

Harley came a few minutes later, a couple of blondes on his arm, kissing goodbye. The Russians, Earl guessed. He watched him run across the car park and vault into the pink Cadillac, throwing his overnight bag in the backseat.

'You'll rip my damn wing mirrors off,' Earl said.

'Harley has still got it, baby.'

For the first few miles, they didn't speak. The whole journey would only take about two hours. They were soon past Wilson Lake. There was already nothing here. Bush, desert, telegraph poles, leafless trees. Smokey sleeping in the back. Earl turned the stereo on.

The song relaxed his mind and he thought about his car. A 1956 Cadillac De Ville.

A two-door coupe.

Automatic three-speed gearbox and he didn't care he was doing near one hundred mph in the dark.

Facts like this eased him. He liked to recite them. Over and over.

'I'm a simple guy,' he began. 'I don't want to be recognised everywhere I go. I don't want a thousand women hanging off my arm. I don't like people taking liberties.'

Harley turned his head.

'I have your back buddy, don't you ever forget that.'

'My back? You like me driving you around.'

'What?'

'Nobody else will ride with you.'

'Here's something you might not like to hear. I can get a ride wherever I like. Goddamnit, I'm so hot right now I could get Walker to drive me there by limousine while I entertained a whole troupe of Kansas City Chief's cheerleaders,' Harley said. 'I ride with you because I'm one of the few guys who likes you. I get it man, I get what you're going through.'

The night was chilly and now totally dark. Already ten-thirty. Earl kept one thumbless hand on the wheel. Blends of streetlight captured on the pink gleam along the fenders and tailfins made it seem almost afloat. The car made a moaning sound. Brake pads still sore.

Earl answered, 'I'm not going through anything.'

'You need to see the bigger picture, no matter how much it hurts.'

'And what is the bigger picture?' Earl was disconsolate. 'I didn't realise you were some kind of shrink now too.'

'Smokey is holding you back man. In every way imaginable. You don't go out. You don't get bookings. You've let your act become a sideshow.'

'She is not a sideshow.'

'If you even cared about her, you wouldn't drive her round in the fucking car like one.'

'What did you say?'

'I mean, she's a wild animal. You gotta let her go. You gotta let go for your own sake.'

Earl pulled up. This time he snatched the revolver from the glove box and pointed the weapon at Harley. Snubnose to his head. 'Get out,' he said. 'Get out of the fucking car.'

'Whatever.'

'Get out and walk.'

He felt the gun's cold scorch on his skin. His neck tightened for the pulsing metal.

'I'm going, man. You're fucking beyond help.'

Harley loosed open the door. He looked back shaking his head. Then set off, overnight bag in hand, down the roadside.

Earl sat in the car playing the same song on a loop. He couldn't get past it. Earl clambered into the backseat and reached both arms around Smokey. He thought of Rebecca. He nuzzled his face in Smokey's blue-black fur, finding solace there. She made a motor-like noise and they butted heads in a friendly way as if they were wrestling. She could never be his daughter. After Rebecca died he drove through deserted streets every night, alone, until he found Smokey, a bear cub, still blind, lapping her fallen mother, a totalled pickup rolled on its side, blood-spattered like a horror scene.

Smokey moved a single comforting paw across his face, claws stubby shorn though still scratchy, and he looked at her eyes dark with sadness. Humans are animals too. He opened the door: unmuzzled, she ran into the night. He looked up at the stars, recalling some things he had hoped for and some things he hadn't.

*

A few weeks later I was buzzing, having made amends for my shit story last time, got good feedback for the pathos in the relationships, the promising way in which my experience of this world was being turned into stories, and, of course, Smokey, who broke everybody's heart. The next Saturday after,

I was taking training at the Dojo as I had done since Trev had bought the gym from Renegade, who were focusing more on other schools who were more indie, and talents who Wrestle World USA approved of. They had some kind of business relationship that everybody knew about, and nobody was quite sure of. There were rumours that Renegade had been co-opted by Wrestle World, some fans were agitating about how punk rock pro wrestling could get into bed with the Trump-donating billionaire run corporation and there were rumours that the Renegade video archive would become part of Wrestle World USA network, my matches included, but these kept being talked about but never seemed to materialise.

I had worked some of the main 'battleground' shows for Renegade with Trev until they lost faith in us after a tag-title match against The Blood Masons. Trev took it better, was bolder about approaching management about what we had done wrong and what it is they wanted, but I squirmed whenever he did, lacking the confidence he had in our ability, and I had long since consigned myself to the idea that I had a better chance on the undercard as a singles wrestler.

We would turn up for the next few months, show after show, Trev in charge of the ring crew, me helping with the ring. The pleasant circus world of wrestling had begun to meet the performative outrage and polarisation of the real one as the Brexit referendum came up and divisions began to flare up online. At one show, the compare, Josh, opened one show moaning about Tory cunts and getting a cheap pop, one fan bit and Jim had him thrown out.

I voted to remain, but was it not possible to tolerate somebody else's views?

This was the guy who first shouted Default at me during my first match, had been to almost every show since 2015. And here he was, removed by security for supporting Brexit.

Everybody's welcome, I thought.

Until you're not.

In bed with billionaires yet still indie, taking money from the man but still punk, everybody welcome as long as you stayed in line.

In any case, even if I was booked by Renegade and signed by Wrestle World USA, I knew this wouldn't be enough for us to get by, not compared to Grace's head of department salary. With a baby on the way, her going out to work and me pretending to fight people didn't sit right with me.

I applied for a job teaching English at Grace's school which was due to start the next academic year. I was unqualified, but that didn't matter, with my experience at university and the school being so hard up for teachers, I could work and train on the job.

Having done rope running, how to take a headlock and how to bump, over the past few weeks, I stood in the ring and demonstrated how to do the spot called The International I had first tried in that session in Liverpool, walked it through several times, told them what to do, what not to do, one guy takes a headlock, the other slingshots him off the ropes only to get knocked down as he lassoed back to him and so on. Then watched as everybody made a mess of it, one after the other, all fooling about like goons.

And these were the ones, like all the others, like me, who turned up on the first day thinking wrestling owed them something.

I would ruin them.

Only the strong would survive!

The ones who would respect the business and honour its codes.

I had sometimes thought in my more pessimistic moments, which were frequent, that anybody could do what I did in the ring. There was no merit in what I did. It was just that most wrestling fans were geeks, overweight and living their lives as meta-fans, engaged in shows as genuine spectators but also *playing* the role of fans during the show and doing what they could outside of the shows to analyse and shape the narratives around what happened in the ring, both kayfabe and real.

But there was reassurance in training these shit bastards. Whatever they did in life, doctors, actors, teachers, comedians, athletes, delivery drivers, whatever they were, almost all of them were shit and all of them knew more about the business than you did, and had bigger dreams than those to which you could aspire.

People ran off the wrong way.

Others ran into each other with their heads bowed and collided like idiots.

Most were incapable of completing the simplest sequences or even moving around the ring without looking like donkeys.

The few who could do it had no sense of performance, it was boring and lifeless.

I must have had *something*. Despite everything I did being generic, there must have been something that got me booked on all these shows and not somebody else, something that meant I was the sole survivor of my training course, one of the few trainees to make it onto a battleground show. What it was, however, I had no idea.

It was like being a writer. What was it that made one arrangement of words superior to another? Especially writers who used a plainer prose style, what was it they included and omitted that elevated their sentences and therefore perceptions above some other guy using the same vocabulary? The same ideas? A sense of style, perfected, repeated and *authentic* was what linked these thoughts, but what was it that meant one writer's voice was better than another's? One was more authentic while another was not? What if you burrowed into your authentic self and spoke with your voice only to find it wasn't any good? You were *authentically* bad?

When Saul Bellow wrote *The Adventures of Augie March*, he said the book came in floods, all he had to do was be there to catch it. Why not anybody else? I looked out across the ring and two guys attempted the same spot we had worked on all day and all last session and still ran like a pair of bone-headed dinosaurs.

Well, this was the drizzling shits.

I called one guy in, walked him through the sequence while the rest of the class watched from ringside.

'The whole thing with wrestling is, it's not in here,' I said, closing myself up and making the headlock tight, 'it's out *there*.'

My eyes gazed out somewhere in the distance, in gestural space, this was where a wrestling match took place in the imagination of the audience.

Now run me into the ropes, I said, holding the headlock as I was crab-walked to the side of the ring and slingshotted off the ropes. From here I bounced back and knocked the guy down with a tackle. He bumped in stages, then rolled onto his arse like a sack of shit.

'Get out,' I said.

I pointed at a young kid who was looking eager on the apron. 'You, get in.'

He looked around as if to say *me?*.

Then climbed in through the middle ropes. Before we locked up, I circled him and he burst out laughing.

'What are you laughing at?' I said.

'I don't know. I'm sorry.'

We circled again, eye to eye, his fingers outstretched as if he was pretending to be a tiger.

Then he laughed again.

'What are you doing?' I shouted.

Ha-ha, ha-ha.

Laughing, again, like a clown, like the business was some kind of joke.

I grabbed him round the neck, took him over and synched on the headlock. From this position, I squeezed just hard enough for it to hurt, and shouted, 'You get in this fucking ring and you treat it with respect. You did that to me in a match and I'd knock you out for real.'

On the way home I knew I had gone too far, he was just a nervous kid but the point was I was terrified of Marilyn walking through the shutters, seeing me being soft on trainees and destroying me himself. The old boys would never let it down. I was a strawb leading strawbs. I tried to be tough but fair but knew there was no need for things to be this way, why couldn't I be gentler?

I had hated the business being so hard when I broke in and now I was making people pay their dues, not by getting the crap kicked out of me like Marilyn did, but through a process of proving themselves and showing respect.

In wrestling, respect had to be earned.

I had earned mine. I hadn't broken my balls, sweated blood and taken my bumps to just give it all away to idiots who though they were the next big thing.

It was becoming difficult to tell where I ended and Earl Black Jr began, but I didn't care. I liked feeling his black blood in my veins, like a poison, a Venom symbiote I had invented, made up of parts of myself I had repressed. The darker blood of Earl Black Jr had bonded with mine.

We were one and the same.

*

I had pitched a singles match on a new training show and wanted Joe to see my Strong Style. I had impressed enough in some tag-matches and bookings elsewhere to main event and he said I would main event with Paddy 'The Baddy' Malone. I had taken with the World of Sport legend Steve Gray and learned to run sequences like World of Sport wrestlers, and the opening of the match began that way, usually, a babyface is a better wrestler than a heel, though with Paddy's East End gimmick and side talking mouth and street slang, it made sense that I would out wrestle him and he would get on top by being a hard bastard. The match started with a collar-elbow tie up, grappling from post to post and then trading holds and counter-holds, outmanoeuvring one another with pinning combinations.

His shine was a right cross, a knee to the gut and generally beating me up. I cut him off with a gut-wrench suplex; when his back bounced off the canvas and he was sitting upright, I sprung off the rope and booted him in the face.

He rallied. A punch to the gut. A slap to the face. Just when he was about to stand up, I caught him with a boot to the nose. He fell to the ground, crumpled. It was too good a sell not to be real. Something was wrong. He crawled into the corner, and when he turned around, his scowling face was covered in blood.

Shit.

I held his head in my hand, bottled it and clubbed him with a weak forearm, soft enough to cause no further damage, hoping the knock wasn't too bad.

Fight back, I called.

He lay there, inert, and I clubbed him again.

Blood pissing from his nose.

'Hit me like a fucking man, you slag!' he shouted.

The crowd cheered.

Thank God, they were coming back round.

I looked across the ring at his pale skinny body as he pointed at me and shouted, hit me again!

A trail of blood ran down his torso. Gore dripped about his nose into his red beard and bloated eyes.

Fucking hell.

Harder.

I hit him harder.

Harder!

Harder.

Again.

Harder! He shouted. Harder!

Harder.

Again, again.

Did he want me to fucking kill him?

For fuck's sake, I summoned up all the anger in me and smashed his skull I felt his teeth rattle with every strike and the blows dulled my forearm.

He was consenting but it wasn't fake.

We had lost the plot and were just fighting each other, in some kind of weird, non-competitive spectacle.

We somehow transitioned into the end sequence we had planned, exchanging moves and strikes until he dropkicked me into the corner, ran to the side of the ring, spring boarded up to the top rope and dived at me foot-first. He pulled down his kneepad in preparation of his trembler, and I crawled out of the corner ready to be met with a knee driving through the side of my face.

One. Two. Three.

The bell rang and I lay there. Surely that was it? My career over?

The ring announcer raised my opponent's hand and shouted, 'And the winner, of this *WAR*, Kieron Gillespie!'

I slid out of the ring and walked away from the ring, looking back to see Paddy being crowded by trainees.

In the back, I sat down on a cold step, head in my hands. A minute later, Paddy was carried in through the door, arms around Luis Rodriguez.

'Sorry mate,' I said. 'I don't know what happened.'

'Leave him.' Alonso snapped. 'Do you want some water?'

Paddy stared groggily at him and nodded.

'I didn't mean to do it,' I said.

Alonso opened the side door and Paddy stood outside. The night was dark and starry, and moonlight carried across the alleyway.

Paddy asked for a cigarette and sat there smoking with a dead glare in his eye. He looked like he had been in a gruesome feeding frenzy, glowing blood smeared across his beard and chest.

The guilt was unbearable.

My head throbbed, probably concussed, but I felt none of it, only the burning shame.

It was the dream I had, where I buried some guy I killed in the garden.

The shame was physical.

'Was the match good?' he smiled.

I said nothing, went back inside and sat on the step.

A pale rinse of my sweat flooded across my skin and his blood was on me. I flicked it away with the back of my hand as best I could.

What was I thinking?

Grace came through the door ready for a fight.

'What was that?' she said.

'It didn't look as bad as it was.'

'That's Strong Style, is it? I basically looked like you were beating the crap out of each other.'

I shrugged.

'Pretty much. Yeah.'

'I didn't like that match.'

I looked up.

I could tell. Non-wrestlers weren't allowed backstage. Only something horrible would have brought her back here.

'Sorry,' I said.

I went to get changed, buzzing as if I had just been in a fight, remembered Dad was meant to be here, and went out through the main bar with my head down.

It was seen as beneath us to congregate with fans, but I couldn't stomach talking to anybody right now, I brushed past them if they got in the way, not making eye contact, not wanting adulation for nearly killing Paddy Malone. I walked across the bar looking for Dad and Grace, head down, avoiding the fans who were annoying at the best of times.

'King of Strong Style!' somebody shouted.

I looked up.

It was The Preacher. His face filled with glee. Mischief in his eyes. He was slightly crazed at the best of times, but in his post-match state, high on life, his beard sparkled in the light with a manic intensity; his huge eyebrows seemed even bushier.

I smiled, held out my hand and he pulled me in for a hug.

'Was it okay?' I asked.

'Mate, it looked stiff as hell,' he said. 'I loved it. Marilyn and Will are over there, go ask them.'

I looked over to where he was pointing.

My stomach lurched.

I didn't much fancy doing that, but I knew that if I didn't there was a risk of disrespecting them and I'd never hear the end of it.

I made my way over and stood beside them like a child. I knew they saw me but made me wait for a break in conversation.

Assholes.

'Did you guys see my match?' I asked.

They laughed.

'You must be fucking kidding me?' Marilyn snarled.

'Oh,' I said.

He smiled.

'Ease up, I'm only joking. It looked like a fight,' Marilyn said. 'There was the issue with the knee to the face, but we got through it.'

'Thanks,' I said.

'Just one thing though,' Will said. 'Sometimes you give somebody a stuff one. That happens. But for a few minutes you looked like a deer caught in the headlights, you know? You should have carried on. Just beat him up a bit until he recovered.'

I shook their hands, smiled, filled with excitement that the match hadn't bombed and going off script had given the match an air of unrehearsedness. It was spontaneity that was wild and raw and more than a little dangerous. Strong Style. I fucking loved it.

I wanted more. It was a shot of testosterone, a bravura feeling of serious manliness like I had the power to batter whoever I wanted, fear nobody and fuck anybody I desired.

I stopped and looked around for Grace and seeing her talking to Dad at the bar, and thought I better go rescue her.

Dad had lost weight and the gastric bypass gave his face a ghoulish look. He leaned over the bar, throwing folded twenty notes and tipping loose change because he didn't have the movement in his fingers to pull out the right amount.

'I'm just ordering,' he said. 'Want anything?'

'Just a quick pint. We'll have to go soon.'

He chucked some more coins across the bar.

The look in Grace's eye said it all. Dad had been in full flow. God knows what he would have said to her.

'So who's this delightful young lady you've been keeping from me?'

Grace flushed red, looking downward to conceal her grin which looked more embarrassed than flattered.

It would have meant something to her though.

'Dad, this is Grace. Grace, Dad.'

'Bit late now!' he laughed.

'Your dad has been telling me all about Vietnam,' she said. 'Sounds like a really cool place.'

He handed me my pint.

'Oh dear,' I said. 'Hope you kept it clean?'

He spluttered.

'Of course I bloody did, what do you take me for, some kind of maniac?'

I sunk half the pint.

'Did you see my match?'

'I had a nightmare getting down here.'

I could see where this was going.

'I didn't get here until a few minutes ago,' he said.

He stared blankly.

In his dark jacket, across the large expanse of his back, he shrugged, and his neck muscles bulged, the last remnants of his size. There was the bull neck and the mallet fists and everything else was string and flesh.

'Did it go well?' he asked.

'It was a war.'

'Sorry I missed it.'

I shook my head.

'What time did you set off?'

'Two,' he said. 'But we hit traffic.'

'You'd have never made it in time. You should have told me. You missed the best match of my life.'

'I liked the one with you and The Dude.'

'You saw that on YouTube.'

He shrugged.

'They'll be other times.'

I looked at Grace and she gave me a stare.

'I've been telling her about the star fruit and rambutan you get out there,' Dad said. 'Beautiful.'

'At least he hasn't shown you his pictures of girls on his phone,' I said, looking at Grace.

Her eyes narrowed.

'Oh, he has,' she said, half-smiling.

I drank the last of my pint.

'Do you want another?' Dad said.

I checked my phone.

'I don't know,' I said. 'It's already pretty late and we need to get back.'

There was a lost look in his eye. A grin flashed across his lips and was gone as soon as it appeared.

'I don't want to keep you,' he said. 'I know you're busy.'

I looked at Grace. She stared back.

'One more can't hurt,' I said.

Dad threw some loose change at me with his immobile fingers. It went all over the bar and I picked the coins up, sticky on one side. I ordered us both a pint, sank mine instantly and bearhugged him goodbye, feeling all his frailty in his embrace but also the ancient strength of his grip. I followed Grace out of the pub and onto the street, which hit us with a sudden blast of night.

*

On the way home I begged Grace to let me stay and drink, said it was the best bit, going through all the turmoil to sink a few pints with the boys after a match, but she said we had a long way to go and I sulked as we drove east out of London, along the docks and the University of East London, which I had left at the end of term when my contract ran out. On we went, with the small engine going as hard as it could, as we slowed alongside haulage trucks that sailed like ships through the dark night and we were a blue Ford KA-shaped dot beside them. This was supposed to be the greatest match of my life; the moment that would define me and maybe it would, but not in the way I might want.

I just wanted to get hammered. What was the point of going through all that ordeal if I couldn't sink a few pints afterward? I loved to have a drink, it would begin with one, the sudden glint of lager on your tongue and the thrilling rushing satisfaction that the wait was over I could pour drink after drink into the black hole and everything disappeared.

It was who I was, what I was entitled to: I had a right to get as hammered as I liked. Drinking was the only way for me to be me. Necking shot after shot, until the lights dimmed, I was full of good feeling and only vaguely aware of who I was and that felt good, it felt good to not be me and live with this reeling, never-ending sense of punishing self-awareness and nervousness and shame. Then I didn't stop until I was stopped: not until I fell over, passed out, or was hauled away in the back of van. I had woken up on benches, in cells, in beds, on lawns, anywhere I lay my head. When I was drunk, anything was possible and it was the over self I kept within, a shadow of the paltry one who lacked conviction, whereas this wild man could be anybody he wanted, could do anything, without the burden of conscience until I woke up with the fear and was too afraid to leave my bedroom for days at a time, hangovers that came like whirlwinds and aches deep in my lower back that felt like I might be terminally ill.

I thought this: listening to the playlist made up of Grimes, Metronomy, Wild Beasts, Bloc Party and our own thoughts hushed by the movement of the car and the steady waves of tiredness.

Coming down from the show, my body began to return to a more natural state, and I could feel the beginnings of aches and cramps that would be stiff in the morning. My eye would be black. I could feel a crust of sweat, mingled with Paddy Malone's blood all over my body that still thrummed with the muscle-memory of every bump and smash. I would have to wash my hands before I ate anything. In the rhythm of the car and the grey oncoming road, the music made its own mood, it seemed unnecessary to speak. The suburbs were disguised in the dark and places I would recognise during the day were black holed by the darkness of the fading streetlamps. Glimpses of a street I was only aware of because I had attended a barbecue somewhere round here a year ago, in which I had spent the morning making a chimichurri sauce to impress Grace's friends, but nobody really ate any, other than me. There was a gentle hum in the car. Songs changed and I barely heard them. The road glowed and the points that were distances on the horizon soon came to the foreground, replaced by a new façade of scenery and the distant glow of a fluorescent yellow 'M' in the distance.

The white blur of the word *McDonald's*. It gave me a shiver of nostalgic joy. For the while my parents were together before they broke up, the highlight of our week was to go to an out-of-town retail complex built on a former landfill site and after a long afternoon of shopping, go through the McDonald's drive-thru, order our meals via the intercom and eat them as a family in the carpark. Dad always told the joke how when they first went to the drive-thru, the customer thought Mum was Dad's daughter – and how we all laughed.

Grace was always worried about kids from school being in there. In Medway, all the under eighteens are excluded from pubs but all drive souped-up hatchbacks with extra-strong beams, blaring drum and bass.

'Are we going inside?' she asked.

'It's gonna be hard to eat in the car. It's like eleven-thirty, no kids are gonna be in there.'

'You wanna bet?'

'If there are any kids in there we can leave, okay?'

She nodded.

If I couldn't drink, I would binge eat. All the restriction of dieting and self-denial had to be let out somewhere.

We went inside and fingered our orders into body-length touchscreens Grace pushed the images for a double cheese-burger meal with a Coke Zero. I added a double cheeseburger, Big Mac meal, McFlurry ice cream, Chocolate Doughnut and a Chocolate Cookie.

About five thousand calories all in all.

I put my card to the reader when the sum had been totalised, pulled out the slip of paper and took a seat. No sooner than I had sat down, I remembered to wash my hands, made my way to the bathroom to have a piss, doused my hands in liquid soap, thought against floating them over the hand-dryer in a cyclone of other men's dirty humidity and dried my palms on the back of my jeans instead.

One guy came in and was doing something I couldn't abide. Pissing with dick resting on his bollocks, hands behind his head.

What kind of gesture was that?

It was reckless, for one. His twizzled little dick spraying away on the mound of his zip squeezed balls.

Then he left without washing his hands. Spreading dick bacteria wherever he touched.

I caught a glimpse of myself in the mirror, expecting to see a wrestler with chiselled features who filled a T-shirt like the WWE superstars I watched in the 90s. Instead, I was skinnier and gawkier – athletic-looking at best.

I made my way back out to the table.

'I got some sauce,' I said.

'Thanks.'

I wolfed down the double cheeseburger in two or three bites and then moved onto the Big Mac.

Grace was staring at me.

'What?' I asked.

'I don't like *Strong Style*,' she emphasised the phrase with incredulity, as if it were some kind of scam, less a style at all and more a method of taking things way too far.

'Why?'

'You were really hurting each other out there tonight, weren't you?'

'No.'

She frowned.

'What about Paddy's face?'

'That was an accident.'

'Like the rest of it?'

'It was just one of those things. You can bump your nose anywhere. His head was too low. I shouldn't have gone for a kick. But there you go. I thought it was my best match otherwise.'

'I don't like violence. It's the same in films. It makes me feel sick.'

'Nobody was really getting hurt.'

'Really?'

I nodded, though my head was heavy and probably concussed.

'That's the work. We make it look real, the more visceral it is, the more real it feels. But it's not, it's completely fake.'

She rested her palms on the top of my hands.

'I love you,' she said.

'I love you, too.'

I hadn't thought about anything much else other than this match for days. I trained like an athlete for these big matches, as if it was real, upped the cardio at the gym and worked out the macronutrient breakdown for each day. My diet consisted of a set number of fats, proteins and carbohydrates. I had lived like this for three years. Yet despite dieting, training and decent genetics, I still didn't look like the steroidal heroes of my upbringing.

Where to start?

I ate another cheeseburger like a dog, inhaling it whole, then chomping on the way down

Then onto the Big Mac.

The soft bread began dissolving on my palate like candyfloss. Grace, meanwhile, pulled out one chip out at a time and studied her burger before taking a sensible bite.

This space-food inauthenticity was what I loved about McDonald's. It was a bonfire of liberal pieties. The meat that tasted like meat-substitute, plasticky cheese, the peculiar aftertaste that was now a commodity in its own right, known simply as *burger sauce*.

I sipped fizz from my Coke Zero.

The thing without the thing. Fat-free mayonnaise. Alcohol-free beer. Sex with condoms. There was some enjoyment in it but not the thrilling danger and therefore pleasure of the original, of the authentic.

How was pro wrestling any different?

The traditional role of men and the masculine had been sidelined in the Western world. At least on the face of it, in discourses of what was correct and right, macho was crude and backward. Pro Wrestling gave these men a world and a status to occupy beyond the mainstream where the fictions of masculinity they played become performances of who they were in and out of the ring. A simulacrum of what people wanted without the danger, though what if there was a danger in the performance, even if there shouldn't be, and what if there was a danger in the glorification of violence for the performance and the audience. I had no idea, nor did I particularly care, it made me feel alive and that's when I felt most authentically like who I was. Pro wrestling offered the opportunity for people with low status in real life the chance to play the type of masculine hero who they were not and could not be. It was a fantasy of wish-fulfilment. The only thing separating me from Earl Black Jr was how I chose to identify; really there was becoming increasingly little difference. The parts of the performance which resonated most with people *were* me. But then I could only do that when I was performing as Earl Black Jr.

Then the bits of Earl Black Jr come out in everyday life. The other week I was getting off a train with Grace and some guy bumped into me. I reared up to him and got in his face. He backed down. Two minutes later, somebody tried to beat me to a turnstile, and I squared him up, the performance knew no bounds and was becoming my real life.

Grace ate at a civilian, *strawberry mivvy* pace, which meant that she was only halfway through her meal while I was already moving onto desert after inhaling three burgers and a box of fries.

She sucked on her straw while looking at her phone.

'Can I ask you something?' she said.

What was it? There was something frank in her expression that worried me, go on I said, and she just said it was to do with wrestling.

Go on then.

'I'm not being funny or anything,' she said. 'But do you actually enjoy being a wrestler?'

I turned and stared at her.

'Of course I do!'

'Was just wondering.'

'You think I don't?'

'Well, just you never seem happy with your matches. Even if it goes well you find something to moan about. There's all this effort you put into it and you don't seem to get much out of it.'

I slurped some Coke Zero.

A lot of what she was saying was right. Why did I put myself through this?

I moved onto desert, inhaled a doughnut, no time to savour its sweetness, before spooning mouthfuls of ice cream into my face.

'I've just got so used to it. I've trained hard to get where I am, you know? There's the loyalty to the people who've stuck their neck out for me. And, if I left, you know what wrestling's like, I'd be out of it. That would be that. I wouldn't still be friends with these people.'

'It's not just a social club though, is it?'

'I don't want to go back to how I was. And what would I do with myself?'

'You won't.'

'How do you know?'

She smiled. 'I don't,' she said.

I took another slurp. With all the sugar in my mouth, Coke Zero tasted even more like Coke without the Coke. It was an empty, gassy simulacrum of a dark liquid that tasted like Coke but wasn't the Real Thing. But to me it was, because I didn't drink the other Coke.

'If you took wrestling out of me,' I said. 'What's left?'

She put her hand to my face. 'Everything else.'

More teenagers arrived in pimped-up hatchbacks. A security guard mouthed something into his radio.

Light grinned on the tinted windows.

*

I went upstairs as soon as we got home. I hadn't noticed Grace get changed, but suddenly she was in a green satin chemise beside me in bed, while I was lying in the sodden sports briefs I wore under my tights.

Did I need a shower?

I couldn't be bothered. I was barely able to keep my eyes open. Concussive, woozy.

I wanted to sleep and not have the match alive in my mind. All the blows and sequences were reeling through my thoughts, almost as vivid and physical as they had been the first time round.

My knee raising as I went to kick him but finding it flush against his nose.

His body collapsed in the corner, me striking him in the head while he was totally punch drunk

The brainbusters. Oh, no.

It was idiotically dangerous. The most dangerous thing I had ever done in my life.

I literally could've killed him.

In bed, I lay with my body humming in pain and I could smell his scent on me, which was robust and orangey; the aroma lingered around me like an apparition, and I felt guilty about how much I fucked him up, wherever he was.

I held Grace in a clinch thinking about the baby concealed within her body, the thing that was a tadpole floating about in fluid but would have all it needed to grow into a person in its own right. I lay behind her, touching my hand to her belly, reaching around for a half nelson to hold her closely. We had recently had our three-month scan and for the first time I saw that the contour of the face on the ultrasound looked just like a mime. The little heart thumping. The slender fingers like a bush baby's, with round dotted pads at the end. The child's snub nose and square forehead were mine, how odd to see those features transplanted onto a prehuman form. I hoped it was nothing like me, that she would be content in who she was, not have to suffer to become herself. My head thumped. I rubbed my neck. Everything was starting to cramp up and there was a sharp pincer in my hip joints like my tailbone had snapped off and the lower spine was superglued together. Every bump or collision with the turnbuckle pads meant jolting the neck muscles, the impact stacked every disc of your spine, juddering the wingnuts. The after effect was sore hips. A gnawing ache in my lower back. Elbows that were blasted and worn. But there was a pleasure in all of this, hell, it was satisfying to feel this blasted and worn, properly embodied and living as blood and flesh, rather than intellect.

The fabric of Grace's night dress sketched the curves of her body which contained my baby, and the light made strange, elusive patterns on the silk.

I put my arms around her and pulled her closer, still smelling of other men.

*

The next morning I woke up feeling like I'd been beaten up. Had a vague sense of Grace pulling a dress over her body, getting Eliot ready for the bus, having several short conversations before I fell back asleep, in a daze of exhaustion.

The bumps that seemed like painless artistry when your body was hot, and the moment was live but now could be felt as bruised or stiff areas of your body. During the planning of a match and then the performance, all you can think about is giving it everything, throwing your body into every move, not the shock on the body after.

The heavy weightlifting sessions and lack of sports massage, ice baths, yoga and warm downs elite athletes would utilise to recover, my body was beginning to break down.

All the demand was on the posterior chain: the heavy lifting involved in deadlift, squat and bracing for the bumps. The wrists, joints and knees. The slams that riveted and sent blast waves through the body.

Then the travelling around the country every weekend, dry heaving, arguing about the composition of the routines like angry dance choreographers, going over them by rote until they stuck, waiting around backstage for hours, before a ten-minute match and back in the car for a round trip that wouldn't end until midnight, was it even worth it?

No, not really.

Grace was right. I didn't even enjoy it anymore. Not since things got serious, which meant every match was under greater scrutiny. First there was the crowd to please. Then the promoter. The guy you were working. The critics online. The people running the podcasts. The fans on social media. Then the veterans who would grasp any opportunity to bury me and tell me how shit I was, that I shouldn't be wrestling and didn't know what I was talking about.

Earl Black Jr was a self-portrait of suffering on canvas. But how much of yourself was worth giving up for in the name of realism?

How much suffering was enough?

And what was it all about, this asceticism, as if a performance could be a self-expression of the true self beneath with all its uniqueness.

In 'The Hunger Artist', a short story by Franz Kafka, an artist captured the attention of the crowd by making an exhibition of his starvation.

He sat in a cage wearing black tights, pale skinned with his ribs sticking out, forcing a smile as people watched on. Some were suspicious of his fasting, doubted what he was doing was real, while others delighted in keeping him under observation in order to try and catch him out.

When he met his challenge of forty days without food, he only pushed himself harder.

Why stop when he was on good form, why not become the best hunger artist of all time?

In time, fashions changed, and the crowds were no longer interested in The Hunger Artist's self-denial. He ran away and joined the circus, although his act grew stale there too and he was almost forgotten about and near death when his supervisor discovered what he thought was an empty cage and asked why he was still fasting?

The Hunger Artist explained as he lay there dying, that nobody should admire his fasting because he couldn't do anything else, and that he could find no other food that he enjoyed.

I had a girlfriend, a stepson, and a baby on the way.

It was stupid and selfish to live like this. I never intended on wrestling forever; a few more matches, a few more attempts at finding a Strong Style and I would be done.

Even though I knew this, to think of giving it up made me sick inside, however much I hated trying to remember the choreography, the nerves before every match, all the politics and the bullshit, it was the performance in-ring, like The Hunger Artist in his cage, longing for the gaze of strangers that made me who I was.

I staggered into the shower, ran the hot tap and felt my body slackened by the water.

Steam rose, and the crust of sweat and blood that had formed around me was washed away.

I held my arms out against the tiles, bent forward and let the water pound my back.

I got dressed in black jeans and a wrestling T-shirt, brushed my teeth and went downstairs for the first of many coffees that day. The TV had been left on. I looked under the sofa cushions for the remote, turned off the cartoons, then back into the kitchen to tidy away a box of cereal and dashed away some crumbs with a wet cloth.

I pulled open the handle on the coffee machine, loaded a capsule, filled the tank with water, put my cup under the nozzle and pressed the button.

My head was thick with headache, and I had just forgotten what I was thinking about.

Maybe I just forgot?

Oh no.

Maybe it was something else. The blows to the head. I got this a lot, I got cracked around the head a lot, I didn't know if I had been concussed or it was fine. I could have been concussed thirty or forty times for all I knew.

I had read the mortality rate for pro wrestlers was up to 2.9 times greater than the rate for men in the wider United States population. I googled concussion and found the effects could lead to confusion, vomiting, headache, nausea, depression, disturbed sleep, moodiness, amnesia and being a cunt, all symptoms I routinely suffered from.

Fighters like boxers and MMA competitors only fight a few bouts a year. If they're any good, they will protect themselves, bob and weave, absorb the worst impact with their guard. Clinching when the blows are precarious. Sensing danger, they brace, move and defend. The referee will stop the bout as soon as a combatant fails to protect themselves. Pro wrestlers often work four or five nights a week or more, collecting injuries and cumulative impact. Vulnerable, you open yourself up undefended for somebody to hit you. Like bumping, falling backward not knowing where you're going, it's unnatural yet compulsive, like living by your own rules. It involves you having to unlearn a lifetime of experience and a million years of genetic coding. To fall. To entrust yourself to fall into oblivion and know you will be okay.

Usually, the guy you're working with is skilled enough to protect you. Some guys work so light you barely feel anything but the deftest of glances. It can be hard to know when to sell because it's so light. Sometimes they're not. Even if one in fifty is a *potato*, a real one, that's a lot of blows to take over a career.

The impact of being hit in the face, bumped, slammed, beaten, bruised often leads wrestlers to become addicted to painkillers. They can't afford to be injured. They don't want to lose their spot. There's no off-season. When self-medication is combined with steroid abuse and recreational drugs, wrestlers often die of heart attacks, suicide or overdoses.

Was realism worth the cost?

Chris Benoit had one of the most realistic styles around. He was described as a killer in the ring; everything he did was with fierce intensity, he made himself jacked with steroids, did the diving headbutt off the top rope which ended the career of Harley Race and ruined the neck of his hero, The Dynamite Kid, who lived out the last of his days in a wheelchair before dying at the age of sixty.

There was no corner Benoit would cut. He was an artist, committed to the real. He took unprotected chair shots to the head. Did a suicide dive through the middle ropes. Had to have neck fusion surgery after a ladder match. But what was it for? Because it made fanboys like me exhilarated with the thrill of the real? People who couldn't quite buy into an art form without it being real in some way, or feeling real, even if that realism was verisimilitude at best.

Over a three-day period in 2007, aged forty and after a twenty-year career, Benoit killed his wife by breaking her back across his knee, he then strangled his son to death and left bibles beside their bodies before hanging himself in his gym.

The autopsy revealed Benoit had suffered countless concussions over his career and had the brain of an eighty-five-year-old Alzheimer's patient, this, combined with years of steroid abuse and his increasingly emotional and paranoid state after the death of his best friend and fellow wrestler, Eddie Guerrero, was enough to send him over the edge.

Benoit, like his hero The Dynamite Kid, were innovators of what was to become the *Strong Style*. Incredibly similar in-ring, Benoit took what Kid had and pushed it further.

Daniel Bryan, a wrestler who adopted a similar style and the flying headbutt of Benoit, was retired for several years due to neck injuries. Katsuyori Shibata split his own head open during a hard-hitting match in the Tokyo Dome and ended up with near life-threatening injuries.

The only thing stopping me from doing a diving headbutt was I couldn't keep my body straight enough mid-air. Otherwise, I would use it like I did everything else, full-blooded, I liked to hit harder, get hit harder, and had already had my bell rung enough to have started to forget things.

Even many of the generation of World of Sport wrestlers who favoured a technical, low-impact style now suffer hip and back problems, living the reality of faking it.

Dad broke his back in the ring. Somebody had planned to use a trap door in the main event and during his match, the boards slipped out of position, and he took a suplex across a girder which shattered his spine. His back was fused, leaving the massive muscle around his neck to have a hunched look like a bull. Otherwise, he had bumps and bruises but nothing serious. The stories he told of being hit with chairs and suitcases full of bricks were all worked. Kayfabe for Dad was about the magic of having *other* people believe, not deluding yourself. Whereas for somebody like Marilyn, kayfabe was a much more dangerous thing, not just about having others believe but having them believe so he could be somebody else. If it meant pouring lemon juice onto bare cuts, stapling his face, falling from a balcony, then so be it.

Because that was the only way he could be Marilyn fucking Draven and why, fundamentally, he was a babyface at heart to the wrestling fans. He sacrificed himself for them. While outwardly, a heel is selfish, in the context of the match they're selfless. They exist purely to get the babyface over. To be the antagonist. Whereas a babyface was about looking good, the way the fans connected with them was by them allowing themselves to be vulnerable. Not everybody was man enough to let this happen. But a babyface has to suffer, to put themselves out there and be brave enough to show their pain.

The biggest drawing wrestlers of the modern era were Hulk Hogan, Stone Cold Steve Austin and The Rock. None of them worked a particularly realistic style. But they were all great characters. They were over. They were storytellers. The realism of Benoit and Lewis was a purist fixation. It will gain respect from the hard core of smart marks at any wrestling show in the way that actors starving or gorging themselves can win awards while somebody getting jacked for a role is seen as vanity. The big draws in pro wrestling only needed enough realism to get by. Most people recognised the thing was not the thing, bad guys didn't really die in movies, nobody should get hurt, and it was only an obsession with ritual sacrifice that made performers go the extra mile, to make people believe at least *something* was real in the performance, to add that thrilling element of risk like Tom Cruise doing stunts for real his *Mission Impossible* films.

No matter how good or stiff a strike might look, how much more plausible it might look, it will never be *real*. A real wrestling match would look just like a real wrestling match. The boring grappling of legitimate enterprise. Just like a map the size of the world would be as useless as it was accurate, art could never be art by replicating the thing it was replicating exactly. Yet there was something else I hadn't been able to articulate and I felt like I was getting close.

If I was going to retire any time soon, which was something that seemed increasingly appealing as well as necessary, I wanted to go out having achieved the Strong Style I was searching for.

I had a message from Andrew Krupp, the promoter of Slam Nation, which surprised me, given that he usually made a point of not booking Dojo guys and had repeatedly asked me to train at his school despite having already been trained.

ANDREW KRUPP

Hey

Weird question. You know that knee strike thing you did before the ground and pound. Can you do that again without killing somebody?

WES BROWN

Ha, very niche!

The answer is yes.

I can.

Draven said it should be my finish.

ANDREW KRUPP

Draven and I agree then. I want to offer you an opportunity.

The idea was to book me over a period of several months to establish me in as a Strong Style heel who would brutalise jobbers in a realistic way and then finish them with the running knee strike. Rather than pin or submit them, as is the convention of pro wrestling, I would win by total knockout like an MMA fight. Meanwhile, one of Krupp's rookies who was a trainee Mauy Thai fighter would be knocking people out with his whirlwind kick.

This would be months of bookings developing the Earl Black Jr character and in-ring style the way I had always dreamed of.

ANDREW KRUPP

We'll see how it goes, but if it comes off in the right way, I can see it getting really over. Big things ahead.

WES BROWN

Absolutely

Everybody would be so jealous! EBJ getting booked at Slam Nation and doing the kind of wrestling I had been warned against ever since I set foot in a ring. I knew people said Krupp was dodgy, or that he treated people badly, but there was barely a promoter in the business who didn't.

Take the bookings.

This was my chance to prove the doubters wrong and become who I had always dreamed of being.

What else was I going to do?

*

In the meantime, I had started going to Marilyn's 'psychology' sessions again on Friday nights over the summer. Only a few people would ever show up for his sessions and one night Jay Langston, the Bollywood Superstar Shah and a fantasy kind of warrior queen called Boudica all stood on the apron while Marilyn, who was in a terrible mood, marched around the ring in his baggy cotton joggy bottoms, flicking his tail of hair.

'Which one of you wants to get in and cut a promo on me?' he asked.

Nobody moved.

'C'mon, am I that fucking scary?' he laughed, 'if you can't intimidate me in an empty ring, where can you?'

Marilyn Draven had trained as a schoolteacher himself; he had a degree in film and taught media studies, but you'd never know it from his persona in the Dojo. What would this guy do in a classroom?

When I was nineteen and nuts, part of me believed I would never be a man unless I had seen action in a war or gone to jail. Mum threw away my application to the army and I never spent more than a night in a slammer, and it was this same part of me that was drawn to Marilyn's session. I didn't want it easy. Underneath all abuse, Marilyn was a brilliant wrestler, an interesting guy and knew exactly what he was doing in the ring. In some ways, I thought of Marilyn and his pornstar girlfriend as shadows of me and Grace. While we dressed like the majority of people in gender-conforming clothes and highstreet brands, Marilyn and his burlesque dancer girlfriend were tattooed, with punkish hair and dyed undercuts. While I had studied literature, Marilyn had a PhD in gender studies, and while Marilyn had gone to train in Kent when he was sixteen, I had gone to college and had my heart set on becoming a writer.

His life was performance art, he was like Lana Del Rey but ultraviolent, playing the role of the monster in his own horror movie and everybody else was extras. It was hard to tell where he ended and his persona began. I'm not even sure he knew. We all played up to it though, it was part of being one of the boys. We were over with Marilyn. It was the only way you were ever truly over.

Being one of Marilyn's boys meant something. It was tougher and harder; it was letting people know you were the best.

Jezebel was first in. She poked her head through the middle rope, climbed in and confidently ran through her snobbish insults, hands on hips. Her parents were Iranian and Indian, and she was well brought up; she had a posh accent and told him she was insulted by his fashion choices.

I whispered across to Jay who was standing beside me, 'I don't fancy this.'

'Don't worry mate,' he answered.

We looked at Jezebel standing in the ring, hands still on her hips, fearless, and then at each other. At the other side of the ring, Queen Boudica blew a wisp of hair from her face in relief. Marilyn laughed. He seemed at ease. He had trained Jezebel and he was more likely to give her an easier ride than one of Trevor's trainees I guess, but who knew? I was here now, but hardly anybody else ever turned up to his sessions because they were fucking terrified. Maybe that stood for something?

'You,' he said, pointing at me, 'Earl Black Jr, let's see what you've got.'

He sat on the top turnbuckle.

'What do you want me to do?' I asked.

'I want you to intimidate me.'

'What shall I do?'

'You tell me.'

Okay, I said. Shuffling on my feet, the ring creaking and aching beneath. Just a silence between me and Marilyn Draven as we stood in the ring, under the damp bricks of an archway. A train rattled by overhead, and when the vibrations stopped I cut a promo on him about being the best technical wrestler in the UK, how I was the second-generation sensation, the Innovator of Old School Violence and was going to bring respect back to the industry.

He beat the turnbuckle pad with laugher.

'So you're better than Bruce Logan are you?'

I shrugged. I did my nervous smile, feeling wimpy and a million miles away from Earl Black Jr.

'It was only a promo,' I said.

'Well, you must be, because that's what you fucking said. Isn't it?'

I looked over at the others on the apron. Blank faces. I sighed, this was ridiculous.

Fuck it.

If he wanted it, he could have it.

I growled in my deepest voice, 'Marilyn fucking Draven. The fuck do you think you're looking at? You are nothing, sunshine. You've won one or two titles, yeah. But you can never have what I have. I had wrestling in my blood. In my veins. My dad was a champion around the world before you were anything. And me, only three years into my career and I'm going to be a champion. I didn't have to spend a decade fighting ten people in a sports hall in the other side of the country. Soon, yeah soon, you'll be retired, finished, a skinny little runt, and I'll be the man.'

He stood up and slow clapped, walking toward me with a little smirk on his face.

'Fucking never have what you have?'

I nodded.

'You are a fucking cunt,' he said.

'Yeah?'

'Your old man was nothing. Nobody's ever fucking heard of him, mate. He was a jobber for the Hart family, so what? Wrestling was shit then. You think you're a technical wrestler? Wrestle me.'

He stared me dead in the eyes.

Bobbing up and down.

'C'mon. Show me what you got,' he said.

The others held onto the top rope with both hands. Not moving.

I knew they thought this would be a bad idea, could feel them desperately trying to warn me away telepathically, but I took a fighting stance. Fuck him I thought, as I swept around, gut-wrenched him off his feet and down to the mat hard. He didn't like it, I could tell from the way he bucked and wriggled violently under my grip, but I held on. As he tried to work out of it I shifted my weight and began riding him. He spun out and I transitioned into an armbar, not knowing whether he would be impressed or try to kill me.

Back to his feet, hair across his face, he looked exasperated and I let him take my neck, where he snapmared me with force and began stomping the back of my head. Were we working? I didn't know as I fed around to the corner and he stalked after me, the sole of his boot in my face, over and over.

It was weird, not quite a proper fight, but the blows were grazing, bruising, invasive. A violation of one body on another. He was using wrestling strikes but with too much force to be working me. Should I have just grabbed his leg and snapped it?

What then?

I could've easily grabbed him and fucking killed him with my bare hands, but where would that lead?

Suck it up, I thought, it'll make for good prose if nothing else.

But as I lay there, trying to protect myself, I was full of shame: I had never had never let anybody hit me before.

A toe of a boot came in against my ribs.

'You're fucking dangerous,' he shouted. 'What are you playing at? Taking me down like that.'

He was kicking at me, having a wild tantrum.

I kept thinking the whole time, whatever he did wasn't that bad, fear of Marilyn was worse than anything he could do to me. Kick me in the head for all I cared. It meant nothing. I could take a beating.

After a while, he gave up, punched himself out and started rubbing his knee. I rolled out of the ring. Queen Boudica came over and put her hand on my shoulder, but Marilyn said not to show me any mercy.

I tried not to look at her, but she saw deep into me as we exchanged glances. Everything was in there. My watery eyes.

Marilyn limped about in the ring saying didn't I know he had a bad knee? What if I had injured him for his match on Sunday?

I apologised and wiped my eyes. Jay was next in the ring and the session moved on.

I stood at ringside with a big fake grin on my face, pretending nothing had happened. But in the ring, everything I saw looked fake and rotten. The stupid characters and the fake strikes and the moves that didn't make any sense and the way the wrestlers gave one another so much space. The way they didn't guard or cover themselves. You would have to be a moron to believe this was real or willing to accept a vast suspension of disbelief. The routine that Jezebel and Queen Boudica went through was a good one, it would have popped people on shows, but I could see the structure, the same seven stages that underlined every match.

I held onto the top rope. It swayed like a lasso in my grip as Jezebel slammed Queen Boudica and she writhed around on the canvas in agony. Marilyn prowled around as a referee one minute, a trainer the next, giving tips to the pair of them. He had calmed down and was compensating for his behaviour. Cracking jokes, offering slivers of advice, a forlorn glance from time to time.

It was too late.

The symbiote was beginning to eat away from my skin. This dark pool of Venom that I had masked myself in to become Earl Black Jr. In the Spider Man comics the symbiote bonds with a host to provide superhuman strength, speed, agility and endurance. It gains and amplifies the powers of the host. What would staying in this industry any longer than I had to do to me? All these old boys, thirty-something men, pretending to be characters they invented, still living at their parent's homes, never growing up and living a perpetual adolescence. If the symbiote provides new abilities in pro wrestling, its cost was the state of these people lives and mental states, and, eventually, they would no longer have their symbiote, or anything else to show for themselves.

When I got home to Grace, she met me at the door and we kissed. I didn't' mention anything about what happened; instead, we watched *Seinfeld* and ate pizza.

In the night, I woke from a dream just as Marilyn's boot was closing in on my face. What hurt wasn't him stomping me, it had been the fact that I didn't fight back. It didn't bother me that the other trainees hadn't intervened, they were petrified, and it was a fear I felt myself, it was why I had to act in a particular way, why I was too embarrassed to say anything to Grace because that would break the veneer of my persona and the cocky belief I had let be known that Marilyn would never pick on *me* because I was somehow more credible than the other dickheads.

Why hadn't I hit him back?

In school, one guy went around with a hitlist of who he wanted to fight. We had been friends and he was a boxer, but after going on a rampage for months that involved him punching almost everybody I knew in the face, he came for me. When we were alone in the locker room he thumped me in the kidney. I wanted to cry. But it was the shame that hurt the most. And while I didn't have a gang like him, or fearless, the next time he came for me, I ducked his jab almost involuntarily before returning with a combination of my own, taking him down to the floor and pounding his head until it burst.

He never touched me again. Nobody did.

Once, playing five-a-side as a teenager against a team of men, one of the blokes punched my mate in the face and we did nothing. Walking away, I couldn't leave things like that and went back and mauled him to the ground, pounding my fist into his face until his mates pulled him away.

But eventually, the time would come for me to get out of wrestling and have to be me again. There would be nowhere to hide, no kayfabe beyond the fiction of yourself.

*

Lucky for me, Krupp had booked me on every other Slam Nation show until the end of the summer. All the other guys were jealous of the ones who were booked week in, week out and I was on a run of working two or three times a week for various promotions across the country, posting up my match graphics on social media and creating a lot of buzz, getting over as a 'good hand' like Dad, had realistic matches more in the way

I would have liked with 'Karate Kid' among others. Even if I was greener than them, I was taking something from every match, getting better, and refining my own Strong Style.

In one match, somebody had bitten my head in training before and as I shoot-style wrestled with James Bliss the cut opened up and I finished up the match with a series of rolling German suplexes, arms around his waist and popping my hips to slam him back over my shoulder, then drag him up again only to repeat the movement and throw him upper back first into the mat. When I hit the running knee, I slapped my thigh as I made contact, giving the impression it had cracked his rib. As the bell rang, I prowled around the ring, arms aloft, blood running across my face, a tableau worthy of a scrapbook like Dad's, horrified casuals and kids in the front row wondering what they were seeing. Backstage, I sneered for some photographs and wiped my head down with a towel. I was panting, bent double, high on ego when Krupp came in and told me wanted to put the belt on me and it would be against Bruce Logan.

I could have said no. But the idea of me going over against Bruce Logan, becoming a legend killer, was too good to pass up.

At any rate, I had been smashing through jobbers for Krupp on a monthly basis, alternating my technical knockout due to the running knee with Mark 'The Hurricane' Brody's spinning heel kick which was laying guys out cold.

It was insane to think I had even been considering retirement, but if I won the belt, it would be a great achievement and, as I said, I could leave at the top of my game.

'So what do you think? That cool?' Krupp asked. It was funny, in his oversized Slam Nation T-shirt and sober, he seemed polite and respectable, not at all like he was when he was drunk, or the stories I had heard about him.

'I can't wait,' I said.

*

A few weeks later, I got a coach up to Leeds in the spring morning sunshine of Victoria Station, and by the afternoon I was sitting at a table outside a café which was inside the glass dome of a shopping centre.

'Can't see a word of that,' Mum said and passed me the menu. 'Can you tell me what's on?'

I read the names of the dishes.

When the waiter came over, I ordered a Goan curry and fish and chips. I don't think we'd eaten together before, definitely not alone. Maybe a McDonald's, something in and out, and in the flat there were other distractions and other people usually.

Mum could talk like no tomorrow, but with me, there was always a hesitancy, perhaps from me too. How much to give, how much to tell one another about yourself.

But maybe this is what she wanted now?

I looked at my phone.

It was early in the day and when I looked around the restaurant wasn't very busy. This place had once been an open-air street with a church at the end. When I was a kid, Mum used to bring me shopping here: we'd look at film posters in Athena before trawling through C&A and walking past the showrooms in Habitat. There was a swoop of glass roof above us, the cross section of balconies on levels, all open, escalators intersecting at points and the small figures on lower levels moving this way and that.

All glass and metal, like everywhere was glass and metal, but I still had a kind of pride to have a place like this in Leeds.

I could buy myself some sneakers, slim fit jeans, zip-top hoodie, put a filter on my camera and load up an avatar online, find out who was the heel for the day and pile on or make babyface statements myself for likes, then I would be winning in the kayfabe of being myself.

'You've not got much to say,' Mum said.

'Was just thinking.'

'Oh.'

I smiled. 'What've you been doing then?'

'Not much. I see a therapist every week. It's not been that long since I could go anywhere by myself.'

'You're doing well.'

There was a silence.

The waiter brought over our meals. I thanked him like a middle-class dude, ate a spoonful of curry, looked up and saw Mum's butch face staring back at me. It was like mine, but softer and rounder, more chins.

'Any news?'

I paused. I knew what she was angling at but how could she possibly know?

'I've got a girlfriend called Grace,' I said.

'So have I,' she said and we laughed.

She splattered vinegar across her chips.

'Mine's nothing serious but I've seen yours. She's very pretty, very clever and a teacher in Kent.'

'How do you know?'

'I saw her on Facebook and googled her. You've done well there.'

We laughed.

The food was decent enough. I lifted a spoonful to my mouth and felt a pleasant burn across my tongue.

I had always worried about Mum's exacting standards. But she had always been good with the few girlfriends of mine she had met and tended to be on her best behaviour. This normally meant siding with them and correcting whatever I said or did to better suit them. Mainly it involved taking the piss out of me, but that was fine and how we were. So, it was good to get her approval, but I was still unsure as to what she would make of Eliot and had a fear that she would think I was being taken advantage of.

'Curry is good,' I said.

'Fish and chips are fine. Just no scraps. I don't know.'

'You and your scraps.'

'Anything else to tell me?'

'No.' I shook my head.

She gave me a hard look with her eye.

'What about Eliot?'

I stopped chewing. 'Grace has a son.'

'I know.'

'You should have said.'

There was no malice or anything, she was pleased, I was relieved, it wasn't something to hide.

'So I'm a grandma?'

'Well, yeah.'

'You'll have to bring them both up as soon as you can.'

I smiled.

'Well, there may be four of us.'

Her eyes lit up.

I had never seen her so happy. She was already talking about baby clothes, when she could come down and help out. What names did we have? Did we want a boy or a girl?

She was so proud. It was good, everything was good. She would be Nana Shirley and I would be a daddy.

She said she had 'suffered from problems' and I said I know, we all have, and that I hadn't forgotten all the good she had done either.

It was nobody's fault.

We walked around town for a bit, looking through some clothes shops and ready meals from Marks & Spencer's. She didn't drink, smoke or do drugs; she ate high-end food, bought hand-made furniture and played Candy Crush. Already, there were plans for Christmas and she wanted to know what kinds of things Eliot was into. She saw me down to the coach station and waved me off as we pulled out of Leeds. Then onto the motorway, plugged into an insider wrestling podcast and trying not to smell the other passengers, who were grubby, the sort of people who travelled to London for a fiver. The sky turned into mauve, twilight purples and clouds that eventually deepened into a darker night, where I fell asleep, nodding awake every time the bus stopped, dreaming of a baby that kept slipping from my arms, and the terrible feeling of loss as it fell.

A few weeks later I finished my MA and submitted the beginning of a novel about pro wrestling which was based on life. It was some kind of corollary of Strong Style, as close to life as possible.

The story would be structured like a wrestling match in a way: it would start hot with some action and then shine up the babyface, get him over as a sympathetic character before a couple of heats, and then take things home with a big comeback. Except the book would come in two parts, the first part where the protagonist is more of a babyface before the second half, engrossed in the world of wrestling, threatens to turn him heel.

Like Strong Style, it would have the appearance of reality. It would get as close to the real as it could, but ultimately, like any narrative art form, it would be a work of kayfabe with the only reality being behind the appearance of reality, and if the audience pretended to believe in the fake events and characters as real, they would feel genuine emotion.

*

The next weekend was a battleground show run by Renegade in Camden and it was a few months away from the Clark 'The Hurricane' Brody match. I hadn't been on a battleground show for months but still turned up to watch from the gantry until Renegade management said we needed to be on the guest list to come. Jack Tanner was one-half of the tag champions and invited me as his plus one. We spent most of the show in the rafters, drinking from cans of lager from a carrier bag we smuggled in through the back. Apparently, I had heat with Kurt Skoll for showing a kid how to do his finger-snap gimmick. In training, he begged me to show them and I eventually gave in. Then it turned out he immediately messaged Skoll, who reacted as if I had given up a trade secret; I had been hiding from him for months.

I watched the end of the show through a small rectangular window from the upper stalls, hidden away at the back of the venue, which was an overflow bar. It was full of oxblood seating booths and when Jack had finished trying it on with some girls he went back on the offensive.

'I don't know how you're going to get over this,' he said. 'I mean, Skoll was not happy.'

'How pissed off is he?'

Jack mouthed an explosion.

'I've never seen anybody get so much heat with him.'

'Does he know I'm here?'

He shrugged.

'Whatever happens,' Jack went on, putting his arm around me strong enough for me to smell under his armpits. 'I've got your back.'

Then he started laughing.

'Are you ribbing me?'

'Nope.'

He passed me a can. I tapped three times and eased off the ring pull with a gasp.

I was alright about ten cans in, missed lunch and was totally pissed.

When the show finished, I went with Jack, Luis Rodriguez, Romeo McClure, Paddy, and The Dude and some others for a Chinese buffet. I didn't even realise it was vegan until The Dude pointed it out to me, and I examined the chewy meat on my fork, tasted it, and saw that it was fungus. Deep-fried, covered in sweet and sour, black bean or whatever sauce, it was indistinguishable from the real thing.

I wolfed it down. When we were done Jack said The World's End was out because the punters had sussed out that's where the workers drank, which then meant The Black Heart was where the workers were going after shows until the punters caught up.

Now the bar of choice was one full of distressed Americana and served cocktails in teapots.

The bar was still empty by the time we got there. Pink neon everywhere. Soon the workers and their entourages would pour in. I went to the bar with JT and ordered a shot and a cocktail sharer for myself.

We clinked glasses.

'This is to Earl Black Jr,' he said, and we nailed the Sambuca before walking over to the back row of tables the wrestlers had taken up.

Even though it was quiet, Jack was drunk and getting passionate about his feud with Skins.

My cocktail pot was a bone china floral teapot. I had to hold the lid closed as I moved and there was a picture of the Queen on my cup.

'The guy's a strawb,' he said to everybody as they crowded over the table. 'Doesn't know a thing about the business.'

The Dude was sitting opposite us and squirmed before trying to disagree. I sipped my cocktail and my stomach churned. I had this sometimes: ulcers in my stomach gnawed away at the centre and got better once I got going.

'I don't know, dude. His work seems pretty sweet to me.'

Jack wasn't going to give up easily.

'Did you see his match? How many things are you going to hit him with, and what does he win with?'

'A roll-up,' I said.

Jack poked me in the ribs to affirm its accuracy.

'Yes. A. Roll. Up.'

We all laughed.

'The job's fucked,' Jack went on, 'these boys are just as bad as the punters.'

The backstory to this was Jack had wrestled Gearhead and they had blown a spot. Skins blamed Jack for being out of shape; Jack blamed Gearhead for planning too much. A few days later, Skins arrived at Jack's training session and took over to make a point about in-ring storytelling. I never said anything to Jack, but Gearhead did know his stuff. I learned more about how wrestling was a mime in that short session than I had the whole year before.

The Dude sucked on a straw and then looked up.

'Hey Senor Black Jr,' he said. 'I heard your match with Paddy 'The Baddy' got pretty gnarly?'

I held the teapot lid down as the brown liquor filled a dainty teacup then raised it to my mouth with my little finger sticking out.

My stomach burned.

'We went a bit too Strong Style,' I said. 'I just caught him with my knee and he was near enough out. The match was fight-y, but in a good way.'

'But you're gonna be a champion right?'

'Yeah.'

'Ah, nice man!'

'Got a lot of heat for it.'

'Ooh that's brutal.'

'Some people take this business far too seriously.'

The Dude laughed and fist-bumped me.

I turned to my left and Luis Rodriguez was ribbing Jack about being out of shape. I poured another cup of Long Island.

'I'm not being funny,' he said. 'But I could see you blowing in your last match against Tommy End.'

The blood rushed to my head. How dare he?

Who was Luis Rodriguez to mug off Jack?

I leaned in between them. Then stared a hole through Alonso. He stopped speaking.

'The fuck do you think you're talking to?' I growled.

He raised his hands in protest.

'Hey man, I'm just playing around.'

'This man has achieved more in this business than you, you cunt. You got that?'

His face went white.

Jack put his arm around me and changed the conversation to Grace. She had wanted to start training, wrestled a few beginner sessions with him and he looked out for her. But of course, she had to give it up when she knew she was pregnant and was sad never to realise her Cyndi Lauper gimmick. This didn't mean that the baby hadn't already taken a bump or two in the ring before we found out.

There was an explosion of cheering and table slapping as the pros from the show walked in. Suddenly the bar was heaving with some of the best wrestlers in the world, wives, girlfriends and hangers-on. The show crew and special guests were cramming in too. I pulled my jacket from my chair and gave it up for the workers on the card.

I drank and drank and drank. Where it once opened up the world, all the fear and anxiety about being who I wanted to be, saying the things I wanted to say, dissipated and there were only the fantastic possibilities that booze offered, like being able to say whatever I wanted without over-thinking it, or just feeling things or thinking things without fear of upsetting people.

Then when I drank, everything was different and all the worry disappeared down the hole and for a while it was all joy and fun, but these days I bypass that. My body isn't stimulated by the alcohol in the same way and any hint of a fuzzy elation is swallowed up into the hole until I carry on drinking and even all the darkness and all the light and everything is sucked into it, who you are, where you are, when you are, all destroyed and there's nothing left but matter falling into the singularity of a collapsed star.

When Marilyn Draven walked in, he went straight for the bar and then held court with his coterie of burlesque dancers and a silver-haired make-up artist who followed him around. He had dropped the Renegade championship in the main event to a spot monkey who wrestled in the new international style, and his mascara had run around his eyes, which looked the same as his porn star girlfriend's. I had never seen anybody so sad and, even though I had gotten over with Marilyn, especially when we'd had a few, Jack said to stay away as he wouldn't be in the mood tonight.

This was how real wrestlers would respond to dropping a title, but I couldn't wait for mine to be taken from me.

Yes, every so often the thrill and testosterone would flow through me, the adrenaline of the performance and the camaraderie of being one of the boys had sustained me, revived me even, but I knew it wasn't for me.

Last week only confirmed it. The feeling was just the same as when I had found out Mum was sectioned. Then she got cancer. I got a book deal, a job in publishing, for the first time in my life I had money and a nice flat in a metro liberal area but I didn't know who I was. When I was reeling, crushed by my attempts at being a contrarian intellectual and lacking the inner core for it, when pushed, there was nothing.

I was a liar, a bullshitter, a charlatan.

I pulled up a metal stool and sat by the wall with Jack who was putting the moves on some girl wrestler, along with some trainees, and the room was circling around me.

'Hey buddy, do you need to go home?'

'No,' I said.

My phone started ringing. It was Grace. I slid the screen open and turned the call off.

'Hey, that's your missus. You want me to call her back?'

I shook my head.

I poured another teacup full of liquor.

When I was done, I staggered to my feet and followed some others outside where there was a drunken commotion.

A guy was rowing with his girlfriend.

He had her by the arm, screaming at her. She tried to get away, he yanked her hard and shouted in her face. She was crying.

People had stopped on both sides of the street but nobody was doing anything.

I stormed across the road, shoved him hard enough with both hands on his chest to send him flying several yards behind on his arse.

'Come on, you cunt!' I yelled.

He sat up, utterly bewildered, nothing but fear in his eyes.

I ran at him, smacked him across the face with a fist and blood trickled down his shirt.

I sat on his torso, raining fists across his stupid face until it disfigured, and chunks of flesh blistered around his eyes.

My hands were throbbing. Somebody called me a *psycho* as they tended to the guy on the street and The Dude pulled me away. I rubbed my knuckles, pounding with violence, and had to hold them to stop them shaking. I was only annoyed that I didn't get more of a chance to hurt him. I knew I had it in me to kill somebody if I wanted.

I went back into the bar but the bouncer wouldn't let me in, so I stood on the street in my Earl Black Jr T-shirt, broad-shouldered, arms pumped and waiting for the others.

Jack and some others came out to see what was going on.

'Hey dude, you okay?' The Dude asked.

I nodded, explained what had happened and how that dickhead had it coming. I looked through the glass to the bar and saw Marilyn Draven's figure staring back, slowly darkening through the glass.

I sat down with The Dude for a minute by the kerbside. Things had got too far. All this anger just made me hate myself.

*

I knew it was time to go and saw a bar on the way to the Tube, thought about one for the road but knew I would spend all night in there and something else had started going on in my guts: I felt drained, like I was hungover already, the poison had taken hold.

I walked down the street uneasy on my feet, and all the light dissipated into monochrome. I slumped onto the Tube, headed for St. Pancras. When I got there, I ordered a truffle burger in a paper bag, boarded the carriage and collapsed into a seat. I inhaled the burger, then started on the chips and fell asleep before the train set off.

I woke up along the way, the light and movement felt sudden and startling. As soon as I became aware, I was overtaken by a deep acidic sickness, vomited into the paper bag with enough force to blast through the bottom of it all over my T-shirt.

Then fell asleep.

Whatever time later, I opened my eyes and had a sense that the train was slowing.

Where was I?

I looked up at the board. Oh no.

The conductor's voice came over the tannoy. *We will shortly be arriving in Faversham, where this train terminates. Please remember to collect any belongings you may have and thank you for travelling with Southeastern this evening.*

Oh, shit.

Shit. Shit. Shit.

I looked down at my T-shirt. The vomit was bright orange, it flowed all down my top like a blast of fire. I rubbed it off but the chunks only disintegrated into stringy, neon fibres that reeked of bile and innards.

As the train stopped, I waited for the other guy waiting in the vestibule to exit before walking sideways, hands trying to cover my midriff and running off.

I stood on the platform in the dark. Everywhere seemed to be the night, enveloping everything as far as I could see.

A text rumbled and illuminated my leg.

It was Grace asking where was I?

I didn't reply.

I carried on up the staircase, walked through the open turnstiles and out onto the street.

The phone lit up again and she was calling.

I swiped it off.

She rang again.

'Yeah?' I said in a gruff voice.

'Where *are* you?'

'It doesn't matter where I am.'

'What do you mean it doesn't matter?'

'it doesn't matter.'

'Where are you' Who are you with?'

'I'm in Faversham.'

'Why?' she asked. Her voice wasn't angry, more tired and concerned. 'How are you getting home?'

'Don't worry about it,' I said. 'I will sort it out.'

'What do you mean?'

'This is all my fault.'

'What are you on about? What's your fault?'

There was panic in her voice but there didn't need to be. She wasn't hearing what I was saying.

'Everything. It's all my fault but I will sort it out.'

A taxi pulled up.

The guy wound down his window. I asked him how much it would be to Chatham, he looked me up and down, and said normally it would be forty-five quid, but for me, it would be eighty.

*

By mid-June, I was booked to defend the vacant UK Light Heavyweight Championship for Slam Nation in a match against Clark 'The Hurricane' Brody, a kickboxer who was green as a wrestler but did have a decent hurricane kick. I had bookings all weekend, every week, across the country for months into the future and getting close to the kind of Strong Style I had been looking for. I had been smashing my way through hand-picked jobbers for Krupp at Slam Nation and laying them out with my running knee strike. Brody, on the other hand, had been booked in parallel to me, knocking guys out with his kick on shows I wasn't on, and vice versa. Eventually, both of us undefeated, buzz had grown around the pair of us having a match. Who would win? Wrestler or Kickboxer? Knee strike or hurricane kick? It was presented like a legitimate fight and there was a fake fight fever in the air during the build-up, some hard-eyed stand-offs, but before all that I had to take the belt from the reigning champ, Bruce Logan, who had discovered he had been wrestling with a broken neck and had decided to retire. I had only met Bruce Logan once, and getting myself eliminated by him in a royal rumble match had been an honour to me. This was totally different.

It was Earl Black Jr vs Bruce Logan and I was going over.

So much of wrestling was about choreography and remembering the other guy's stuff. Most of the time it was just guys trying to get their shit in. Nothing made sense. Every so often you got somebody who knew what they were doing, the spots just stuck and everything was easy to remember.

I was under no illusion that Bruce was a better wrestler than me, but all those 'TV action' sequences he liked to do just seemed like filler and meaningless action for the sake of action. But what about *realism*? Why did so few people care about that in pro wrestling? What I wanted was a Strong Style that wouldn't convince anybody wrestling was real, but that made them forget it was fake.

The days before I was due to face Bruce 'The Bone Collector' Logan were long. I could barely sleep. I lay there on sleepless nights, thinking about how the match might go. What if I fucked up? It didn't stop me from inviting everybody I knew. Everybody would be there and whatever happened, I would rise to the challenge. I had to, what else could I do? I woke up with a knot in my stomach on the day of the match. I rolled over and held Grace who smiled, eyes closed.

When she went to work I sat around, sent Dad the picture of me with my fists pressed into my hips at thirteen, all skin and bone and then the one taken a few weeks ago where I looked jacked, eyes menacing, and body ripped.

'Today London, tomorrow the world,' he said.

'In the new one, I'm ready to take Bruce Logan on,' I answered.

Dad said he was on his way. I felt sick again. Got up, looked out of the curtain at the grey day, I watched a crisp packet sidewind down the street in the breeze and sat back down.

Why could I never enjoy it?

One day this would be over, and another day it would all be over. I wouldn't have to worry like this.

I took a deep breath.

When Grace had pulled into the drive a few hours later, I got in the car beside her and high fived Eliot in the backseat.

I lay my head against the backrest staring into nowhere.

'What's wrong with you?' she asked. 'You're still going over, aren't you?'

'Yep.'

'What's the problem?'

'Don't know,' I shrugged. 'Guess I never thought I'd be beating Bruce Logan and winning a championship. I've become the guy I used to stare at in the photos, except it doesn't feel like what you think it might feel like. It just feels normal. Now that I'm here, that kid I was is the one who feels a million light years away, like when you climb a mountain and look down at where you started, only it's so far away it feels like somewhere else entirely.'

She struck a shrewd look and turned the engine on.

'Well, this is what you wanted though, isn't it?'

'I don't know,' I sat my legs on the dashboard, arms folded. 'I thought I'd feel like whatever Dad felt like. Those pictures, all my life, I don't know. I am the man in those pictures now but it doesn't feel like it should.'

'In your dad's stories you mean?'

'Yeah.'

She leaned across the handbrake, touched my stubble and kissed me.

'You worry too much,' she said.

'I know.'

We drove through the streets of terraced houses, Grace talking about what happened with the kids at school that day, out onto the green-shrubbed motorway. Half an hour later we stopped outside the tree-lined semis of Strood waiting for Jack. How could he live here?

Maybe he was ribbing us? I asked Grace who laughed and said he probably was a posh boy.

Wrestlers were just like children. Lots of the veterans, Jack included, had got into the business as a teenager, earned enough to get by in the bar if he lived at home, and knew nothing else of the world. I texted him that we were outside and got out of the car, ready to take the backseat. When he appeared, he was beardy, bear-like, dressed in black suit that he still somehow made look scruffy, cricket bat in hand.

'Jack Tanner,' I said, pulling him in for a hug.

'Earl.'

He shook my hand and passed me the Tommy Gun, which I slid beneath my seat. It had VIN written across the back of it in black tape. The same gun he was waving around when he won the tag-team championship with Big Jake.

I offered him the front seat out of respect, but he declined, got in the back, made an effort to greet Grace and always made a fuss of Eliot. He was kind, gentle, good with kids. When we set off I remembered where we were headed, but the presence of Jack on the backseat was a comfort in itself.

Trevor Morello was a more sober mentor than Jack, who was a bad influence but fun, and had his own things to teach about the dark side of the ring, like how to get booked at the bar or get over with the boys.

He had looked out for me on shows where I was a stranger in the locker room and made sure I didn't get screwed over by Krupp. We were drinking buddies, even sometimes against my wishes when he would pour drinks into my mouth, knowing just the taste was enough to get me going.

'You got Bruce today haven't you?' he asked.
'Yeah.'
'You'll be fine.'
'I am a bit nervous. I was reading about this guy in PowerSlam fifteen years ago. Looked up to him for years.'
'I wrestled him a few months ago.'
'How did it go?'
'Terrible,' he said. 'I botched a spot I'd done a million times. All the best.'
We laughed.
'I'm over too.'
Grace smiled.
Jack stared silently past me then said, 'You're winning the belt?'
He slapped me on the back from the backseat and gripped my neck with both hands.
'No pressure then, eh?'
Like a lot of full-time wrestlers, Jack lived at his mum's house in a state of permanently extended childhood. He refused to drink coffee or read a newspaper because he thought it would make him grow up.
He laughed again.
'What?'
'Your dad is the best,' he said, looking into his phone.
My heart sank.
'Oh no. What's he done now?'
'Nothing bad. Look.'
Jack showed me the image and narrated the gag that he had posted a picture of Earl Black Jr on a video game and captioned it, unironically, with 'you know that you've made it when they make figurines of you'.
It was amazing.
'Big pop,' he said.
'That just killed me.'
'Your dad is so crazy,' Grace said.

Jack laughed and then found a more serious tone.

'I showed Susie the pictures of your old man dressed as a Nazi,' he said.

'And?'

'She showed it to some of her right-on mates and you're getting heat.'

'I thought some of it seemed more legit.'

'Don't worry about it.'

'I'm not. I just don't get it?'

'You know what they're like.'

'I mean, that's mental. Do people come out to have a go at Michael Fassbender for playing a Nazi? Or some of the families of people in Indiana Jones?'

'As long as they don't find out you're a Tory!' Jack shouted, slapping me on the shoulder and falling about with laughter.

'I'm not a Tory,' I said.

'You wait until I tell Bruce Logan,' he laughed, then made the chugging noise he did when he was bantering.

'You're a twat. Do you know that?'

He smiled.

'I love you really, mate. Seriously though,' he said. 'Get your old man's jackboots on and then you'll get some heat, ha.'

When we got there, Grace parked up and we got out. It was a bright and warm June afternoon. I could be anywhere in the world but here. Instead I was choosing to put myself through hell. My stomach lurched, churned, and the anxiety was so intense I was exhausted after matches and beginning to worry about the stress effect of being constantly adrenalised.

I couldn't eat breakfast on a morning without wanting to be sick.

Drinking coffee made me burp.

There was a constant gnawing in the centre of my gut.

But in the run up to this match, I had avoided drink for six weeks, had started feeling somewhat better and was else was I going to do? I could live my life without testing myself and then what would I have to show for myself?

On the other hand, Jack had gone off to get a sandwich and was totally at ease.

I looked around for Grace, who was coming back after paying for a parking ticket. I kissed her goodbye and stood outside the venue alone.

*

There was a picture of Earl Black Jr snarling on the poster by the exit and I stared at it before I went in the side door to Cinderella's, a nightclub in the centre of Rochester and one of the biggest venues in Kent. Some of the crew were smoking outside but I didn't talk to them. Wrestling outside Renegade still felt like a foreign country. Somebody else's kingdom where you were never truly welcome.

I walked down the hallway through the rear entrance, and it was all concrete, smooth corridors like the shots of wrestlers arriving live on WWE RAW I watched twenty years before. Of course, the shots were staged and the wrestlers had been there all day. It just gave a sense of expectation and excitement: who would arrive next?

I held my holdall in one hand and took a deep breath as I pushed through the exit door and walked onto the main dancefloor.

The ceiling was covered in rigging, lights dangling from above, flaps open and hard white light beamed over the canvas. Some of the boys had taken up positions by the ring, talking through their matches in their hoodies and street clothes. The boards banged as another pair ran a spot and slingshotted from one side to the other. I walked through slowly, shaking hands as I went and looking round at the rows and rows of empty plastic chairs, the empty booths and the empty standing space that would soon be full of two thousand people, broadcast online across the world on Wrestle Tube.

I sat on a cabaret table with the nerves starting to get to me. What would Bruce be like? What if I messed up?

I looked up and Jay Langston appeared.

'Hey man,' I said, we shook hands and hugged. 'Who you got today?'

'Sammy.'

'Nice.'

'Who you got?'

'Got the championship match, haven't I.'

He laughed.

'Enjoy it mate,' he said.

'I'm shitting myself.'

Jay had competed for Wrestle World USA in the past few weeks. He still had something robotic about the way he moved, but he was amazing on the mic and obviously looked like a body guy; his in-ring had come on a lot too.

'You've got no need to,' he said.

'Easy for you to say, big man.'

At that point, I heard a mad scuffling of plastic wheels on the concrete and saw Marilyn barrelling towards us in a leather jacket, his sideswept hair flaring around his face and his eyes fixed on me.

He looked totally mental.

'Who's going over in your match?' he snapped

I didn't speak. Jay pointed at me.

'You?' he screamed. 'You must be kidding me?'

I shook my head.

He was kidding, right?

He held his stare. I smiled but was full of rage. Before I could say anything more, he turned on his heel and walked away, muttering to himself.

I looked at Jay. He looked at me.

About twenty minutes later, Krupp called a team meeting and I followed Roy across the room to discuss the finishes for the matches and what he expected from the performers. Bruce

Logan walked in, the same man I'd watched on the tapes and shows all these years, buzzcut, barrel-chested, red-skinned except a bit shabbier, grizzled stubble on his cheeks, denser and even larger than he had been twenty years ago.

Having survived so many wars in the ring and rehabbed himself from a broken neck, he looked grizzled and had a wild look in his eye like he'd been surviving in a wilderness for the past few decades, but he was only in his mid-forties. He had a tough old man body, thick-veined and hairless, a round belly spilling over at the edges and a craggy face with two-day stubble. He was the first wrestler I had seen who looked like a wrestler, precisely because he was a wrestler from TV. In the way that models angular faces can look good on camera but weirdly geometric in person, he was excessively masculine, comically so with his jutting jaw and big potato head, a curl of silver-blonde marooned at the centre of his balding forehead and his eyes sadder and older than they appeared on screen, a hard glint in his vodka-blue stare.

He was the real-life incarnation of the video game character I had played as a child, whereas I was a fanboy of pretending to be the avatars I used to invent on my PlayStation.

He took a seat in the front row and started eating his burger and fries from a brown paper bag, leaning over it, broad-backed, trying not to spill any.

In my head, the way this worked was he would shake my hand and we'd talk things through, get on as we had in the dressing room in Woking and plan a few spots at the end and improvise some British grappling at the start, see how it went, maybe even do the three quarters of the match like that.

There he was.

Bruce Logan eating a burger.

When the crowd dispersed into their pairings, dancing through the steps of their matches, I stood toward the back of the room with Jack while Logan carried on eating.

'Do you think I should say hi?' I said.

'Go on.'

'I'm scared,' I said.

Jack laughed.

'You're working him aren't you?'

'Yeah and he might think I'm being disrespectful if he has to find me. But what if he wants to eat and thinks *that's* disrespectful?'

'You're going way over the top, mate.'

'Oh it's not so different from when you ran away from William Regal, is it?'

'Hey,' he smiled. 'That's different.'

I set off. Two or three small steps at a time, creeping close until I edged into his eyeline

He looked up.

His brows were ridged and forehead slightly protruding. He looked like the manliest man you could imagine, a commando, a fisherman, a lumberjack, somebody's rock-hard dad all rolled into one.

'Hi,' I said. 'I'm Wes. I'll be working with you tonight.'

I extended my hand.

'And?' he said.

I faked a smile. He stared hard at me, the whites of his eyes showing, all his stubble silvery as his expression dropped.

This was a guy who had spent thirty years propping up British wrestling almost single-handedly. He had worked Ric Flair at Wembley. Now he had the dishonour of laying down for me.

I understood that Logan would be pissed off, but it didn't ring true with anything anybody had said about him.

Was it *me*?

Was there something arrogant in the way I had approached him? I racked my brain thinking about things that might have upset him. The other guys I knew who had worked him had all jobbed to him, was *that* it?

'What do you do?' he asked. 'Do you have any ideas?'

I told him I mostly did suplexes, T-Bones, German, butterfly, my thing was realism, Earl Black Jr was a grappler. I didn't do any moves that were created post-1970. Did I do anything off the top rope? No. Did I do any powerbombs or anything like that? No. I said. Just suplexes.

Let me have a think, he went on, computed the few moves and sequences I had given him into a match that made sense, it was a Bruce Logan match, a pro wrestling version of the *monomyth* with lots of take one and feed round, duck the clotheslines, hit the buckle and eat the boot, feed round and take a move, take a move, take a move, all action.

He didn't want to wrestle, or *realism*, he wanted a spotfest, an indie match with an indie wrestler so he could carry on getting booked for the top promotions in London.

I took a seat and now the guy from the poster on Dad's wall all those years ago was not only sitting next to me, but he was also about to *lay down for me*. It was incredible, a revolution, and whilst I was pleased to have this opportunity and looked forward to word getting out, it was something I didn't deserve, just Krupp getting ahead of himself. It felt like a crime against the natural order of things.

He ate the last of his Big Mac, wiped orange sauce from his lip and stared at me hard in the eye.

'You got the match?'

I nodded.

'I think so.'

Like fuck I had it. As if I could remember all of that, as quickly as that.

'There's really not much to it,' he said.

'I know.'

It was only *wrestling*, I thought, and strolled off toward the back with my heart thumping and my arse about to fall out. 'It's not *real*.'

But nothing could have mattered more.

*

Some of the other wrestlers were getting changed backstage, which would ordinarily be a bar on a club night. Jack walked in, eating a banana.

'You get a good spread here,' he said. 'Energy drinks too.'

'I don't know what to do. Bruce's just told me the match and walked off.'

'Go and ask him, he'll be fine.'

'Yeah but I don't want to annoy him, and I literally can't remember anything of what he said. I'd need to go through it about fifty times.'

'Go and find him.'

Jack was right. What else could I do? Better to annoy him now than forget everything when I got in the ring.

Backstage was like a house. There was a technical area immediately behind the curtains, a fire exit which led to an alleyway where wrestlers congregated in the sunshine, while the corridor led to a room with sofas and lined in floorboards which led upstairs to several floors, each with similar rooms, bathrooms and showers.

Some rooms you weren't allowed in. The guys at the top of the card tended to be on the top floor and I was only really welcome on the bottom floor. I was desperate to find Bruce though, and go through the match.

I went outside into the sunny afternoon where Big Barry Bartoli was chatting about the old days with Bruce Logan over a cigarette. It was good to see, two legends I had so much respect for getting on like that. Barry was about six-three, with a shiny bald head, a thin white handlebar moustache and prison tattoos around his ringed fingers, gripping the end of his cigarette.

Maybe Bruce wouldn't think I was such a moron if he saw that I was pals with Barry?

He was stood smoking beside his big yellow van like the carnie he was.

'You alright, Wes?' Barry said. 'Big match tonight.'

'Yeah.'

'You got the match?' Bruce asked.

I walked slowly towards them.

'Sorry Bruce,' I said. 'Do you mind going through it again?'

Fucks sake.

I could see it in his rolling eyes.

'There's not a lot to it, you know?' he smiled.

'I'm sorry. I just don't want to mess it up and it's, you know, it's a big deal for me to work with you.'

He told me the match. 'You got it?' he said.

'Yeah, thanks,' I said. 'Got it.'

The moment I turned back I had forgotten it. I knew there was no chance I could ask him again and writing it out on a bit of paper or my phone would make me look even worse.

This would be it, this was finally it. The match where I shit the bed. All those other times I had somehow managed to wing it, but, no, not now, this was it, the end was coming.

I typed what I could remember into my phone and spent the next two hours pacing around, trying not to shit myself, thinking about the bits of the match I could remember. It wasn't really as bad as I thought, was it? Maybe Bruce was just riding me because he liked me?

Nonsense.

All I had was self-regarding delusions. It was all I ever had.

I got changed and went to sit behind the curtains on a speaker in the dark. The show had started, and the place was rammed. As wrestlers came and went for their matches, I peeped through the curtain at the stage, the top of the stairs I would soon walk out on, and out at the mass of people, the sprawl of round heads and bodies, the searching beams of stage lights and fake smoke that permeated the air.

Krupp walked past fast, out of character for his lumbering way, belly jiggling. He turned back and gave me a wave before carrying on.

Other wrestlers came in and out, some pre-match and dry, smelling of Tiger Balm, talking through what was to come; others who had been out there were wet with sweat, reeking of aerosol and adrenalised, gasping for air. Dad would be there, getting in from his Megabus on time. Lauren was coming. Grace and Eliot and her brother and dad. Everybody was coming to see the champion.

The problem was it wasn't me.

By the time my match came along I was exhausted, and the adrenaline had already rushed from my body, leaving a husk with shaky hands and feet, my whole body feeling bloodless and pale. Being in the main event looked amazing from the outside – it was the match everybody always most looked forward to – but on this side of the curtain most of the other wrestlers had been and gone, the crew were all out watching the show and the locker room was deserted. I cut a lone figure, just my heart in my mouth and the inadequacy of my soul and somewhere Bruce Logan lingering in the building. Fuck knows where he was or what he was doing.

Was this what making it looked like?

I didn't know.

I was wearing my black tights and *Black & Son: Wrestlers since 1966* tank top, with a large knee support on my left leg. I got up and paced about. It was the first time I had worn the tank top and was really proud of it. It had my silhouette, in Dad's V-shape pose against a white backdrop, 'Black & Son: Pro Wrestlers since 1966' in a Jack Daniel's typeface.

I paced back and forth.

I knew I had it in me. I could do this.

The crowd popped for a spot. Then another, bigger this time and again. One. Two. Three. The bell rang.

It was time.

My music hit. 'Trickfuck' by Blacklisters. I waited for raging guitar and then stepped through the darkness. I looked around with a mad stare, prowling like a maniac toward the stage and then raising my arms in a default way.

All eyes turned my way and the spotlights lingered warmly on me. People seemed to be everywhere, spilling out of the rafters, up on their feet and chanting.

I took the long route around the whole of the ring before sliding in, making eye contact with one or two to create a ripple effect of staring into them. By showtime, the nerves had gone and I was on autopilot, in pure performance mode. Everything I did was hyper-conscious of nothing but the story I was telling, striding about as Earl Black Jr.

I climbed to the second rope, raised my arms aloft and stared out into the crowd.

The crowd responded with boos. It was funny: the bigger the crowd, the less nervous I got. I owned them. The more noise, the more response, the better. Amid the blur of faces I vaguely knew where Dad, Grace and the others were sitting, and I couldn't help but break into a quick smile when I saw them booing me. But then I heard a small group in the front rows weren't playing the game, the ones who had uncovered Dad's old photos as 'Mr X' dressed in a bodysuit adorned with swastikas were calling me Nazi scum, righteous with indignation.

My music faded and a few chants of 'default wrestler' rang out. I paced up and down the slanting canvas, rocking on its suspension, soft underfoot. There was a pause, an agony that went on forever as the crowd anticipated the arrival of Bruce Logan, the reigning champion of Slam Nation, and cries of 'let's go, Logan' rang out across the crowd until it was a demand. The tension was palpable: 'let's go, Logan' they chanted, and I held my hands over my ears, like Dad did, only making them louder.

When his music hit, a hard rock riff I had heard for twenty years, and his likeness appeared on stage, a feeling of pride came over me and I gazed back at him ready for war.

As Bruce made his way to the ring, he slapped palms with the fans, exchanged a knowing look with Dad, who was sitting on the front row, stiff leg outstretched, watching with the strained, slightly dim look he had, and continued around each of the four sides of the ring.

I slid outside as he entered, giving him the adulation and roaming around outside to give the crowd something else to moan about.

At the bell, I slid back inside, and as we circled, my eyes on him, his eyes on me, I took a determined step forward. It was go time. We locked up, hard, in a collar-and-elbow tie-up like gladiators; even though we were working, there was a degree of one-upmanship. He was larger than me, bigger and heavier, but not stronger, I felt, as we waltzed around the ring. Neck and biceps bulging. Somehow, he narrated the match to me. It was going alright, I thought, as we ran through the early spots and I remembered enough to follow his lead.

I whipped him into the corner, ran in, ate a boot fed round into the middle and he launched himself at me with a diving uppercut from the second rope. The spot I had seen so many times over his twenty-five-year career blasted through my chest like a memory, as he gestured to the crowd, which he had brought to its feet.

I cut him off with a jumping knee. Worked him over hard. I didn't care who he was, made sure every stormy and forearm was as snug as I could.

Fuck him.

I grounded and pounded, felt him tense below me, as if all this grizzled strength would unravel if I smacked him just a bit harder, all that folklore would just burst out of him and ooze all over the canvas. I smashed his head into the apron hard enough to bust a myth. Pushed him into the ring. Roped my arms around his waist and then slammed him over my shoulder into the mat. His body bounced. He was working with me but there was something corpse-like about his deadweight. All red and tanned, the heavy muscles holding it all together, the snarling cartilage and years of bumps that had taken their toll.

I looked up at the crowd, recognising many of the faces booing me from other shows.

Nerds. Geeks. Kids.

All intensity escaped my pose. I stared right into the eyes of a fan. Created a ripple effect, seeing discomfort etch across his face, which was real, and his jeering spread around the rest of them and remembered to pretend.

Was anybody still with this match?

I wasn't. I was dead inside, all my life leading up to this and there was Logan rolled around, reaching out his outstretched palm to the crowd. Begging for their admiration. It was all so puerile, a pantomime and all the people who get genuine heat with me were making it known. Boos and sneers rang out from the smart marks who didn't think I was up to it, and the ones who thought I was a Nazi and the wrestlers in the crowd and behind the curtains who wanted my place on the card.

I knew every suplex was hurting him but he wouldn't have it any other way. I was going to be the champion and I would take what was mine.

I clocked him hard with a forearm.

Snatched a waistlock, popped my hips and chucked him over my head.

He somersaulted, landing with a dead thud. The years of bumps had calcified his body. There was no bend or give in it. Just a slab of dad-bulk, dead meat tied together by old cartilage, memory and connective tissue.

The ring creaked and sighed.

He bounced up off the mat. Even his bumps looked knackered.

I teased the crowd. Here, in this moment of darkest night, the hero began to come back to life. His hand began waving. Inside I sighed, disappointed by how fake this was. But he had wrestled around the world, the crowd began to chant and he let loose a flurry of uppercuts and an exploder. I bumped and fed. Bumped and fed. Not knowing where to go next, Bruce pulled me around the ring.

He sent me into the corner, ran at me with his knee, brought me out to an exploder and, as I lay on the floor, signalled for his Rolling Tiger.

The crowd cheered.

When he grabbed my waist, I flicked my heel back, giving him a low blow and in the meld of our bodies sweat and warmth, slipped out of his waistlock into my own. Bearhugging him from behind, I popped my hips, sent him crashing into the mat again and signalled for Old School Violence.

I looked out at the fans. Drew my thumb across my throat and growled. I sensed the diffidence, a silence in the atmosphere as I ran up and drove my knee into his side. A gasp came from the floor.

I wasn't winning was I, surely not?

My thigh collided with his side and I slapped the firm of his back. His body buckled.

I lay on top of him and hooked his leg. One. Two. Three.

The bell rang. Nobody moved in the crowd. The silence was eerie as the announcer shouted my name and declared the winner of the match and new UK Light Heavyweight Champion.

I held the belt above me and screamed. With the belt still aloft, I walked over to the side of the ring where Dad was and pointed at him, mouthing, 'this is for you'. His expression didn't change. I'm not even sure he could see me.

'You're not as good as your Dad,' somebody shouted. 'You're an embarrassment!'

I didn't know if this was heat or legitimate but I didn't care. I smiled and blew them a kiss.

Where was Bruce?

After the loss, he was supposed to hit his finisher on me but he was still selling in the ring. I went over, clubbed him in the back and told the referee to tell him to attack me.

He didn't. The referee said he didn't want it and when I got to the back, some of the boys hailed me with high fives but as soon as I passed the curtain I knew things were bad. The match was awful. Nobody would look me in the eye. Something was wrong.

I scanned around for a seat, none of the veterans would give their seat up for me so I sat on the floor and placed the belt beside me.

Marilyn came up to me.

'The fuck was that?' he screamed.

'I don't know.'

A crowd of veterans formed around me. My neck was burning. I knew I was in over my head.

'You take the belt from a guy like that, fucking injure him and then you don't know?'

'Strong Style is the wrong style,' one of them said, and they laughed, I had suplexed him too near the rope another said, and another tore into me before they all laughed at another wisecrack, and I tried to move away.

'I'm sorry,' I said.

'No good being fucking sorry,' Marilyn said.

At that moment, the curtain billowed, and Bruce Logan limped through, covered in sweat and looking ruined.

'You're dangerous,' Marilyn said.

I nodded.

Bruce walked over.

'Leave him alone,' he said, reaching for his sides; his ribs were tender. Sweat dripped from him, making a gloss around his forehead. 'I could feel the anxiety on you. You've got a lot to learn.'

Marilyn stared at me like he was evil. So crazed with anger, he was like something out of a horror film. His eyes black with mascara and face stubbled beyond shadow.

'I don't even know what to say to you. You're a cunt!' They all laughed again.

There was no insult they could throw at me that I wasn't already thinking about myself.

Everybody laughed, by now not about anything to do with the match, more at how pathetic I must have looked.

I sat around on the cold step, surrounded by everybody but nobody near me. It was incredible how much guilt and shame I felt. I had expected some heat for going over but anticipated more elation and that the sensation of upsetting the boys would have been nothing compared to the feeling of being a champion.

My stomach churned.

All the drinking I did wasn't helped by all the worry I had before matches, and my stomach acid was up and burned most mornings, or, like now, when I got into a state about something.

Anxiety knotted inside me.

I didn't even want to think about what Grace and her family would have made of it; nor Dad, for that matter, and whatever performance I put in he would say he was proud, though I knew when I had let him down.

The remainder of the show was playing on the screens above the empty bar. Wrestlers in states of various undress, some between costumes as their gimmicks and their selves, chuckled at what they saw, winced at the big bumps and the veterans scratched their heads at anything dangerous or didn't make sense. Billy Storm was cracking jokes, his lycra vest pulled down over his overhanging belly, his head shaved and mask hanging from his hand.

I held the championship belt in my hands, saw my reflection blurred in the curved gold and felt every pound of its weight. Instead of getting changed, I just put my glasses and T-shirt on, looking half like me and half like Earl.

This should have been just the start of my career, I couldn't think of anybody who had retired *after* winning a championship. It was such a difficult thing to achieve and few people could without the proper dedication. It wasn't something an amateur could fake, but that's what I had done. Tonight it was the real me that everybody had seen.

When the show was nearly finished, I left through the side door. It was still light in the car park, which surprised me, but it wasn't even late of course. I held my hand above my head like a visor against the sunlight and bumped into some fans who wanted a selfie.

'Great match,' one of them said. I smiled. He must have been an idiot to think that stinking pile of horseshit was a good match. It really was terrible.

Another wanted me to sign his T-shirt, and I did, in the scrawl of Earl Black Jr, which was similar to but not the same as my own. I grabbed a headlock on the kid, grinned evilly and flexed my arm for a pic. Around us was just another day in Rochester: the cars rode past down the main road; people came to and fro from the bars and cafes; none of them knew of the mad carnival that was going on a few hundred feet away from them and the colossal shame which was about to explode inside me and shatter who I was. I kept trying to reassure myself: I had come a long way since that night I was knocked on my arse, barely able to feel anything and totally depressed; I was being oversensitive; it would feel better in the morning. There was still the match with The Hurricane to come to prove myself.

All this, I knew, was bullshit.

As the kids raced back to their mums, I looked up and saw Grace smiling and Eliot trailing beside her. His little face was stuffed with pride; it had puffed out his cheeks and he could only stare nervously at the object around my shoulder.

I was an inch taller in my boots and Grace leaned on her tiptoes to kiss me.

'Are you pleased?' she asked.

I pulled the belt from my shoulder and passed it to Eliot.

'No,' I said.

With that, all the joy and excitement fell from her expression, and I realised my mistake.

'Everybody loved it,' she said. 'My dad thought it was hilarious and we thought you really hurt him at the end.'

'I did.'

Oh dear, she said with a grin, an expectant look on her face. Eliot stared at the belt.

'You champion, Wes!' Eliot shouted.

I nodded, watching him hold the belt in his hands as if it was magical, the gold reflected back under his chin and cheeks.

I looked over at Grace, 'You seen my dad?'

She pointed with smiling eyes to him wearing his camo vest and cargo shorts, his bad leg bright purple, speaking to some fans with beards and wrestling hoodies who looked like hard rockers.

He was in his element, eyes alive, throwing his arms back and forth to tell the stories he had told me and everybody else, over the years, The Ancient Mariner telling his tale that may be based in fact but was so exaggerated and fantastical in his eyes it belonged more in the realm of folklore than anecdote. I didn't step forward, I left him there to enjoy being remembered again, the crowd growing larger as they listened. It was as if Dad was compelled to teach the word of wrestling by his own example, adding more layers to the legend, and everybody was pleased to hear it, just like I was as a child, to be a part of it.

When he spotted me, a smile blossomed across his face and he hobbled over like a one-legged dog.

'Today London, tomorrow the world!' he said.

He was wearing a black polo shirt with a green combat vest over the top of it, a *sao vàng* of Vietnamese and Union Jack on the chest pockets.

'I see you still have some fans.'

'It's amazing. I wrestled fifty years ago and they still know all the names, these guys know who I am.'

'Did you like the match?'

He laughed.

'You're bloody stiff!' He winced as if I was about to hit him. 'I stopped wrestling with you when you were fourteen because you were hurting me.'

He saw Eliot with the belt, smiled so hard his cheeks bulged, and patted him on the head.

'So young man,' he said. 'Are you going to grow up to be a champion like your dad?'

Eliot's eyes were full of amazement. As I slung the belt over his shoulder, he nodded and grinned.

*

In the car after the show, the conversation was flat, with Dad asking Grace about what she taught, and when she said history he launched into a fifteen-minute monologue about the history of Vietnam and how the people were a warrior race. Dad was in the passenger seat, his army attire smelling a little fetid. Grace slid the window down an inch or two. I sat in the backseat with Eliot, the championship on my lap, gazing into its dull lustre.

I looked at my phone and a wrestling critic congratulated me by direct message, told me to wear the belt with honour; the news of a title change was going round social media.

The streets and cars coming past us all blurred into the twilight. My head was thick from the match and Grace played Bruce Springsteen on the stereo to cheer me up, I thought. It annoyed me that she had to put up with my artistic vicissitudes, good match, bad match, all the soul-searching and discontent. I had never known somebody like that. She was the same with everybody – the kids she taught, Eliot, me, always putting others first. It heartened me when she sounded off about somebody or had a go at me sometimes to bring her down to the worldly level everybody else seemed to operate on and to give herself something sometimes. I did my best to treat her and do romantic things, but when I had got what I was searching for from pro wrestling, I would repay her for the love she had given me.

Something had snapped after the match. It was like a fracture, a bone that had broken.

Bruce Logan was as legitimate as they come and a black belt in *jiu jitsu*. As 'Devil's Arcade' played, I thought about one of

Jorge Luis Borges' short stories I had read a few weeks ago. It was called 'On Exactitude in Science' and only one paragraph long. In it, the art of cartography had attained such perfection that a map of a single province occupied the entirety of a city, the map of an Empire occupied the entirety of a province and the map was therefore useless, tatters of it were left in the deserts for years to come. A map the same size as the expanse it depicts is no use to anybody, in the same way as a pro wrestling match that is real is not a pro wrestling match

When we got back, Dad sat at the kitchen table with Eliot.

'You ever learn how to tie knots?' he growled.

Eliot shook his head.

'He might find this tricky, Dad,' I said. 'He's dyspraxic.'

Dad had a loop of rope in his hand, that he had brought with him.

'Right, make a loop like this, and then left over right, right over left and around. The Rabbit comes out of its hole, around two trees and back into its hole.'

'I'm not sure I could even do this.'

I remembered this from own childhood and I couldn't do it then. Dad had his arthritic hands outstretched, still plate-large but rusty looking, barely any poseable possibility in his fingers, just shakes.

Eliot took the rope and made a fair attempt at feeding the rabbit through the hole but lacked the co-ordination himself to move his hands where he willed them.

'Let's start again,' Dad said.

He was as calm as ever. Exactly the way I remembered him, soft and growling, with an infinite capacity for patience.

'This is how you tie knots like a sailor,' I said to Eliot and he smiled, about ready to give up.

Dad's eyes were bright and green, the moment had a warmth and contentment to it that was a salve to how I was feeling about the match and the burden of wearing the belt.

'Do you have any bags you want me to bring in or clothes you want us to wash?' I asked Dad.

His furry eyebrows raised in astonishment.

'No, I travel light.'

'Well, what have you brought? What's in the bag?'

Eliot pushed his seat under the kitchen table, sensing danger, and went into the living room to find his mum.

'Not a lot,' he answered.

I picked up the bag from under the table and rifled through it. He wasn't wrong. It contained a razor, some medicine, a packet of polos, some cigarettes and a loaf of bread.

'What the fuck?' I said.

'Like I said, I travel light.'

'There's travelling light and then just not bringing anything.'

'I spend months at a time in Vietnam with just a couple of pairs of shorts and a vest.'

'Yes, and no wonder they smell.'

'They don't.'

'So you're going to spend the weekend in the same clothes?'

'I have a fresh pair of pants.'

'Great.'

'You're always sneering at me, always telling me what to do, you're just like your mother.'

That night, Dad insisted on playing a detective show called *Inspector Montalbano* on full volume between loud staggers to the balcony to smoke. Climbing up the stairs to the living room had jarred his knee and he shouted ooh and ah as he moved about.

I came downstairs and set up BBC iPlayer on the desktop in his room on the ground floor and reminded him that we were trying to sleep.

'Sorry,' he said.

'No problem,' I answered, explaining I hadn't been away with him for years and had forgotten how difficult it was for him to move around.

By the morning, the house smelled of smoke and I went downstairs to see him in his room, which was usually my office. As I approached the door, I heard a buzzing sound and went in to find him shaving his head all over the bed.

'Dad,' I said, 'Just do that on the floor and I can sweep it up.'

He looked puzzled.

I was starting to get that feeling of somebody else's projection of you. I was joyless and fussy and unmanly in his eyes, but it was my house and all he needed to do was act with some consideration.

'It's electric, there are no bits going anywhere,' he said, carrying on, silver glints of grey hair and dry scalp shaved all over the bedsheets.

'Why can't you just do it on the floor? I'd appreciate that.'

'I'll clean up any mess.'

'Why not just don't make any mess?'

'There is no bloody mess!'

I left him to it. During the day, we had planned to go see the ships in the Dockyard and look around the maritime museum. I told Grace to loosen up around him, but they both seemed wary of one another. She didn't know how to react to his stories or feel comfortable telling him to shut up or take the piss out of him, which he loved. While Dad wasn't sure what to say to her and kept launching into historical monologues about the Stuarts, Vietnam or World Wars.

Despite showing him how to do knots like a sailor, Eliot and Dad seemed similarly cagey about one another. 'My dad used to wrestle with The Rock's granddad, you know?' I said to Eliot, who was momentarily impressed before Dad just mumbled in agreement and the conversation ran dry. I had been looking forward to this, he'd only really met Grace and Eliot in snatches, I thought him being in a more relaxed environment would let them see how funny and charming he could be, but the reality was much more awkward.

The next afternoon, after mainly staying downstairs and smoking, Dad went for a nap and when I heard water splashing a little while later, I went downstairs to see what was going on. He was running water from the tap into a bucket and throwing water all over the bathroom and floor.

I ran toward him.

'Stop, stop!' I shouted. 'You don't clean up like this!'

He carried on filling his bucket and throwing water everywhere.

'Dad, for fuck's sake! Stop!'

He was like a zombie, an undead look in his eye and carried on filling the bucket before I pulled it from his hands.

'You're going to flood the floor,' I said.

'You said you wanted me to tidy up my mess.'

'Not like this!'

I looked around at the bathroom, it was under about an inch of water and the walls were soaked.

He turned and hobbled into his room. 'I'll go if I'm not welcome,' he said.

'You *are* welcome.'

He started packing his thing away: the medicine, the rope, the loaf of bread.

'This bread is lovely,' he said.

'Look, it's not that we don't want you here. But you can't just throw water everywhere. And you want everybody to listen to you and your stories, but when do you listen to anybody else?'

'I get the message. I'm going home.'

His eyes were sad and his lip hung low; there was a shadow over the cheek and chin of one side of his face.

'Why do you have to be such a baby? Why not just compromise? Why not just at least try to show some consideration for how people behave when they're in somebody's house?'

'I'm a cripple. It hurts me to be outside my comfort zone. You've turned into Mr Grumpy.'

My hands were shaking.

'I'm not Mr fucking Grumpy.'

'There you are. You only call me to tell me off.'

'What do you mean?'

'I ring you and just get a tirade. You never say Dad, how are you?'

'Yes, but when do you ask after us? You don't even want to come down to see your granddaughter when she's born.'

'I am an old man.'

'Well, we can come to you.'

'I am fed up arguing.'

'We can come to you.'

'I don't want you to come to me.'

'You could show some fucking gratitude. I'm offering to bring up my family to see you and you just want to sit up there thinking we don't like you. It hasn't always been easy, you know? That shithole flat you lived in, all the mad shit you do, these things have an effect. I used to think you were a god, you were my hero, I wanted to be just like you.'

There was a pause. Soapy water ran slowly down the bathroom tiles. Dad narrowed his eyes and said, 'None of that would have happened if your mum hadn't thrown me out. I lost everything.'

'But it's always about you, isn't it? I couldn't see it all these years, but maybe mum was struggling because of you and whatever depraved shit you got up to.'

I knew I was being aggressive, partly to let out some anger and partly to see how far I could push him and what he would do, but instead of fighting his corner he just turned away like his heart was empty.

'I got mixed up with a bad crowd,' he mumbled.

'C'mon, Dad.'

'Your mum could start a fight in an empty room.'

'That's probably true,' I smiled.

'I've tried to put it all behind me,' he said as he turned back to me, searching for something he couldn't find from one of his many pockets. 'I swore I would never leave my boys.'

I put my hand on his shoulder.

'I know you did,' I said.

'My health, my job, my car, my kids.'

'I get that.'

'I'll be dead soon, so you won't have to worry about me.'

'No, you'll live forever. You've got decades in you.'

The sparkle had gone from his eyes. His bulk just seemed wasted and he dropped down onto the bed, old and tired.

'Half of my heart has stopped working. Arrhythmia is still affecting it. A couple of months ago I couldn't breathe. I went to hospital and they told me.'

'Why didn't you say?'

He shrugged.

Then said in a low growl, 'You don't want to know about my health.'

'That's bullshit.'

'I'm just old and get in the way.'

'Yes, but it doesn't mean we don't love you. How long do you have?'

'I don't know. I don't have all the answers.'

I pulled him close for a bearhug, tears in my eyes, and held him, like a wrestler, for what felt like hours.

*

The next morning I sat down at the kitchen table. The light was a bright summer-yellow and the leaves of the trees high across the road held some of its colour, swaying in the river breeze. Grace was already up, her bump zeppelin-shaped in her Blondie T-shirt, as she moved around trying to clean up for Dad's sake. Eliot was watching wrestling in the living room. Given that we were living in a townhouse, the kitchen was on the first floor, and outside there was a metal staircase to the garden and the yard outside the ground floor where Dad was staying. He had chosen this route as his preferred way to try and climb stairs. You could hear him coming before he arrived, the growls and groans as he hauled himself up.

By the time his emerged at the French doors, in a pair of shorts and a vest with his shoulders rounded and hulking, he had already worked up a sweat, panting, with a cigarette in his hand.

'Fuck me,' he said. 'Those stairs nearly killed me.'

'You need to be careful,' I said.

'If I were a horse, they would have shot me,' he grinned, all the charm still in his eyes but the power faded from his body.

We laughed.

'Cup of coffee, lots of cream please,' he barked. Then he put on a pair of reading glasses. I put mine on and we exchanged glances at one another, with the same shaved-head-and-goggles look.

'We don't have cream.'

He opened his mouth and eyes wide in shock, slapped his face and shook his head.

'What kind of establishment do you call this?'

'I'll make you a coffee,' I said.

Grace walked into the room and started filling a bottle of water at the sink.

'How are you this morning Frank?' she asked, in her unassuming and sensitive way, rounding up some cups for the dishwasher.

'All the better for seeing you,' he smiled.

She looked away, not sure how to take a compliment.

'You don't need to keep tidying up,' I said. 'My dad doesn't care how clean the house is.'

Dad looked inquisitive as the light caught the sparks of grey in his eyebrows. He said, 'When Wesley's mum was pregnant with Cal, he was so big he was right up to her throat. When he was born, he was thirteen pounds and when I came into the hospital after a shift on the doors, he had a bull neck, about this thick,' he said, making a ring with his hands and laughing. The nurse just looked and said we know who yours is!'

'Poor Shirley,' Grace said.

'They were both big babies,' Dad said.

'You'll have to come down when this one's born,' I said.

'I'll see if I'm still alive.'

Grace seemed taken aback by his directness and went about loading the dishwasher. I kissed her, one hand on her belly, and she gave a little smile and a shrug of her shoulders before leaving the room and going for a bath.

'Do you think she likes me?' Dad asked.

'Yeah.'

'She's awfully quiet and I'm not sure she knows how to take me being a geriatric eccentric maniac. When it comes to me, you can love me, or hate me, but I'm not somebody you'll forget.'

We laughed.

'She's just shy and you're a bit much as a character.'

'Having a family suits you. It's good to see you being a dad with a lovely wife to keep you on the straight and narrow.'

I filled the kettle, moved over to the sink to clean some mugs and stared back at Dad.

'So they can't operate?'

'Not at my age.'

'Have you got any medication or anything?'

'Beta blockers and some other things. But they make me very tired.'

A pain was searing through my lower back. It was something I lived with now. Something between cramp and the wingnuts of my spine being pulled apart. I leaned over the counter and tried to stretch myself out like a cat.

'Your back playing up?'

I nodded.

'Now you know what it feels like to be a wrestler.'

The kettle boiled. I made Dad a coffee with plenty of milk and took it over to him and then made my own. I hadn't had a drink since I had been in the hospital and already things were starting to feel better. I was seeing things more clearly, but the other reasons I had always drunk were more apparent now and couldn't be hidden from, you had to take life on without pulling the punches. All my problems, whatever they were, would have to be confronted, no holds barred, there was no choice other than to learn to live in my own skin without pretending to be myself.

'Not just a wrestler,' I said. 'I'm a champion.'

'That's my boy.'

'I have the match coming up against The Hurricane. Any tips?'

'Don't do anything illogical or do anything unlikely. You have solid moves. Make it look like you're always trying to beat one another. Everybody knows the fight is fake but you need to help them believe it could be real. Nobody wants it to look *fake*.'

I thought back to the long summer when I learned to fall. The wrestling fundamentals that were so old school now that nobody knew them: leg picks, inverted spins out of hammer locks into top wrist locks, stepover toehold variants, it was beautiful and nobody used this stuff. It was all vintage. What was old was new.

Dad had learned to wrestle in the mid-1960s and the way he taught things hadn't been hampered by age. There was still a closer link to sporting wrestling styles and wrestlers were often shooters – guys who had a background as legitimate fighters – the 'true life' tough guys who lived rather than played their parts.

The thing I had missed at the time was it wasn't about just learning to fall. Dad had got into a state after he broke up with Mum and left the house, but in the years since he had got himself back on his feet.

I thought about my own fall into drinking.

'Before I started wrestling, I was drinking way too much. I've stopped now.'

'That's good. Drink and drugs are a mugs game. Drink is the only drug designed to destroy every organ in your body.'

'When you had those dark days after you moved out, how did you pick yourself back up?'

'I don't know, I kind of drifted away from it.'

'But that's not easy?'

'It took a long time. I got mixed up with a bad crowd. I had nowhere to live. Slept in my car all winter. Finally got a flat but it was in a bad area. I lost my job, my home, my kids, my health, my car. I couldn't work, got jailed for something I didn't do.'

In his sadness, he seemed more frail and childlike. Lucy the cat appeared and leapt up onto the table in front of him. He stroked her head with a stiff hand, which she butted her head against.

'I thought you ran a butcher over with a car?' I asked.

'I did.'

'So what did you get jailed for that you *didn't* do?'

He looked puzzled for a moment. 'I can't remember.'

He was sitting hunched over the table, his palms smoothing over one another, wearing the thick-framed spectacles he had bought for a pound.

I hadn't spoken like him this before, broken the kayfabe of the shit we had been through and how we had fallen. It had never even really occurred to me how he had got himself straight again after going off the rails.

'How did you pick yourself up?' I asked.

'You've got to know what you want and go for it.'

'But what did you want?'

'To get myself together.'

*

In the coming weeks, I changed my kit from trunks to black tights like Dad, changed my music to 'Here to Stay' by Korn, and was completely straight edge. Already, I was sleeping better, not spending half the week hungover, and able to train harder and recover quicker. There were no fights. No waking up at the end of the trainline covered in vomit. Grace said she was worried sobriety might have made me boring, but it hadn't. In a few months, I would have a baby in my arms and I needed to be ready. One Thursday night I skipped one of my MA seminars to do one with the ex-MMA fighter Randy Lewis instead. I opened up to let him into the Dojo and we chatted about his approach to wrestling. I liked his unpredictability, it kept the jeopardy up; he was cool about it and said he wished promoters would let him do it more often.

Just like MMA, any strikes at any moment could knock out an opponent. There wasn't the sense of having to run through all the stages of a narrative and then endless near falls, which quickly lost their shock value if *every* match had them. Some of the excesses in the choreography owed themselves in part to indie boys wanting to get themselves over and wanting to always have their best match, but it was also the way video games and CGI movies were, explosion after explosion with seemingly unkillable antagonists and a debasing of the effect of violence. The problem was near falls meant nothing if you didn't believe they could end the match.

Lewis took the session, how he put together his strike sequences and some of his in-ring psychology. He didn't like rope running or comedy spots and after the session, he singled me out to speak to me. He said I had good intensity, I told him about how the old boys tried to block me wrestling Strong Style and he said *fuck them*. Easy for him to say with his legitimate fight background and in-ring talent, I thought, though I knew he was right and went home on the train from Brixton pumped with excitement.

I rang Dad the next morning and he said he couldn't come down to the see the match. I told him I understood why and he said to not get drawn into anybody else's match and to call it on the fly.

On Saturdays, after leading training at the Dojo, I came back to Kent to take MMA lessons at a combat academy, given that he was interested and we had a match coming up, I invited Trev along. Upstairs, we rolled on the mats with a black belt in Brazilian *jiu-jitsu* called Mick. In some ways, it was totally different from pro wrestling: it wasn't about building sequences or theatrics in any sense, but the grappling and technical skills were similar in some respects. We learned side control, front mount, rear mount, how to switch between and escape chokeholds in a realistic way.

One afternoon, we tussled, I took Trev down and transitioned slick as anything into a cross armbar.

I squeezed my legs and pulled back. Trev tapped out.

'Well done,' Mick said, clapping, encouraging and professional in a way that we weren't necessarily in the wrestling gym. Pro wrestling, where it was fake, and everybody had to act tough otherwise the fiction of ourselves might fall apart, led to us all acting like tough guys all the time and needing everybody to pay dues, lest it be known that all we were doing was a form of dance.

A trainee had been eyeing us up the whole time, eager to get in and roll with us, but we declined.

After the session, I walked outside with Trev.

'So, Andy put the belt on you?' he said.

'Don't know how I've managed that,' I laughed.

'You're good.'

'Don't feel like it after the Bruce Logan match.'

He smiled.

'At the end of the day, just remember, it's only wrestling.'

'It's only wrestling.'

On the train home, I pulled up an article on my phone. The one about Dad in Slam magazine, 'Earl Black: A Career Cut Short'. A doctor once explained that every fall in a wrestling ring is like 'getting rear-ended by a car travelling at 20 mph.' Frank 'Earl' Black, the Australian who toured the world as a pro wrestler from 1966 to 1973, begs to differ. 'Forget that,' said Black, 'it feels like 60 mph!' Indeed, here is a man qualified to give judgement, for pro wrestling injuries would almost cripple him at only 27 years of age.

There was the picture of him inset in black and white, one of the ones from the scrapbook that he carried with him and had shown everybody for decades after. Of all the things Dad had done, being a wrestler was the role that defined him above all else. He gazed across the distance, hair in a blonde quiff, fists pressed into his hips, back muscles flared like a cobra, the Far East Championship wrapped around his waist. He was twenty-seven when he retired. The same age that I started. Now I was going to defend my title and put an end to this. I was strangely restless, my body already stronger and leaner with the increased testosterone; the thought of performing in a match was unvarnished, in part unrehearsed, raw and spontaneous, alive with the thrill of the real and lifelike character, and narrative drama filled me with excitement every time I rehearsed it in my mind.

Heavy is the head that wears the crown, I thought. I was proud of having won the belt and it was a defining moment in my life and career, but wearing the belt brought new scrutiny and pressure; there was a target on my back. I read the reviews of my matches online and couldn't help but notice the small coterie of diehards who didn't buy into me, didn't think I was good enough – I didn't kick, flip or do complex sequences. I listened to the podcasts and what fans were saying on forums. Some preferred my comedy shtick from earlier in my career, felt that's all I was good for. My every move was analysed as if I was a nothing more than a text, a grammar of signs and symbols to be deconstructed. Then there was the heat from the boys, not all of them, but it was there and palpable every time I walked into a venue, each of them fancying themselves in my position;

even though it was only a secondary belt I held, they were sore that they weren't the ones who had been given the gold. Then there was the pressure of delivering as a champion. A champion needed to perform like one. They needed to be a draw on the card. They needed to have the best matches. All the while, I remembered the fundamentals of what Dad had taught me, the intricacies of chain-wrestling, and knew what I wanted, which was to nail a match in the Strong Style I wanted and then retire. After the humiliation of the Bruce Logan match, I had wrestled good matches every week but even then, something of the shine had gone from pro wrestling. The confidence had been knocked out of me, but there was something more than that, as I realised I had gone as far as I could go as a wrestler artistically. Realism required a lot of artistry. To be any better would mean going full-time, being on the road every week only to make marginal gains and no matter how good I could become, there would still be the limit of my memory and my inability to remember anything.

No, I had nearly found what I had been searching for in pro wrestling.

There was another booking which involved the culmination of a storylined feud between me and Trevor, in which the match would be interrupted by ninja turtles. It was ridiculous, but part of some kind of blend of docu-soap and *Twin Peaks*-style surrealism that one promoter wanted to try. I got top billing. I wasn't too upset by that. In any case, I had negotiated a 'death scene' in which Earl Black Jr would be murdered by the turtles.

It seemed a fitting way for a madness to end.

When I got back into town I stopped off at a tanning salon, went inside, and waited for a booth to come free. When I got inside, I undressed, made cones out of the stickers they gave me that barely fitted my eyes, I got inside the booth and watched the tubes of light beam around me like a nuclear reactor. As the heat warmed the air around me and my skin glowed up, redolent of that fleshy burn you smelled when you walked into one of these places, I thought about my upcoming match with The Hurricane and what needed to happen. There needed to be realism, but that was born of artistry. What was it that enticed me to want to wrestle this way? That made me feel *incomplete* until I achieved it?

Oh, I needed this to become my true self.

It was some kind of latent Romanticism. In 'The Artist and the Beautiful', a short story by Nathaniel Hawthorne, a watchmaker was trapped in a world of 'coarse' utilitarianism.

Everything had to be orderly and precise in their world, like the mechanisms he engineers for people. But what the watchmaker wanted was to be an artist and to spiritualise his machinery and make something beautiful. His contemporaries mocked him and he was considered mad.

Nonetheless, after great personal turmoil and sacrifice, he created a robotic butterfly, magnetised with the filament of life. When his detractors encountered it, they were initially impressed, before decrying how useless his creation was.

The butterfly is crushed at the hands of a child. But the watchmaker is not bothered, for he knows he has risen high enough to achieve the beautiful, and the butterfly was just a symbol of what had been made perceptible to him. He could live with his spirit possessed in the enjoyment of his reality.

As my skin began to burn, and the air whirred around me, I held the lasso grips above me and stood there in the shape of my life in the windswept hum of blazing light.

*

The next Saturday I sat beside Grace in her car as we were about to set off. Today was the title defence against Clark 'The Hurricane' Brody.

I slumped in the seat.

'You ready?' she said.

'Yeah.'

She turned the key in the ignition and stopped.

'Just seems like you're always moaning,' she said. The matches never go the way you want them to go. Even when they go well. When they're bad, you're all over the place. All you do is moan about the politics and not getting to do what you want to do. We spend every weekend driving all over the place and then waiting around. Was just wondering why you did it?'

She looked at me.

'I don't know,' I said. 'I don't want to go back to how I was before wrestling, you know? I've been good lately, but I don't want to fall into another depression and not get out.'

'Do you think you will?'

I shrugged.

'No.'

'It just seems a lot of work and effort for something you're not interested in.'

'It is.'

'You've been really happy the last few weekends you haven't had a show.'

'Yeah.'

'I'll be happy doing whatever you want, but it just doesn't seem like you want to do this anymore.'

'I mean, I only got into this for one match, and I did that. Then I wanted to see how far I could take it, you know? It was like falling down a rabbit hole and not knowing where it ended. I wrestled on big shows. I won a belt. I wrestled up and down the country, had the kind of matches I had wanted, got to do storylines. I did everything I wanted to do.'

'Sounds like your mind is made?'

I nodded.

'It's a shame your dad's not coming,' she said.

'It is. But this one's for me.'

We talked about everything but wrestling on the way over, the way teaching was a performance, the things we needed for the baby, what would happen if we lived our lives by making the opposite decisions like George in *Seinfeld*.

About thirty minutes later, Grace dropped me off at the leisure centre in Swanley. I had spent night after night planning the structure and thinking of strike and submission sequences that were realistic, made sense and Clark would be capable of doing.

I walked through the double doors with my sports bag and title in my hand, unnoticed but conspicuous, and turned past the main counter, a corridor overlooking the swimming pool and up a staircase at the far end towards the sports hall.

In the upstairs changing rooms were windows looking out onto the space which was currently being occupied by a roller hockey match. Two teams of teenagers in full-body gear and padded suits.

I dropped my bag and sat cross-legged on the floor, people stopping as they walked by to shake my hand. This room was used for martial arts - the whole floor of was padded with judo mats - and I leaned against a pillar.

I looked around at the rest of the locker room. Most of the vets, even though they gave me shit sometimes, were on side and I had earned their respect by working with them, putting up with their shit and being deferential. In the end, they dropped the act and I was just one of them. Unless, that is, I was on somebody else's patch and the whole process would begin again.

Some of the trainees were having their first shows. They paced about nervously with pale faces, while the more experienced guys dicked around, were totally at ease and mainly gossiped about the promotion being bought out, what it would mean for our spots and a new brand of low-carb protein bars that tasted just as good as proper chocolate.

I watched it all unfold around me in a breezy way, just touching the mat and feeling the pillar behind me and knowing that this might be one of the last times I shared a locker room as a wrestler and still, as much as I was done with it all, how hard it would be to give up.

I waved at Jack who pulled a funny face and carried on planning his match. He was wrestling against the Wrestle World's Ryan Murphy tonight.

Ryan was maybe the best wrestler in the world right now. He was the reigning Wrestle World UK champion and had made a name for himself as *The Shoreditch Shooter*. He was an exemplar of the modern British Strong Style, had a joint manipulation finger-snapping sequence that got over everywhere, and had come back from being buried by the old boys when he first broke through. He was a vegan, not a twat, and ran a promotion in the midlands. This was the way many of the wrestlers were going now, indie in style, and more laid-back and respectful as people.

The Old Guard was being flushed out and it was a good thing.

I did another round of handshakes to people spilling into the room before finding Brody and making our way down to the sports hall to walk through the match when the hockey had ended.

'You remember everything I've sent so far?' I asked.

He nodded as if he didn't.

'So I was thinking,' I said. 'We start with a kind of worked shoot. Get the story over that I'm a wrestler and dangerous on the ground and want to keep you there. But on a standing level, you're 'The Hurricane' and I can't get near you. We'll keep this part pretty fluid. But don't back off me. Come at me as if you were sparring for real, just kick me in safe places. If you come on too strong, I'll get my guard up and back off.'

We practiced this for a few moments, getting a feel for the rhythm of our offence.

'Then,' I said. 'Hit me with a few hard ones. But there's risk involved, and I take you down like this. Then bam, right away, I swivel from side control looking for an armbar.'

He lay on the ground, and I took side control and showed him what I was looking for.

I heard a voice, high-pitched, whiny and disbelieving which made me shiver.

You're not gonna fucking do that are you?' Marilyn said, laughing.

We shook hands.

'So what are you idiots doing? Think you're better than pro wrestlers?' Do you?' he shouted.

Brody shook his head.

I raised my hands.

'Not at all,' I said.

'So what's all this shoot shit then?'

I got the sense he was joking but with Marilyn you never knew.

'Just something we're trying,' I said.

'Know your crowd, how are you two gonna get over a shoot match here? These people are mutants.'

I shrugged.

'It's what the promoter wants I guess,' I said. 'We've been building up to this.'

'Just work smart,' he said, then smiled, wished us luck and sloped off in his hunched way.

*

We opened with sparring, Brody on a standing level working his kicks and strikes that I couldn't compete with.

Soon as he came near me, I grabbed a clinch and pulled him into the ropes, stealing a knee strike as the referee intervened to break us apart.

The idea was that as a kickboxer Brody would be better on a vertical base, while I would dominate on the ground and look to take him down to the mat.

Brody would get his shine in the form of a kickboxing series of strikes; when he shaped up for his tornado kick I would duck it and snatch a double-leg takedown where I would dominate him in side control and transition into a far-side arm bar that he would fight out of and strike a number of kicks and a leaping double-footed stomp.

Back to our feet, Brody returned to his kicking game, lashing me with kicks that burned lightning across my chest, backing me into a corner where I began to kick back at him and exchanged a few elbow strikes.

Brody sold round and as he fed in a circle back toward me, I ran and hit him with a flying knee across his face and tried for a German suplex, which he blocked, elbowed me in the face to break my grip, hit the ropes, baseball slid between my legs onto his feet and hit a series of kicks and strikes that were easy to sell because they were real.

Quicker than my guard, he hit a high kick followed by a low leg sweep and showed his fist to the crowd to g-up the tornado kick.

Sensing the moment, I sold up and round and as the kick came toward me, ducked, slapped on a sleeper hold and sunk him into the mat.

Just when it looked as though he might drop his hand for the submission, the fist was shaking back to life and he fought me upright and going for a Pele kick, I unloaded with a sequence of German suplexes, With him writhing around below me, I signalled for Old School Violence with a cutthroat gesture and ran knee first into his ribs. Yet there were still signs of life.

I hit the running knee, Brody was down on the floor, arm crooked against his stomach, writhing but not out. The referee hadn't called the stoppage. I ran over to him, grabbed him by the arm and stomped his head as it popped up and down like a punch ball into the sole of my boot.

The mood changed.

A woman in the front row held her face in her hands

Angered, prepared to go to any length to win, this was when my boot came down like a piston banging down on his head.

His cheeks reddened as I stomped furiously on his face. A howl of rage came from deep within me, the horror of the inner darkness escaping, the fury of all the anger and self-loathing I had carried all these years.

At that moment, stomping on Brody's face, however real it looked, it wasn't real and I was glad of it.

I stomped and stomped and stomped but left no mark.

The referee backed me away into a corner. My theme song hit and I had my arm held aloft.

I was the champion.

Out of the corner of my eye I could see I had popped the boys watching from the balcony above.

Having done what I set out to do, I staggered out through the doors into the sports hall that was now empty. It was over.

A few moments later Brody was carried through by some trainees, possibly a medic but it was all kayfabe by the looks of it, I was sure I hadn't hurt him and as soon as the door was closed he was back on his feet, racing toward me with his arms outstretched.

We hugged.

'Thank you, man,' he said.

'That was just what we needed,' I said.

When I climbed the staircase back into the foam-matted martial arts space we were using as the changing room, I saw Marilyn and walked right up to him.

'Did you see my match?' I asked.

Marilyn's eyes were evil and full of his casual hatred. The other old boys didn't speak. The heroes of British wrestling I had worshipped as a kid. Everybody in the room turned their gaze on me.

'Did I see your fucking match?' he hissed. Then, easing into a smile, eyes suddenly jovial and posture relaxed, he patted me on the shoulder and said, 'I did. It was good. Well done mate.'

*

A few weeks later, Krupp sold the promotion and the new promoter booked me in for a match that I was due to lose within five minutes, with no offence and the belt would be gone. I had other offers, more bookings for other promotions and some wanted to put more belts on me but I knew it wasn't for me.

The morning after dropping the belt, I went into the cupboard under the staircase, unzipped my holdall, pulled out my kit and held my tights, knee strap and T-shirt in my hands. It was unwashed, smelled of another time when Earl Black Jr trod the boards.

The shine on my boots.

A stray thumbtack still impressed into the rubber sole from the hardcore match at Super Strong Style. The worn, muffled left knee of my black tights where I delivered the running knee strike, heard the oohs when I fingered the seam.

I pulled out the T-shirt and unfurled its stench.

The silhouette of me in my dad's signature pose, fists on his hips, and in black and white Tennessee font:

Black & Son. *Pro Wrestlers* since 1966.

I had never thought I would wrestle forever, I hadn't even thought I would last more than a match, but here I was all these years later having done far more than I ever set out to do and going out on my own terms.

Winning the title was the end of my story in pro wrestling. It wasn't for me.

I had only ever been faking it as a wrestler.

While teaching was hard, I was winning some of the kids over, getting classes under control and got the same buzz from a good lesson with my new Mr Brown gimmick as I did from performing in the ring.

And there, I got to be a babyface, at least in my own mind.

I didn't want to travel the country, sitting around for hours backstage, given the silent treatment or criticised a lot of the time, dealing with the hierarchy and honour culture, all the politics of planning a match, remembering it, how you performed in the ring, the anxiety and pressure, I was happy to do without it. I was going to be a dad. I had a family.

I folded away my kit and put it in my bag. Then I posted from my Earl Black Jr account:

> It's so long but not goodbye. I have a baby and full-time teaching to wrestle with for now. Hopefully EBJ will see you down the road

By the end of the day I got 171 likes and Marilyn Draven, among others, sent me a message saying he wished me the best and that my break would only be temporary.

I knew it wouldn't, I just couldn't say I would definitely never wrestle again, it was too final.

But I knew I didn't want to wrestle anymore.

I took the bag up to my bedroom.

What I was giving up wasn't the choreographed fights with the macho culture based on respect, itself based on the fictions of fragile egos, no, it was the make-believe world that had become folklore, it was the fairy tale world that Dad once belonged to, that I had been a part of, that was the business, with its rites and rituals, the mythic realm of men.

I put the attire in my holdall and slid it under the bed.

*

Being outside the business and coming up for air was like surfacing with the bends. All the iron in the haemoglobin in my blood had been disturbed.

It was dizzying, what was I going to do? Who was I going to be now?

I wasn't entirely sure. I had stepped out of Dad's shadow, the world ahead of me without wrestling was a more serene place, covered in a bleached light. One where I could be a writer, a dad, a husband, somebody more like myself.

Somehow, several weekends had gone by without drinking and by the summer, every day got a little bit easier and I enjoyed being a family man even more, it gave me something to feel good about, and this kind of life contained its own rhythms, the rise and fall of the sun each day in our little family that seemed like its own world. Then I thought about Dad, I knew Dad wasn't going to be around forever, but how long?

Nobody knew.

I tried to keep in touch with him as much as I could, even if I lived 200 miles away and he could be awkward to talk to. A human heart beats more than 2.5 billion times in a lifetime. I imagined the chambers of Dad's whale heart, the big slow beats that were slowly coming to a halt. He had been given months to live before, was even clinically dead at one point, told he would be wheelchair-bound about twenty years ago but he still soldiered on, his bulk in his black coat, lumbering about, telling his stories, and I heard he had recently added a new one to his set, about his boy who grew up to be a champion.

One of the matches I had filmed as part of a web series with a docu-soap element for Renegade had finally come out of post-production and given that Mum had come down to visit, I was going to premiere the show by streaming it on the TV.

I hadn't been able to watch wrestling since I retired. Dad used to do this and now I understood why. I got everybody together in the living room, Mum sat in my sixties-style armchair, the rest of my family squeezed on the sofa, Eliot on one arm, Grace on the other, her bump between us and I looked around, barely able to conceal a smile. I got the main event ready to go, pressed pause, went into the kitchen and came back with a non-alcoholic craft lager for the premier.

Mum had a dazed look in her eye as the ring entrances began. She had shaved her head and wore glasses like me. The scars on her arms had faded into a soft pink, barely there, and she always seemed hot, sleeves rolled up in a workmanlike way, arms thick and bulging, as if she was about to knock up a fence at a moment's call.

'Want to sit on nana's lap?' she asked Eliot.

He came over and hugged her.

Since she had been sectioned and got the help she needed, Mum had calmed down and had a new persona as Nanny Shirley, just like her gran who had raised her when her mother couldn't, and she loved spoiling the kids.

As I watched Earl Black Jr enter the screen, LIVE IN NO MAN'S SHADOW across my tank top with my silhouette within a shadow of Dad's V-shaped pose.

'Is he any good then?' Mum whispered to Grace.

I looked over.

'I can hear you,' I said.

'Yeah,' Grace said. 'He was really good.'

'Oh, really?' Mum answered.

'Why wouldn't I be?' I said.

'Shut up you,' she said. 'Good at everything aren't you, bloody big head!'

We laughed.

'This is on the Internet Movie Database, so, you know, I am an actor basically.'

'What aren't you?' Mum said.

The lights went out and a gang of humanoid turtles in dinner suits attacked all the wrestlers with canes as part of a crazy storyline that was partly inspired by Twin Peaks. It had killed the realism, but this was pro wrestling after all, who needed to take it so seriously? It was fun, it was a show; the only people who had to pretend it was real were wrestlers, for everybody else, it was great as it was. For the fans, this would be my legacy, the fun side of Earl Black Jr, the character, the battle against the mutant rats and not the search for Strong Style.

Earl Black Jr lay in the middle of the ring, looking out, I was on the other side, looking back.

'Who they, Mummy?' Eliot asked.

'Giant rats,' Grace said.

Eliot nodded, happy to believe that his stepdad had battled mutant rats and lived to tell the tale.

'You can't tell me that's real,' Mum said.
'Nobody said it was,' I said.
'Your dad always told it was real.'
I laughed.

On the night, this was where the show ended, but on the broadcast the scenes we filmed months later in the first half term as a teacher, we were chased backstage to an underground lair where Trev throttled me against a wall, accusing me of being in on the invasion, I garbled a denial and, as we agreed to put our differences aside for the greater good, a knife was drawn behind Earl Black Jr, the realisation of death in the film of his eye, he sank to his knees, raised his arms one final time, spat a mouthful of blood and collapsed; a turtle emerged from behind him before the closing shot of his face on the ground.

*

In the coming months, the news came that punk rock pro wrestling had been sold to Wrestle World and then some weeks later Marilyn Draven had signed for a New Japan Pro wrestling where he reverted to 'death matches', putting his body on the line and destroying himself with barbed wire and C4 explosives to keep his place on the card as the rise of Strong Style had brought in a new generation of wrestlers who were more athletic, tended to be vegan, more politically engaged, straight-edged and artistic in-ring. Their performances of manliness were on the canvas mainly, along with more women and other kinds of heroes. Meanwhile, Wrestle World signed up vast numbers of UK talent on non-compete clauses to mothball them and stop UK broadcasters being able to resurrect British wrestling on terrestrial TV, killing the business on an independent level like Vince McMahon Sr had done to the NWA territories in the 1970s before establishing the stranglehold of the WWE on pro wrestling. Now it was Renegade doing Wrestle World's dirty work, squeezing the life out of the independents.

A few weeks later I met Dad in a café in Leeds. When I walked in, he was standing at a tabletop with his long coat on and aged hands overlapping, rubbing them in a Buddha-like repose. He was short enough for me to look down above his head and while his back still had a broad frame, the rest of his size had disappeared into the past.

'Hello, young man,' he said.

'Hello, Dad.'

'You want a coffee?' I nodded and set off to the counter only to be stopped by his outstretched arm. He hobbled over himself, a look of Smokey the bear in his small black eyes, his old man ears red from the cold.

When he came back he put my drink on the table and lifted the lid from his own, blowing life into the foamy lather of his latte.

'When you back in Vietnam?' I asked.

'Few weeks,' he said. 'I have some chores to do and save up a bit more money and then I'm gone.'

'You'll be a grandad again by the time you get back.'

He smiled.

I had always thought he would be dead by the time I had kids, doctors said he wouldn't make it longer than five years after the last big flareup of his osteoarthritis. I had factored it into our interactions for the past twenty years. One time I saw a guy break down in tears on a bus after hearing his dad had died, and with mine being so much older and with his bad leg, figured I would be lucky to get five more years. I prayed to God I would.

I looked up at him, his calm aura with his nut-bald head, softly moisturised skin, his mallet fists glowing pink. Without violence, they were a pair of heavy lumps of flesh.

'What makes some wrestlers dickheads?' I asked.

'Some of them believe their own publicity. Macho is an exaggeration of your own importance. Inferiority complex, ego.'

'And why weren't you like that?'

He shrugged.

'I never needed to be. I liked myself.'

'That's interesting.'

Have I told you about the fruit over in Vietnam?' he asked. 'Oh my God. There's fruit you've never heard of. Beautiful,' he closed his eyes and put his palm on his forehead to summon the past. 'It reminds me of home. Growing up in Didcot where the gables would be so full of gooseberries they would hang low, and you could just take them, and the juice ran down your face.'

'You can remember that?' I asked.

'Yeah.'

I dusted a sachet of sweetener into my Americano and lifted it to my mouth.

'I've quit wrestling,' I said. 'For now at least.'

A look of astonishment came over his face, his eyes became concerned and furrowed like little grey animals.

'Whatever for?'

'I can't get to the gym, wrestle all weekend and teach.'

'Each to your own.'

'I did a lot of things I wanted to,' I said. 'And there's all this remembering, it's too much for me.'

'You were better than I ever was, you know?'

His eyes stared.

I shook my head. I wanted him to be proud of me, not to admit I had outdone him. This legend was what sustained me.

'I'm not,' I said.

'Every man wishes for a son who will be greater than he was,' Dad said. 'And you are.'

I thought of Dad in the wrestling books. Driving the Ford Cortina down the wrong side of the road. Standing beside me, a giant, and me a boy. The bouncer. The wrestler. The father. The times he came to my readings. The weekends he took me to football. The diatribes about Vietnam. How he taught me to piss by standing on a bamboo blind he pulled from the window so I could reach the toilet. The bootleggers and low-lifes.

Deep down, I knew the wrestling of Dad's era was not like the wrestling of today and in that capacity he was right, but I didn't want him to be, as he sat before me at this moment, I didn't want to see what was real: the hollowed-out man, with the bushy grey eyebrows, hooded eyes and old man nose, still similar in appearance and shape to the one he had, but oversized and squashy, a single earring now inexplicably in his right ear that suggested to his vanity and eccentricity. It made me feel for him even more as I recognised that the man I dreamed of being may never have been, so much of my idea of him was dreamed up through his stories, the kayfabe presentation of himself that he revelled in. Yes, so many of the qualities he had were real as they were in me, but the bravado and the spectacle of manhood performed in the ring would doubtlessly be things that Eliot would want to honour and, in turn, he would one day see me for what I really was: just a man, not a hero, somebody just trying to be themselves.

Despite spending my life emulating his success, I didn't want to be 'greater' than he was, if that meant I no longer had my hero, the myth that had comforted and sustained me all my life, the myth of being a man. Dad said he was shy when he was young but playing the villain gave him confidence. Unlike some of the wrestlers he knew, like Bruiser Brody, he didn't need to prove himself all the time because he liked who he was. Some wrestlers always had to show you that they were better than you. Bullies in wrestling, he said, don't last long. Bruiser Brody was stabbed to death backstage in a shower in Puerto Rico and nobody was ever convicted of his murder.

Dad's jowls dimpled when he ran his tongue through his false teeth, hands together, fingers steepling. A look as innocent as Eliot's in his eyes. However old he got, he never became cynical or world-weary. He never got beaten down by circumstance; he lived in a world of folklore and legends about days so long gone they contained the barest trace of the real.

The truth of them didn't matter. Most of what happened had happened, but never quite in the way he described them, it was just his way of seeing things.

'You'll be a dad soon, anyway,' he said.

'Well, I sort of already am.' I nodded.

'Why did you never let on that wrestling was fake? Why did you never break kayfabe?' I asked.

'Why denigrate yourself by admitting it was fake?'

'Because it is?'

'If it's fake then it means you are fake. You need people to believe you are the real thing.'

'Do you mean there's something in there worth defending, about the artistry of pro wrestling that people miss? Or like do you mean you're only real so long as people believe the illusion?'

'It's about having pride in yourself. The people in Vietnam google me and are impressed.'

'But what do you gain from it?'

'In their eyes, I am a hero, almost a God. Why spoil it for them?'

'Because it's not real?'

'I like being crazy. Being normal is boring.'

Dad rested his hands on the table.

While I knew that the self was the illusion that made us human, kayfabe in a sense, I didn't want to live with any more illusion than I had to.

'Did you read the stuff I sent?' I asked.

He smiled.

'I am flattered to see you wrote as much about me as you did about yourself.'

'Well, you're a major character.'

'I am far from perfect, but I tried to be a good dad.'

'You are,' I said. 'You begin as a God and then become mortal. As I will one day.'

'I see.'

'Are you happy with the depiction of you so far?'

I had been writing a novel based on my life but the more I wrote, the more I realised it wasn't wrestling that was fake, it was wrestling that was real and the world was fake.

He smiled with thin lips and nodded.

'It's a very accurate portrait of an old man who has seen triumph and disaster and treated both the same way.'

'I am thinking of including waking up to you washing your clothes having shat yourself.'

'Oh my God.'

His hands pressed flat on the table.

'For the comic value of you saying you 'travel light' but also the pathos and realism of the transformation from myth to man,' I said.

He looked concerned.

'I don't think shitting myself will add to the quality of the book.'

'You haven't read the scene.'

'Leave it in as long as you mention it was because I had an operation. You haven't mentioned my very un-PC jokes and fantastic stories.'

I laughed.

'Okay,' I said. 'I'll get some of those in too.'

'Did I ever tell you about the riot at Jakarta airport?' He broke out into laughter.

He had, but I said *no*.

'When international wrestlers were based in Singapore in the sixties, we commuted to Hong Kong, Taiwan, Thailand, China, Borneo, Malaysia, and Japan. A probe was made into having the first-ever wrestling match in Indonesia and the situation was volatile because the country was run by the army. The match was arranged by Ranjid Singh, the Singapore movie producer who was promoting the wrestling. His excellent contacts and publicity machine ensured full houses wherever we went. I travelled to Jakarta, the capital, with Steve Rickard of Australia, and King Kong from Hungary.'

He paused and his eyes shone, withdrawing from the story for a moment to see the impact of it on my face.

I smiled. He smiled back.

'As we got off the plane and went into the terminal, Steve spotted our opponents, Shintaro Fuji, Charlie Londos from Greece, and Jack Claybourne of France.

'Not one to miss an opportunity, Steve thought this would be a good chance for some publicity if we beat up the other wrestlers in front of the press and photographers. Steve set about Charlie Londos, I clocked Shintaro Fuji, and King Kong bashed Claybourne. We didn't anticipate the riot that ensued,' he said, laughing.

'The airport erupted with a mass of brawling bodies. Many did not know why they were fighting. Security guards fired warning shots above our heads, but by now it had become difficult for the wrestlers to get out of the way.

'The sound of gunfire brought soldiers running, who started shooting at the wrestlers.

'Steve found an escape route, and we fled through it onto the runway, where a light aircraft was taxiing for take-off. Steve jumped in and told the pilot to go, King Kong and I followed.

'The army was still shooting at us, but the pilot could not speak English and was trying to get us out of the plane. When bullets ricocheted through the fuselage, he stopped arguing and took off.

'The army continued to shoot holes in the plane, but luckily we reached Malaysia quite soon after, and made our way back to Singapore. Ranjid Singh was not deterred however and was still looking for a payday.

'The army was placated with golden handshakes, and we were back in Jakarta and wrestling the following week! We wrestled in a field with a curtain round it, having changed in our hotels. The spectators, never having seen wrestling, did not know what to expect.

'I went on the first match with Jack Claybourne, feeling out the crowd, who were quiet to begin with. After a few minutes, I resorted to my usual practice of kicking the shit out of Claybourne like a crazy horse.

'When he made a comeback and drop kicked me over the top rope, the crowd realised what was what, and supported him against me.

'The other matches went off without any drama, but it was not a place wrestlers were too keen to go to. Back to Singapore, and my all-expenses-paid Ambassador hotel in Kallang for a couple of weeks' rest.'

He broke into laughter. 'Those were the days,' he said. He draped his coat over his shoulders, popped a Polo in his mouth, pulled out a cigarette and grinned a grimace. He said he was going for a smoke, and I watched the shape of his still-broad back and upper neck in his black coat, hauling himself away on his leg like a gondolier, as he shuffled toward the door.

Acknowledgements

It turns out you need the help of a lot of people to write a novel about yourself. The original idea of *Breaking Kayfabe* was supported initially by Steve Dearden and *The Writing Squad* who were bold enough to invest in my pro wrestling training as a research project initially, and to CHASE doctoral partnerships for funding my PhD degree in Narrative Non-Fiction which culminated in the finished version of the novel.

To Julia Bell, Toby Litt, Russell Celyn Jones and Dr Katherine Angel at Birkbeck whose input into early drafts of the novel during my MA was invaluable. My friend and former colleague at *Dead Ink*, Nathan Connolly, for his long-standing support and advice. My wife, Becki, for believing in me enough to quit my job and do a PhD to write this novel, for her suggestions and putting up with me. To my friends Lauren Niland, Chris Kerr, Nicholas Hogg, Ben Craig, Helena Blakemore, Dr Roberta Garrett, Chiara Perugia and Dr Gillian Butler for help along the way.

To my PhD supervisory team at the University of Kent, David Flusfeder and Amy Sackville. The novel really took shape under David's guidance; without him, the novel wouldn't have developed in the way that it has. My examiners, Professor Hywel Dix and Professor Vybarr Cregan Reid for offering some much-needed input on the manuscript.

To David Collard for inviting me on his Carthorse Orchestra and without his support I would've given up on finding a publisher for *Kayfabe*. And then to Kevin and Hetha Duffy and everybody at Bluemoose. The word 'persona' literally means mask, and Fiachra McCarthy has captured the idea perfectly with the cover design. My editor, Lin Webb, herself a former wrestler, and my tag-team partner on this book. Without Kevin and Bluemoose, it's unlikely that this story would have found its way into print and for that I am eternally grateful. Serious, innovative, daring literature owes its future to independent publishing.

To Adam Farrer and *The Real Story* for publishing an early extract from *Breaking Kayfabe*, which was a huge confidence boost. Thanks go to *Storgy* for first publishing my story, *Kansas City*, and allowing its reproduction in this book. To Joelle Taylor for allowing us to use a quote from her collection, *C+nto & Othered Poems*. I am also indebted to the many friends, peers and students who have supported me, and the influence of Karl Ove Knausgård in particular.

Finally, I couldn't have written this book without my dad, whose character and stories inspired this story, and for offering his wisdom on matters concerning pro wrestling. The same goes for my mum, to my brother Courtenay, my children, Edward and Eliza, and the many people I encountered during my time as a pro wrestler. While many of these characters and events have a basis, like pro wrestling, in reality, the novel blurs the line between fact and fiction. However real a character may seem, even if inspired by living people, they are not flesh and blood, and never can be. They are fictions, hopefully realistic in effect, but works of *kayfabe* nonetheless.